Shotha Rusthveli

Shotha Rusthveli

THE KNIGHT
IN THE TIGER SKIN

✥ POEM ✥

Fredonia Books
Amsterdam, The Netherlands

The Knight in the Tiger Skin

by
Shot'ha Rust'hveli

ISBN: 1-58963-500-0

Reprinted from the 1977 edition

Fredonia Books
Amsterdam, the Netherlands
http://www.fredoniabooks.com

Contents

7

A Word on Shot'ha Rust'hveli

The Knight in the Tiger Skin by Shot'ha Rust'hveli is recognised as one of the greatest works to have been created by human genius.

Eight centuries separate us from the author of this immortal epic, but even today its life-affirming passion, shining humanity and heroic spirit, the ideas of patriotism and internationalism that it embodies and the elevated human feelings and moral ideals it expresses link this great literary monument of the distant past with the spiritual world of all freedom-loving peoples.

Rust'hveli's epic has become part of the heritage of all mankind. No less than the people for whom it was written, Europeans and Asians, Americans and Africans can gain from this work something more than a romantic, knightly tale brilliantly told in verse.

This is so due above all to the fact that in the past 100 years Rust'hveli's immortal epic has been translated not only into the languages of the Soviet peoples, but also into many world languages.

For centuries Rust'hveli's work, the product of an unknown world and written in a still unstudied tongue, survived only in the native land of the poet, south of the Caucasus mountains in the gorges of the rivers Chorokhi, Rioni, Kura and Alazani.

For world culture the appearance of *The Knight in the Tiger Skin* was akin to a major archaeological discovery. The Russian public figure, Yevgeny Bolkhovitinov, was the first person of the larger world to take note of this priceless treasure. Writing soon after Georgia joined Russia in 1802, he observed enthusiastically of the poem that "the scenes of action resemble those of Ariosto's poem *Orlando Furioso*, but the beauty, the originality of the pictures, the naturalness of the ideas and sensations are Ossianic".

...Bled white by its enemies, Georgia had slumbered for six centuries. Now, through the North, it was returning to the European civilisation to which it had been linked for many centuries through the South before the Mongol invasion.

The Knight in the Tiger Skin was written on the eve of the fatal catastrophe which befell Georgia· in the "golden age" of its history, when this small but powerful feudal country stood at the height of its political, economic and spiritual renaissance. Scarcely had the book appeared than Georgia was for many centuries torn from the outside world, its once famed culture known only to very few.

Even in the 19th century, although Rust'hveli's epic had been noted and many had tried to bring it, if only in part, to the knowledge of the world, *The Knight in the Tiger Skin* remained an enigma to the foreign reader.

It was only at the turn of the century that the veil concealing the work was drawn aside. "As Homer is Greece, Dante Italy, Shakespeare England and Calderon and Cervantes Spain, so Rust'hveli is Georgia.... A people, if it is great, will create song and carry in its bosom a world poet. Such a monarch of the ages, still unknown to Russians, was Georgia's chosen one, Shot'ha Rust'hveli, who in the 12th century gave his motherland its banner and call–'Vephist-kaosani'–*Wearer of the Snow-Leopard's Skin*. This is the best poem about love ever written in Europe, a rainbow of love, a fiery bridge linking heaven and earth."

These words belong to the poet Konstantin Balmont, who translated *The Knight in the Tiger Skin* into Russian. He recalls his first encounter with Rust'hveli thus: "I first became acquainted with Rust'hveli amid the expanses of the ocean, not far from the Canary Islands, on an English ship bearing the name of Athene, beautiful goddess of wisdom. On board I met Oliver Wardrop, who gave me an English translation of *The Snow-Leopard Skin*, of which he had a proof copy, to read. The translation had been done with great affection by his sister, Marjory Scott Wardrop. To touch the Georgian rose amid the immensity of the ocean dawns, with the kindly complicity of Sun, Sea, the Stars, friendship and love, of wild water-spouts and fierce storms, produced an impression which I shall never forget."

Balmont's translation, the first full and truly poetic rendering of the work, began to appear as early as 1916 in magazine instalments.

The English writer Marjory Scott Wardrop visited Georgia in the 1890s. There she met the outstanding Georgian poet and public figure, Ilya Chavchavadze, who introduced her to Rust'hveli's poem. Filled with admiration for the work, she threw herself into study of the Georgian language and in 1912 Shot'ha Rust'hveli was brought to English readers in a prose translation.

Thus this ancient Georgian poem appeared almost simultaneously in two world languages.

*   *   *

In discussing *The Knight in the Tiger Skin* we must inevitably begin by discussing its author. Who was Shot'ha Rust'hveli? Do Georgian historical writings contain any mention of him?

The earliest references to Georgia and the Georgian people are to be found in Herodotus, "the father of history". Still earlier, Homer mentions a Georgian tribe, the Khalibi, while writing of the Trojan war. Descriptions of the state of Iberia and ancient Colchis are contained in the writings of Strabo and many Greco-Roman authors.

The age of Rust'hveli was, in world history, the time when the future captains Dzhebe and Subetey were riding and shooting beneath the burning sun of Central Asia, preparing for the wars to come. Bloody clouds were gathering in the incandescent skies of Mongolia; in the West the third crusade was raging and the terrible Saladin, having defeated the knights of Europe, was entering Jerusalem.

Both the political and spiritual future of Georgia and the life of Rust'hveli himself were bound up with these important parallel processes.

But in the meantime, the "golden age" reigned in Rust'hveli's homeland. On the throne sat T'hamar (1184-1213), a queen famed for her intelligence and beauty. Her state was united and strong, resting on the firm foundations which her great forebear, David the Builder (1089-1125), had laid. David had taken advantage of the crusades to expel the Arabs and Turks from his country after 300 years of domination.

Georgia's renaissance was closely linked to both Western and Eastern culture. It was at this time that "Iranian literature met the literature of the North, of Europe, that Leili met Isolda, Buddha the legend of Ahasuerus. Georgia was the land where these two cultural streams, rushing towards each other, met. The focal point of this meeting, a man endowed with a remarkable lyrical gift, intelligence and passion, was Rust'hveli" (Nikolai Tikhonov).

History has no precise facts for us about the great Georgian poet, but *The Knight in the Tiger Skin* itself and a handful of other historical and literary documents now at our disposal make it possible to form a definite picture of the poet's personality and of the times in which his work of genius was created.

Shot'ha Rust'hveli's life and the time of creation of his poem exactly coincide, according to the events described in it, with the era of Queen T'hamar, down to the dynastic conflicts that reflected contemporary clashes at court.

It is fortunate that the author refers to himself more than once in his poem, introducing himself as Rust'hveli. "I, Rust'hveli, indited a poem.... Hitherto the tale has been told as a tale; now is it a pearl of measured poesy."

Of T'hamar the poet writes:

"By shedding tears of blood we praise Queen T'hamar, whose praises I, not ill-chosen, have told forth."

The lines: "I, Rust'hveli, have composed this work by the folly of my art," and "I am sick of love, and for me there is no cure from anywhere", clearly indicate the poet's unspoken love for the queen. Some Georgian scholars of Rust'hveli consider that the amatory conflict conveyed in the poem reflects the personal relations of poet and queen and it is possible that isolated coincidences occur, but we lack the corresponding historical and biographical documents to conclusively prove this.

In fact, we possess no precise historical information on Rust'hveli's character. However, the life of Queen T'hamar is presented relatively fully in ancient Georgian historical writings ("Kartlis tskhovreba") and, in particular, in the stories by "Basil", the queen's personal historian and court tutor.

Several people bearing the name Shot'ha appear in historical sources of the 12th and 13th centuries and in ancient deeds. Could it be that one of them is the poet? Georgian scholars have long investigated this question, settling now on one, now on another Shot'ha as the author of *The Knight in the Tiger Skin*. (It is only since the examination of the Jerusalem fresco depicting Shot'ha that this dispute may, to a certain extent, be considered settled.)

Who, then, was Shot'ha, the poet from Rustavi?

Two settlements in Georgia have laid claim to the poet. One lies twenty kilometres from Tbilisi, Georgia's capital, and is now known throughout the Soviet Union for its metallurgical industry. Eight centuries ago this Rustavi was a large administrative, economic and cultural centre in the kingdom of Georgia.

In 1265 the town was utterly destroyed by the Mongols. The builders of modern Rustavi were confronted by a striking sight while clearing a section of the ancient ruins: the headless skeleton of a young girl separated by some metres from her skull. An axe was in the girl's hands. She had evidently been defending herself from an invading Mongol soldier, who beheaded her with his sword. Beside the girl's skeleton the remains of her devoted dog were found.

On that day, 700 years ago, the Mongols also beheaded the town which considers itself the birthplace of Shot'ha Rust'hveli.

The second Rustavi is a small village in the south of Georgia, on the border with Turkey. This part of the country is sometimes referred to as Meskhetia.

The cliff town of Vardzia, which dates from the 12th century, is located here. This cave complex served both religious and secular purposes and had remarkable frescoes depicting Queen T'hamar and members of her family. Here, too, are found the multi-level Van Caves, cut in the 13th century, and the fortress of T'hmogvi, birthplace of Sargis T'hmogveli, author of the *Dilarget'hicni*, who is mentioned in *The Knight in the Tiger Skin*. The fortress of Khertvisi and many other historical monuments which played a major role in the political and cultural life of ancient Georgia are also located here. Meskhetia gave Georgia's culture many outstanding figures, writers, scholars, artists and philosophers. Scholars confirm that the name Shot'ha was particularly common in this province in the 10th, 11th and 12th centuries.

According to tradition Shot'ha Rust'hveli came from this corner of southern Georgia and many scholars now consider that Shot'ha Rust'hveli was a Meskh from Rustavi in Meskhetia.

But which of the Shot'has mentioned in historical sources was the poet? The majority of Georgian literary sources name the author of the poem as Shot'ha, treasurer of the court of Queen T'hamar.

Rust'hveli figures in popular tradition as a minister of the queen. He is supposed to have been educated first in Georgia, at the academies of Gelati or Ikaltoy, and then in Athens or on Mount Olympus, where many Georgians studied at that time. The poet became a master of Greek, Arabic and Persian and gained an intimate knowledge of the literature and philosophy of these countries before receiving a high post at the court of Queen T'hamar.

Indeed, his poem indicates that Rust'hveli was well read in the ancient philosophers, including Heraclitus and Empedocles; however, many Georgian scholars now assert that the principal source of his ideas was the writings of such Georgian thinkers as Petrus the Iberian, Ioane Laza, Ioane Moskh (Meskh), Yefrem Mtsyre and Ioane Petritsi, who radically revised the ideas of the ancients.

Academician N. Y. Marr consistently advanced the view that Georgians of the 10th and 11th centuries were studying the same problems which were occupying the most advanced minds in Christian countries of West and East during the period and that they were ahead of Europe inasmuch as they were able to respond before anyone else to the new philosophical trends and possessed a model apparatus of philosophical criticism for the time.

According to the same sources and to popular tradition Shot'ha Rust'hveli travelled widely–as is also evident from *The Knight in the Tiger Skin*–journeying in his old age to Palestine, there in Jerusalem to die.

Georgian scholars now have all the necessary documents to prove conclusively that Rust'hveli was minister of finance at the court of Queen T'hamar.

It is known that as early as the 5th century Georgians founded the Monastery of the Cross in Palestine. For twelve hundred years they carried out a great educational and cultural mission from this monastery until it was captured by the Greeks in the 17th century.

There, in the course of the centuries, a history of the monastery was written and information was compiled on its leading figures, the names of whom were inscribed in a "Memorial Book".

Hundreds of volumes in Georgian, Greek and other languages used at that time by Georgians in Palestine, including the "Memorial Book" and the church calendars, passed into the possession of the Greek church and are now kept in the library of the Greek patriarch in Jerusalem.

Georgian scholars have at their disposal only a number of microfilms, among them copies of the church calendars. One of these microfilms states: "On this Monday the funeral mass of the treasurer, Shot'ha, is to take place." This entry relates to the first quarter of the 13th century.

For many centuries scholars in the poet's homeland knew nothing of this.

In the middle of the 18th century the Georgian public figure, Timote Gabashvili, visited Georgian antiquities in Palestine, among them the Monastery of the Cross in Jerusalem. Gabashvili described his travels in a book entitled *A Journey*, in which the following reference to the Monastery of the Cross occurs: "Below the cupola the columns have been renovated and painted ... by the treasurer, Shot'ha Rust'hveli, who is himself depicted there as an old man." Gabashvili conjectured that Shot'ha the treasurer must have been the poet, Shot'ha Rust'hveli. He based his supposition that Rust'hveli was a minister of finance on the traditional legends of the people.

Who destroyed the cupola and columns of the monastery, restored and painted with the assistance of Shot'ha Rust'hveli, and when did this happen?

The Monastery of the Cross was destroyed and rebuilt, repaired and reconstructed several times in the course of its history. It may be assumed that Shot'ha Rust'hveli arrived in Palestine after the destruction and capture of Jerusalem by the Egyptian sultan, Saladin, during the third crusade. Georgian scholars possess a document written by the Arab historian, Ibn-Sheded, which states that when in 1187 Saladin took Jerusalem, the Monastery of the Cross also fell to him. Queen T'hamar of Georgia offered a ransom of 200,000 dinars for the cloister. Some researchers speculate that the queen sent her minister of finance to Jerusalem on this mission.

Rust'hveli took part in restoring the walls and columns of the Georgian cloister in Palestine, which had been destroyed by Saladin. As a mark of gratitude, Shot'ha himself was depicted on one of the columns of the monastery. Rust'hveli was portrayed in secular dress, kneeling beside St. John Damascene, the great medieval Christian poet, and Maxim the Confessor, who developed Christian philosophy and theology on the basis of neo-Platonism. Of interest here is the fact that in the 7th century Maxim the Confessor opened up the way to the teachings of Dionysius the Areopagite, who was considered a neo-Platonist in the Middle Ages, although he was an orthodox Christian. Dionysius is referred to in *The Knight in the Tiger Skin* as "Dionos"; his thinking is entirely Christian and philosophical and, Georgian scholars assert, it is this view of the world that was the source of Rust'hveli's poem. The poet may have personally chosen a place for this fresco between these two saints.

All these facts have become known only in recent years, since Georgian scholars obtained a portrait of Shot'ha from Palestine, for the fresco of Rust'hveli about which Timote Gabashvili wrote in the mid-18th century and which was described by the members of a scientific expedition in the 19th century disappeared at the end of the last century. Georgian scholars arriving in Palestine failed to find it. How many secrets were buried together with the portrait! Indeed, everything that has been written above has come to light only since the rediscovery of the fresco. Georgian travellers to Palestine at the turn of the century sadly reported that the whereabouts of the portrait were unknown. The fresco seemed, indeed, to have been irrevocably lost.

This problem began to concern me fifteen years ago, when the idea was conceived of celebrating Rust'hveli's jubilee. I resolved to get to the bottom of the mystery surrounding the Rust'hveli portrait in Palestine.

Our expedition, which consisted of Akaky Shanidze and Georgy Tsereteli, both members of the Georgian Academy of Sciences, and myself, arrived in Palestine in the autumn of 1959. I have described the scholarly work performed by the expedition in detail in *Palestinian Diary* and interested readers may refer to this. I shall confine myself here to noting that after careful investigation we succeeded in discovering the Rust'hveli portrait which, fortunately, had been neither erased nor damaged, but was hidden beneath a thick layer of black paint. From the 17th century on, Greek church figures had systematically resorted to actions of this kind to wipe out every distinctively "national" trace from the old Georgian monastery. We cleaned this fresco, which bears the inscription "Rust'-hveli", and brought a copy of it back to Georgia. The Palestine fresco is the most valuable biographical document bearing on the great Georgian poet and thinker that we possess today. The portrait and the Jerusalem church calendar helped to conclusively prove that the poet Shot'ha Rust'hveli and the treasurer Shot'ha mentioned in Georgian historical sources and popular legends are one and the same person.

* * *

The original of *The Knight in the Tiger Skin* has been lost. It may have been reduced to ashes in 1225, when the ferocious Dzhalal-ad-din put Tbilisi to the torch, or later, when the Mongols burned Christian manuscripts in the squares of the city. It could have been torn to shreds during raids by Persians and Turks. During that dark period much was destroyed and lost in Georgia.

"Mose Khoneli praised Amiran, son of Daredjan; Shavt'heli, whose poem they admired, praised Abdul-Mesia; Sargis T'hmogveli, the unwearying-tongued praised Dilarget'h," Rust'hveli tells his readers. Where are the *Abdul-Mesia, the Dilarget'hiani* and many other works now? They have been swallowed up by the black waves of history. Even today we cannot find these literary monuments and traces of them survive only in folklore, in the form of separate fragments, like magnificent ruins of the architectural monuments which are scattered the length of Georgia. It is a cause for great joy that *The Knight in the Tiger Skin* passed through flame intact.

The most ancient manuscript of Rust'hveli's immortal work extant dates from 1646. A number of earlier records have been preserved in the form of fragments, dating from the 15th century. One such fragment, consisting of only a few lines, was discovered recently during the comprehensive excavation and study of the Van Caves. An inscription by the hand of poetess Anna Rcheulishvili was found on a rock. She refers to her sufferings in words from *The Knight in the Tiger Skin:* "I am sitting in a castle so lofty that eyes can scarce see the ground."

As a result of assiduous research work more than 150 manuscripts of *The Knight in the Tiger Skin* have been discovered and these are now kept in Soviet libraries. But not all these manuscripts are suitable for scholarly purposes.[1]

The Knight in the Tiger Skin was first published in 1712 at the initiative and under the editorship of King Vakhtang, founder of the Georgian printing press. Vakhtang had apparently studied ancient manuscripts of the poem, of which far more existed in his time than now and which evidently dated from earlier period. On the basis of these manuscripts he produced a scholarly edition of the poem.

In the absence of the original the text of *The Knight in the Tiger Skin* underwent constant changes at the hands of copyists over the centuries. Many

---

[1] For the history of the poem see: S. S. Tsaishvili, *Shot'ha Rust'hveli's "The Knight in the Tiger's Skin"*, Khudozhestvennaya Literatura Publishers, Moscow, 1966, pp. 117–28 (in Russian).

"embellishers" inserted new passages into the poem at will or in accordance with the wishes of those who ordered copies from them. In the 16th century a revival began in Georgian culture and literature and the popularity and influence of *The Knight in Tiger Skin* grew immeasurably. Copyists of the poem made various changes to the plot, while interpolators were revising the poem to bring it ideologically into line with the teachings of the Christian religion. For these reasons the primary text of the poem is distorted in many manuscripts. In subsequent centuries the poem was increasingly "enriched". The first editor of Rust'hveli's epic had much to do in order to remove obvious insertions from the text and "turn obscurity into clarity". After Vakhtang the great Georgian writer and public figure of the 19th century, Ilya Chavchavadze, did a great deal to discover the genuine text of the poem. However, even today the process of restoring the text to its definitive form is still continuing.

The Georgian people bore its beloved work–*The Knight in the Tiger Skin*– through the flames of the ages, like "a Banner and a Call", whose creator, "conducting his lover heroes through all kinds of trials, made them shine in life with such glory that they could never die. Herein lies the advantage of the Georgian genius over his European contemporaries and later poets, just as the Indian, Kalidasa, stands above geniuses of the drama thanks to his *Sakuntala*. Here, after all, there is no devilish enchantment of death, but a full harmony of happiness, higher and more perfect than of Europe's geniuses..." (Konstantin Balmont).

The people felt the spirit and philosophical essence of the poem–felt it and recognised in it the most precious contribution to its spiritual treasure-house. Generations of Georgians have worked and defended their land under this banner and in response to this call: "What is worse than a man in the fight with a frowning face, shirking, affrighted and thinking of death? In what is a cowardly man better than a woman weaving a web! It is better to get glory than all goods!"

It is characteristic that people were and still are to be found in the inaccessible mountains of Georgia who know all 1,500 verses of Rust'hveli's poem by heart. Worthy of note, too, is the fact that for many centuries *The Knight in the Tiger Skin* was considered a bride's most valuable dowry. Every Georgian kept a copy of the poem beside his bed, together with the Gospels.

Foreign travellers even considered that Georgians had two gods–Christ and Rust'hveli. The priests could not forgive the poet for this and in the centuries to come persecution began of the man whose portrait had, in his lifetime, adorned Christianity's most holy place–the Monastery of the Cross in Jerusalem. According to some dama, in the 18th century almost the entire first edition of his poem was thrown into the Kura River by clerics.

That the love story contained in the poem unfolds in Moslem rather than Christian countries, principally in Arabia and India, was also not to the liking of churchmen. But whatever the forces opposed to it, *The Knight in the Tiger Skin* survived triumphantly through the centuries and is as popular today as it has ever been.

* * *

Rust'hveli considered love the principal sign of human nature and humanity. His immortal poem is a hymn of love and its dominant note, struck by Rust'hveli with characteristic brevity and philosophical profundity, is the eternal truth that "only love exalteth us".

Let us turn our gaze to the cherished pages of *The Knight in the Tiger Skin*.

But first we must clarify, if only in the most general terms, the soil from which the poem sprang, the spiritual atmosphere in which it flowered.

Humanistic ideals and aspirations pervaded Georgia's culture in the age of Rust'hveli. Indeed, if one takes in the whole sweep of the period, one might form the impression that the forces creating Georgian culture before Rust'hveli had, as it were, hastened to erect the walls of this magnificent building so that the poet could crown it with a splendid dome, only a few decades before the fatal catastrophe that broke over his land.

The cultural advance in Georgia was remarkable for the pace of its development, its richness and creative tension. Following the adoption of Christianity, Georgia succeeded in creating more in the period between the 4th and the 12th centuries, amid unending defensive wars and under the constant threat of destruction, than could have been conceived of in so short a span of time.

"During my trips to Georgia I saw the monuments of Georgian architecture, frescoes, etc.," Alexei Tolstoy wrote. "I must say that when I met with these treasures of the 10th and 11th centuries I was convinced that Georgia had created all the prerequisites for the Renaissance and had produced works equal to those of Giotto two centuries before Giotto."

The entire life of the Georgian people was filled with tireless seekings in the field of culture, and especially in that of belles-lettres.

In the very first hagiographical works and soon thereafter in religious poetry and historical and philosophical writings as well, clear signs of an interest in man, in his total spiritual and physical being, emerged. Delight in man's beauty, love, which elevates him, and his search for truth began to come thematically to the fore.

Profound knowledge of the works of Aristotle and Plato revealed by Georgian literature of the time was not fortuitous; nor was the emergence in the 5th century,

20

at the heart of religious literature, of highly developed belles-lettres, written in a rich literary language.

Georgian culture in the 12th century was distinguished by particular variety and richness. The kingdom's two academies—Gelati and Ikaltoy—offered their students a general education while also serving as major centres of science and philosophy.

Moreover, as I have already noted, a lofty synthesis of Western and Eastern culture was brought about in Georgia by virtue of its geographical position.

All this formed the foundation and walls of the magnificent edifice which would have remained incomplete had not Georgia produced Rust'hveli.

Rust'hveli accomplished and expressed with great power that elevated human ideal of which the medieval world—the medieval world alone?—could only dream. He raised man to heights inaccessible to his own and subsequent times.

The Gordian knot which medieval thinking, whether religious, philosophical or artistic, was unable to unravel is known to all. This was the gulf that had formed in knowledge between God and the real world, between creator and created. The best minds of the Middle Ages laboured in vain to find the solution to this mystery, but their conclusion was always the same: the deity alone is real, while the created world is only an appearance, an abode of evil and the possession of Satan.

Mankind gazed with fascination into this chasm and at the two shores of the gulf without finding a way out of the problem. If philosophers were able to glean hope from a rejection of earthly things, placing their trust solely in "the other shore", the fate of artists and poets was far more complex and difficult, for the very nature of their work placed them in the here and now, on the earthly shore, while the message conveyed by religion and philosophy was that only the life of the other world was real and everything earthly was worthy only of rejection and condemnation.

This sense of being in a hopeless spiritual dead-end left a deep and sombre mark on the work of medieval artists.

This, then, was the spiritual atmosphere of the age of which Rust'hveli was a witness.

One preliminary observation should be made. Let us imagine for a moment that we know nothing of Rust'hveli's view of the world and that we have not studied his poem from this point. Nevertheless, it will be clear to everyone who has read it, even once, that the poet who emerges from its pages could not, simply in terms of his psychological cast of mind and spiritual make-up, have been an adherent of a dualistic concept of life.

A world dislocated and divided was inconceivable to the author of *The Knight in the Tiger Skin*, just as heroes with divided souls or split natures were inconceivable to him. The characters of *The Knight in the Tiger Skin* are monolithic, whole, carved, as it were, from huge single blocks of stone. Even when Tariel has lost hope in meeting his beloved, despairs and is on the verge of madness, in flight from life and alone in the desert, he does not cease to be a whole person, for in the situation that has emerged and the circumstances fate has presented him with he cannot act, think or suffer other than as a whole person.

It is clear from what has been noted above that Rust'hveli's position is that of a monist. But what is the nature of this monism? Can we suppose that Rust'hveli overcame the dualism of his age simply by dismissing the question of the other world and of the very existence of "the other shore"? This point of view has been expressed by some Georgian scholars, who claim that Rust'hveli was absorbed by this world alone and that the sphere of his interests did not essentially extend beyond the bounds of the earthly.

I believe that thus posing and resolving the question means its over-simplification. The historical approach to this complex issue should not be neglected: there is little profit to be gained from ascribing to a 12th-century poet conclusions of which mankind became firmly convinced only in the course of the last century. Free, unfettered thought should not be confused with the atheistic and materialistic thought. These domains were quite out of the question in the 12th century. Complex cultural phenomena and philosophical ideas must be explained on the basis of the laws inherent in them and not in terms of laws imposed on them from outside, even if this is done from the most advanced modern point of view and with the best of intentions.

No, Rust'hveli, contrary to the conclusions drawn centuries later by human minds, certainly did not dismiss the question of "the other shore"; but, despite the dominant tradition of his age, neither did he turn away from the reality of "this shore", even in theory. Rust'hveli was able to overcome the apparent contradiction, to bridge the gulf. How?

The gulf was conquered by declaring it–and not the created world–to be an evil which, in Rust'hveli's concept, was illusory. The gulf dividing creator and creation was only apparent. Anyone who wanted to enter into communion with God must demonstrate the illusoriness of the gulf, that separates man from his creator, by conquering evil. Only active struggle against evil would give an opportunity for communion with the Almighty.

The world was not created by God for it to be made an abode of evil. The earth, adorned with incomparable and varied beauty, was created for people, since man himself was involved in God and was a part of him, created by him. Without man the unity and harmony of the world was inconceivable.

According to Rust'hveli's concept of things, love, even in this world, could bring man into contact with the supreme harmony and thereby make him closer to the divine.

Man was given intelligence in order that he might know the world created for him and make his knowledge an instrument for achieving the supreme goal. For the truly wise man there was no gulf separating heaven and earth: he knew it was the gulf, not the world, that was illusory. Apparently essential evil was only the product of ignorance and was overcome by active knowledge, which must not remain "wisdom for its own sake", but which must be wholly directed towards the affirmation of good, towards the supreme goal of communion with God, towards the highest order and harmony.

It is here that the fundamental difference between Rust'hveli's view of the world and traditional medieval thinking lies.

Rust'hveli considered that the world was created by God for man and that man himself was a part of God. It was therefore for man to live, create and act, and not to reside in a prison of evil. The world was illuminated by the sun and the sun was the visible image of the creator. The source of all earthly light was God himself.

The poet was convinced that one must love a real, living being, not a lifeless symbol of God. Love brought us into contact with the supreme harmony, since it was through love that evil was conquered, the fetters broken and the illusion that creator and man are divided dispelled.

Rust'hveli knew that in order to grasp the supreme truth man should not await heavenly enlightenment in a mystical ecstasy. The creator had endowed man with intelligence with the object of embodying in him His own nature. God and man were united by virtue of intelligence and it was for this very reason that the possibilities of human intelligence were limitless.

There was certainly no need for Rust'hveli to go beyond the bounds of Christian teaching for confirmation of his philosophical ethical ideas. If it was true that the objective seeker after truth could find every one of these principles in religious dogma, how much more so was it the case that they could be grasped by the intuition and wisdom of a poetic genius. It is also by no means impossible that Rust'hveli saw and perceived immeasurably more in Christian ideas than was accessible to ecclesiastical commentators. Of course, none of these truths would have been stamped on the poet's consciousness with such clarity and harmony had he lacked the philosophical experience of Pseudo-Dionysius the Areopagite.

Once the gulf dividing creator and created had been overcome and the forces directly raising man to divine perfection revealed (love and wisdom), it inevitably became clear that man's activity had value for existence, both divine and earthly. Hence the vital conclusion that the earthly activity of man as he strives to commune with God is by no means all vanity and confusion in a world of vanity (as was claimed in the theories of the Middle Ages), but an integral part of an inconvertible process of development and movement in an indivisible universe. Ultimately this earthly human activity was contiguous with divine action. But, of course, only that cause which is directed by the active personality, filled with love and wisdom, to the supreme goal, to the divine ideal can itself be divine. Existence unilluminated by the light of love and intelligence is doomed to stagnation and torment in the prison of evil, where everything is short-lived, illusory and transitory, barren and impotent. There all the laws of earthly life as a whole operate with implacable severity, but in a fog of lovelessness and non-understanding, since, as we know, according to Rust'hveli's most important philosophical and ethical conclusion, "evil is in this world for a moment, goodness is immutable!"

This is why, when we say that Rust'hveli raised man to inaccessible heights, we have in mind the idea of humanity and not simply of one man. Tariel and Avt'handil, Nestan and T'hinat'hin and their friends, too, are a living embodiment of this idea. They are truly pinnacles of creation, lords of nature, monarchs of the spirit.

Therein lies the explanation for the constant comparisons between the heroes of the poem and the sun and their frequent personification by the image of the sun.

In turning to a general artistic characterisation of the poem, we should direct our attention to a particular circumstance. While the structure of *The Knight in the Tiger Skin* is extremely complex, being conceived and worked out on several levels, each of these levels is characteristically elaborated with the same thoroughness and consistency. The various levels interpenetrate each other and only by the most painstaking analysis can they be separated.

1 believe that in all literature only the smallest handful of works are as perfectly constructed as Rust'hveli's poem. But even more important is that the poem, as conceived and created, presupposes an unusually wide audience. *The Knight in the Tiger Skin* has always been equally near and dear to the learned scholar and the humble toiler. Both find in the poem words addressed to them, comprehensible to them and dear to them. And each perceives its idea, which today shines with a special light at us, its millions of readers. This idea is simple and great. Rust'hveli reminds us, contemporary men and women, that

man and man alone is the greatest value in the world and that he must be fine and perfectly harmonious. His body and soul, his mind, feelings and actions must be fine. It is man's appointed role and hence his obligation to develop within himself such a will that his thoughts and actions are directed towards good and towards noble ends only.

But Rust'hveli also warns us that for man to be truly great, for him to be elevated to heights which are worthy of him, a contemplative and passive humanism, no matter how noble or well-intentioned, is not enough. For "the road to hell is paved with good intentions". Only activity–and heroic, self-sacrificing activity, if necessary–eternal, unflinching and tireless action can trample evil underfoot and ensure the triumph of good. "Evil is killed by good, there is no limit to good!" This is what makes a man a man and ensures the triumph of a world order in which true harmony reigns.

To liberate Nestan-Daderjan from captivity, incredible trials had to be undergone, intolerable torments endured, insurmountable obstacles overcome and more than human feats, almost inconceivable for ordinary mortals, carried out. This reflects Rust'hveli's moral maximalism: the poet never abased his heroes with petty tasks, difficulties and obstacles. But even if we leave aside the symbolism contained in the story of Nestan's capture and liberation and read Rust'hveli's poem from a purely modern point of view, in terms of what interests us most, the same wisdom that underlies every level of this sophisticated poem will unfold before us: evil can be subdued only by the active force of triumphant good and good can reign on earth only in irreconcilable and victorious conflict with evil.

This is why *The Knight in the Tiger Skin* has become a priceless treasure of the people, why this poem has constantly awakened and sustained man's faith in his own powers and in the triumph of good.

Irakly Abashiadze

THE KNIGHT
IN THE TIGER SKIN

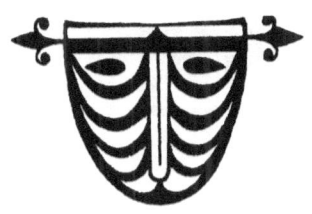

Introduction

1. HE who created the firmament, by that mighty power
   made beings inspired from on high with souls celestial;
   to us men He has given the world, infinite in variety we
   possess it; from Him is every monarch in His likeness.

2. O ONE God! Thou didst create the face of every form!
   Shield me, give me mastery to trample on Satan, give me
   the longing of lovers lasting even unto death, lightening
   the sins I must bear thither with me.

3. OF that lion whom the use of lance, shield and sword
   adorns, of the queen, the sun T'hamar, the ruby-cheeked
   the jet-haired, of her I know not how I shall dare to sing
   the manifold praise; they who look upon her cannot but
   taste choice sweets.

4. BY shedding tears of blood we praise Queen T'hamar,
   whose praises I, not ill-chosen, have told forth. For ink
   I have used a lake of jet and for pen a pliant crystal.
   Whoever hears, a jagged spear will pierce his heart!

5. SHE bade me indite sweet verses in her praise, laud her eyebrows and lashes, her hair, her lips and teeth, cut crystal and ruby of Badakhshan arrayed in ranks. An anvil of soft lead breaks even hard stone.

6. NOW want I tongue, heart and skill for utterance! Grant me strength! And if I have aid from thee I shall have understanding, so may we succour Tariel; tenderly indeed should we cherish his memory and that of the three star-like heroes wont to serve one another.

7. COME, let us sit and shed a never-drying tear for Tariel's sake. In truth none like him has ever been. I sat me down, I, Rust'hveli, indited a poem, my heart pierced with a lance. Hitherto the tale has been told as a tale; now is it a pearl of measured poesy.

8. I, RUST'HVELI, have composed this work by the folly of my art. For her whom a multitude of hosts obey, I lose my wits, I die! I am sick of love, and for me there is no cure from anywhere, unless she give me healing or the earth a grave.

9. THIS Persian tale, now done into Georgian, has hitherto been like a pearl of great price cast in play from hand to hand; now I have found it and mounted it in a setting of verse; I have done a praiseworthy deed. The ravisher of my reason, proud and beautiful, willed me to do it.

10. EYES that have lost their light through her long to look on her anew; lo! my heart is mad with love, and it is my lot to run about the fields. Who will pray for me? The burning

of the body sufficeth, let the soul have comfort! The verse
in praise of the three like heroes cannot but affect the
hearer.

11. WITH what Fate gives to a man, therewithal should he be
content, and so speak of it. The labourer should ever work,
the warrior be brave. So, also, should the lover love Love,
and recognise it. Neither must he disdain the love of
another, or that other disdain his.

12. MINSTRELSY is, first of all, a branch of wisdom; the
divine must be hearkened to divinely, and wholesome is
to them that hearken; it is pleasant, too, if the listener be
a worthy man; in few words he utters a long discourse:
herein lies the excellence of poetry.

13. LIKE a horse is tested in a great race on a long course,
like a ball-player in the lists striking the ball fairly and
aiming adroitly at the mark, even so is it with the poet
who composes and indites long poems, and reins in his horse
when utterance is hard for him and verse begins to fail.

14. THEN, indeed, behold the poet, and his poesy will be
manifest. When he is at a loss for words, and verse begins
to fail, he will not weaken the verse, nor will he let the verse
grow poor. Let him strike cunningly with the polo-mallet;
he will show great virtue.

15. HE who utters, somewhere, one or two verses cannot be
called a poet; let him not think himself equal to great
singers. Even if they compose a few discrepant verse from
time to time, yet if they say, "Mine are of the best!" they
are stiff-necked mules.

16. SECONDLY, lyrics which are but a small part of poetry and cannot command heart-piercing word—I may liken them to the bad bows of young hunters who cannot kill big game; they are able only to slay the small.

17. THIRDLY, lyrics are fit for the festive, the joyous, the amorous, the merry, for pleasantries of comrades; they please us when they are clearly sung. Those are not called poets who cannot compose a lengthy work.

18. THE poet must not spend his toil in vain. One should seem to him worthy of love; he must be devoted to one, he must employ all his art for her, he must praise her, he must set forth the glory of his beloved; he must wish for nought else, for her alone must his tongue be tuneful.

19. NOW let all know that I praise her whom I erstwhile praised; in this I have great glory, I feel no shame. She is my life; merciless as a leopard is she. Her name I pronounce hereafter praising her allegorically.

20. I SPEAK of the highest love—divine in its kind. It is difficult to discourse thereon, ill to tell forth with tongues. It is heavenly, upraising the soul on pinions. Whoever strives thereafter must indeed have endurance of many griefs.

21. SAGES cannot comprehend that one Love; the tongue will tire, the ears of the listeners will become wearied; I must tell of lower frenzies, which befall human beings; they imitate it when they wanton not, but faint from afar.

22. IN the Arabic tongue they call the lover "madman", because by non-fruition he loses his wits. Some have nearness to God, but they weary in the flight; then again, to others it is natural to pursue lovely women.

23. TO a lover, beauty, like unto the sun, wisdom, wealth, generosity, youth and leisure are fitting; he must be eloquent, intelligent, patient, a conqueror of mighty adversaries; who is not all these lacks the qualities of a lover.

24. LOVE is tender, a thing hard to be known. True love is something apart from lust, and cannot be likened thereto; it is one thing; lust is quite another thing, and between them lies a broad boundary; in no way do thou mingle them—hear my saying!

25. THE lover must be constant, not lewd, impure and faithless; when he is far from his beloved he must heave sigh upon sigh; his heart must be fixed on one from whom he endures wrath or sorrow if need be. I hate heartless love—embracing, kissing, loud smacking of the lips.

26. LOVERS, call not this thing love: when any longs for one to-day and another to-morrow, bearing parting's pain. Such base sport is like mere boyish trifling; the good lover is he who suffers a world's woe.

27. THERE is a noblest love; it does not show, but hides its woes; the lover thinks of it when he is alone, and always seeks solitude; his fainting, dying, burning, flaming, all

are from afar; he must face the wrath of his beloved, and he must be fearful of her.

28. HE must betray his secret to none, he must not basely groan and put beloved to shame; in nought should he manifest his love, nowhere must he reveal it; for her sake he looks upon sorrow as joy, for her sake he would willingly be burned.

29. HOW can the sane trust him who noises his love abroad, and what shall it profit to do this? He makes her suffer, and he himself suffers. How should he glorify her if he shame her with words? What need is there for man to cause pain to the heart of his beloved!

30. I WONDER why men show that they love the beloved. Why shame they her whom they love, her who slays herself for them, who is covered with wounds? If they love her not, why do they not manifest to her feelings of hatred? Why do they disgrace what they hate? But an evil man loves an evil word more than his soul or heart.

31. IF the lover weep for his beloved, tears are his due. Wandering and solitude befit him, and must be esteemed as roaming. He will have time for nothing but to think of her. If he be among men, it is better that he manifest not his love.

I

Story of Rostevan, King of the Arabians

32. THERE was in Arabia Rostevan, a king by the grace of God, happy, exalted, generous, modest, lord of many hosts and knights, just and gracious, powerful, far-seeing, himself a peerless warrior, moreover, fluent in speech.

33. NO other child had the king save one only daughter, the shining light of the world, to be ranked with nought but the sunny group; whoever looked on her, she bereft him of heart, mind and soul. It needs a wise man to praise her, and ten thousand times a thousand tongues.

34. HER name is T'hinat'hin; let it be famous! When she had grown up to full womanhood, she contemned even the sun. The king called his viziers, seated himself, proud yet gentle, and, placing them by his side, began to talk graciously to them.

35. HE said: "I will declare to you the matter on which we are to take counsel together. When the flower of the rose is dried and withered it falls, and another blooms in the lovely garden. The sun is set for us; we are gazing on a dark, moonless night.

36. "MY day is done; old age, most grievous of all ills, weighs on me; if not to-day, then to-morrow I die–this is the way of the world. What light is that on which darkness attends? Let us instate as sovereign my daughter, of whom the sun is not worthy."

37. THE viziers said: "O king, why do you speak of your age? Even when the rose fades we must needs give it its due; it still excels all in scent and fair colour. How can a star declare enmity even to the waning moon!

38. "SPEAK not then thus, O king. Your rose is not yet faded. Even bad counsel from you is better than good counsel from another. It was certainly fitting to speak about what your heart desires. It is better. Give the kingdom to her who prevails against the sun.

39. "THOUGH indeed she be a woman, still as sovereign she is begotten of God. She knows how to rule. We say not this to flatter you; we ourselves, in your absence, often say so. Her deeds, like her radiance, are revealed bright as sunshine. The lion's whelps are equal, be they male or female."

40. AVT'HANDIL was Spaspeti,[1] son of the Amirspasalari.[2] He was more graceful than the cypress; his presence was

---

[1] *Spaspeti*–captain of the troops.
[2] *Amirspasalari*–commander-in-chief.

like sun and moon. Still beardless, he was to be likened to famous crystal and enamel. The beauty of the host of T'hinat'hin's eyelashes was slaying him.

41. HE kept his love hidden in his heart. When he was absent and saw her not, his rose faded; when he saw her, the fires were renewed, his wound smarted more. Love is pitiable; it makes man heart-slain.

42. WHEN the king commanded that his daughter should be enthroned as king, gladness came upon Avt'handil; the fire that was burning Avt'handil was extinguished. He said to himself: "Often will it now fall to my lot to gaze upon her crystal face; perchance I may thus find a cure for my pallor."

43. THE great sovereign of the Arabs published throughout Arabia an edict: "I, her father, appoint my T'hinat'hin queen; she shall illumine all, even as the shining sun. Come and see, all ye who praise and extol!"

44. ALL the Arabians came; the crowd of courtiers increased. The sun-faced Avt'handil, chief of ten thousand times a thousand soldiers, the vizier Sograt, the nearest to the king of all his attendants. When they placed the throne the people said: "Its worth is beyond words!"

45. T'HINAT'HIN, radiant in countenance, was led in by her sire. He seated her, and with his own hands set the crown on her head; he gave her the sceptre, and clad her in the royal robes. The maiden looks on with understanding, all-seeing, like the sun.

46. THE king and his armies retired and did homage. They blessed her and established her as queen, many from many places told forth her praises; the trumpets were blown and the cymbals sounded sweetly. The maiden wept, she shed many tears; she drooped her eyelashes, the tail feathers of the raven.

47. SHE deemed herself unworthy to sit on her father's throne; therefore she weeps, filling the rose-garden with tears. The king admonishes her: "Every father hath a peer in his child," quoth he. "Until now the raging fire in my bosom has not been extinguished."

48. HE said: "Weep not, daughter, but hearken to my counsel: To-day thou art queen of Arabia, appointed sovereign by me; henceforth this kingdom is entrusted to thee; mayest thou be discreet in thy doings, be modest and discerning.

49. "SINCE the sun shines alike on roses and middens, be not thou weary of mercy to great and small. The generous binds the free, and he who is already bound will willingly obey. Scatter liberally, as the seas pour forth again the floods they have received.

50. "MUNIFICENCE in kings is like the aloe planted in Eden. All, even the traitor, are obedient to the generous. It is very wholesome to eat and drink, but what profits it to board? What thou givest away is thine; what thou keepest is lost."

51. THE maiden hearkened discreetly to this her father's advice, she lent ear, she heard, she wearied not of

instruction. The king drank and sported; he was exceeding
joyful. T'hinat'hin contemned the sun, but the sun was like
to T'hinat'hin.

52. SHE sent for her faithful, trusty tutor, and said: "Bring
hither all my treasure sealed by thee, all the wealth
belonging to me as king's daughter." He brought it; she
gave without measure, without count, inexhaustibly.

53. THAT day she gave away all she had gathered since her
childhood; she enriched both small folk and great. Then
she said: "I do the deed my father taught me; let none keep
back any of my hoarded treasure."

54. SHE said: "Go, open whatever treasure there is! Master
of the Horse, lead in the droves of asses, mules, and horses."
He brought them. She gave them away without measure;
she wearied not of generosity. The soldiers gathered together
stuff like pirates.

55. THEY pillaged her treasury as 'twere booty from Turks;
they carried off her fine, sleek Arab steeds. Her munificence
was like a snowstorm whirling down from the sky; none
remained empty, neither youth nor maiden.

56. ONE day passed; there was a banquet, food and drink—a
feast of fruit. A great gathering of warriors sat there to
make merry. The king hung his head, and his brow was
furrowed with sadness. They began to discuss this one with
another: "What weighs upon him, and why grieves he?"

57. AT the head sat the sun-faced Avt'handil, desirable to them that look upon him, the agile leader of the hosts; like a tiger and a lion is he. The old vizier Sograt sat by his side. They said one to the other: "What ails the king, and why has he grown pale?"

58. THEY said: "Some unpleasant thought has come into the king's mind, for nothing has happened here to make him sad." Quoth Avt'handil: "Let us inquire, O Sograt, let him tell us why he is displeased with us; let us venture on some pleasantry; why hath he shamed us?"

59. SOGRAT and the graceful Avt'handil arose; each filled his winecup, and with meek mien drew nigh. Then with smiling faces they cast themselves on their knees before the king. The vizier sportively spoke thus, with eloquent words:

60. "YOU look sad, O king; there is no longer a smile on your face. Thou art right, for, lo! your daughter with lavish hand has given away all your rich and costly treasure. Make her not queen at all; why bring grief on thyself?"

61. WHEN the king heard him he looked up with a smile. He marvelled how he had ventured thus, how he dared to speak such words! "Well hast thou done!" He thanked his vizier. He confirmed this what he said: "He who lays avarice to my charge is a lying chatterer.

62. "THAT afflicts me not, O vizier. This it is that troubles me: Old age draws nigh; I have spent the days of youth,

and nowhere in our dominions is there a man who hath learned from me the knightly arts.

63. "IT is true I have a daughter tenderly nurtured, but God has given me no son; I suffer in this fleeting life. There is none to be compared with me in archery or at the game of ball. It is true that Avt'handil resembles me somewhat, thanks to my teaching."

64. THE proud youth hearkened modestly to these words of the king; with bent head he smiled. Well did a smile befit him; his shining white teeth gleamed like sunshine on a mead. The king asked: "Why smilest thou? Or why wert thou shy of me?"

65. YET again he said: "Why dost thou laugh at me? What is laughable in me?" The youth replied: "I shall tell you if you grant me leave to speak. With what I say be not offended, be not wroth, blame me not, call me not bold, ruin me not for this!"

66. HE anwered: "How can I take aught thou sayst as displeasing?" He took an oath by the sun of T'hinat'hin, that contemner of the sun. Avt'handil said: "Then will I speak boldly; vaunt not yourself of your archery, it is better to speak modestly.

67. "I, AVT'HANDIL, earth under feet, am an archer before you; let us lay a wager; let your armies attend as witnesses. 'Who is like me in the lists?' said you—vain

indeed is denial!–that is decided by the ball and the field."

68. "I WILL not let thee thus dispute with me! Say the word, let us draw the bow; do not shirk. Let us make good men witnesses of our rivalry; then in the field it will be manifest whose praises should be sung."

69. AVT'HANDIL obeyed; they ceased their discourse. They laughed, they sported like children, lovingly and becomingly they behaved. They fixed the wager, and laid down this condition: Whoever shall be beaten, let him go bareheaded for three days.

70. THE king commanded, moreover: "Let twelve slaves be chosen to attend us, twelve to give me arrows and wait upon me; Shermadin alone is for thee; he is equal to them. Let them count the shots and the hits, and give a faithful, unerring report."

71. TO the huntsmen he said: "Travel over the plain, beat in many droves, go yourselves to do this, invite the soldiers to look on, assemble and close round!" The festivity and banquet broke up; there were we pleasantly merry.

II

King Rostevan and Avt'handil Go Hunting

72. EARLY in the morning Avt'handil came forth like a well-grown lily; he was clad in crimson, his face was of crystal and ruby, over his face was a golden veil, he was fair in huntsman's apparel. He rode upon a white steed: he invited the king to come forth.

73. THE king was arrayed, he mounted, they set out for the chase. The people surrounded the field, they made a ring round about it; there was much mirth and excitement; the armies kept the ground. For their wager were they shooting and striving together.

74. THE king commanded the twelve slaves: "Come, accompany us, bring us the swift bows, prepare the arrows, compare what is struck and keep count of the shots." Game began to come in from every corner of the plain.

75. HERDS of game, innumerable, flocked in: stags, goats, wild-asses, high-leaping chamois. Lord and vassal pursued them; what sight could be fairer! Behold the bow, the arrow, and the untiring arm!

76. THE dust from their horses' tracks cut off the sun's rays. They slew, their arrows sped, blood flowed through the field; as the shafts were shot away the slaves brought more of them. The beasts wounded by them could not take another step.

77. THEY ran through that field; they drove the herd before them. They slew and exterminated, they made wroth the God of the heavens, the fields were dyed crimson with the blood they shed from the beasts. Those who watched Avt'handil said: "He is like an aloe-tree planted in Eden."

78. THEY coursed over the whole of that plain only they had travelled over. There on the farther edge of the plain flows a stream; on the bank of the stream are rocks. The game fled into the wood, where horse could not follow. They were tired in spite of their strength.

79. EACH laughingly said to the other: "'Tis I that have won Merry were they; they sported, hither and thither they frolicked. Then came the slaves who had tarried, and the king said: "Tell the truth; we seek not flattery from you."

80. THE slaves said: "We shall speak the truth; think not we shall deceive you, O king; we may by no means liken you to him. Slay us at once if you will, it matters not; we cannot help you in any way. We observed the beasts stricken by him; they could not move forward a step.

81. "TOGETHER ye have slain in all a hundred score, but Avt'handil killed more by a score; he missed not even one at which he aimed his bow, but we cleaned up many of your arrows which left blots on the earth."

82. THE king heard this with as little concern as the result of a game of backgammon, he rejoiced so at the victory of his foster-son; he loved him as the rose loves the nightingale; smiling he made merry, all grief was gone from his heart.

83. THERE they both sat to cool themselves at the foot of the trees; the soldiers assembled and stood round them, countless as chaff; near them were the twelve slaves, bravest of the brave. As they sported they gazed at the stream and the edge of the glens.

III

How the King of the Arabians Saw the Knight Clad in the Tiger's Skin

84. THEY saw a certain stranger knight; he sat weeping on the bank of the stream, he held his black horse by the rein, he looked like a lion and a hero; his bridle, armour and saddle were thickly bedight with pearls; the rose of his cheek was frozen in tears that welled up from his woe-stricken heart.

85. HIS form was clad in a coat of tiger's skin with the fur outside; his head, too, was covered with a cap of tiger's skin; in his hand he held a whip thicker than a man's arm. They looked and liked to look at that wondrous sight.

86. A SLAVE went forth to speak to the knight of the woe-stricken heart, who, weeping with downcast head, seems not a spectacle for jesting; from the jet channel of his eyelashes rains a crystal shower. When the slave approached, he could by no means bring himself to speak a word:

87. THE slave was much perturbed; he dared not address him. A long time he gazed in wonder till his heart was

strengthened; then he said: "The king commands thee to attend him." The slave came near, and greeted him gently; the knight wept on and heard not, he knew not that the slave was there.

88. HE heard not a word of the slave, nor what he said; he was wholly unconscious of the shouting of the soldiers, he was sobbing strangely, his heart burnt up with fires; tears were mingled with blood, and flowed forth as from floodgates.

89. BY his head! His mind was wafted elsewhither. Once again the slave uttered the king's message, but the knight ceased not from weeping and heard him not, nor was the rose-bouquet of speech plucked from his lips.

90. SINCE he answered not, the slave went back and said to Rostevan: "I have told him what you said, but he will not listen. Mine eyes were dazzled as by the sun; my heart was sorely troubled. I could not make him hear a word though I have tarried there so long."

91. THE king wondered, he was wroth, he was vexed in heart against him. He sent the twelve slaves standing before him; he commanded: "Take weapons of war in your hands; go and bring hither him who sits yonder."

92. THE slaves went forth, they drew nigh to him, their armour clanked. Then indeed the knight started up, he wept still more woefully; he raised his eyes and looked round,

he saw the band of warriors. But once he said, "Woe is me!" and spoke no word more.

93. HE passed his hands over his eyes, he wiped away the hot tears, he made fast his sabre and quiver, and braced his strong arms. He mounted his horse—why should he heed the words of slaves? He wended his way elsewhither, and healed not their troubles.

94. THE slaves stretched forth their hands to seize that knight; he fell upon them—alas! even their enemies would have pitied them; he beat one against another, he slew them without raising his hand, some with his whip he smote, cleaving them down to the breast.

95. WRATHFUL was the king, and annoyed; he shouted to the slaves. The youth looked not back nor heeded his pursuers till they were upon him; as many as overtook him he made to look like dead men, he threw down man on man; Rostevan lamented thereat.

96. THE king and Avt'handil mounted to follow the youth. Proud and haughty, his form swayed to and fro, his steed was like Merani,[1] the sun shone brightly on the field; he perceived that the king pursued him.

97. WHEN he saw that the king was come, he struck his horse with his whip; in that very moment he was lost, our eyes

---

[1] Merani—the Pegasus of Georgian legend.

see him not; he seemed to have sunk into an abyss or flown to heaven; they sought, but could find no trace of his course.

98. HIS footprints they sought, and marvelled to find no trace. Thus, leaving no vestige, the man passed away like a Devi.[1] The soldiers mourned for their dead; they hastened to bind up the wounded. The king said: "I have seen cause for loss of joy."

99. HE said: "God is weary of the happiness I have had hitherto, therefore He turns my pleasure into the gall of bitterness; He has wounded me unto death, none can cure me. I am grateful, such are His will and desire."

100. THUS he spoke, and returned; he went frowning away. They summoned not to the lists; groan was mingled with groan. Each ceased from the chase wherever he was following it. Some said: "He is right!" Others said: "O God!"

101. THE king went into his bedchamber sad and frowning. He considered Avt'handil like his son and none else followed him; all went away, the household dispersed; merriment ceased, the castanet and the sweet harp.

102. T'HINAT'HIN heard of her father's great sadness. She rose and came to the door; she with whom the sun strove

---

[1] *Devi*—a djinn.

asked the chamberlain: "Sleeps he or wakes he?" He answered: "He sits brooding; his colour has suffered a change.

103. "AVT'HANDIL alone is present; he sits in a chair before him. They have seen a certain stranger knight; this is the cause of his melancholy." T'hinat'hin said: "I will now depart; it is not time for me to go in. When he asks for me, say: 'She was here but now.'"

104. TIME passed; he inquired: "What doth the maiden, my solace and jewel, my water of life?" The chamberlain replied: "She came, pale-faced, but now; she learned of your sadness and went away, but she is ready to come to your presence."

105. HE said: "Go, call her; how can I bear absence from her! Say unto her: 'Why didst thou turn back, O life of thy father? Come, drive away my grief, heal my wounded heart I will tell thee wherefore my joy is fled.'"

106. T'HINAT'HIN rose and came; she did as her father wished The light of her face is like the splendour of the moon. Her father set her by his side, and, kissing her tenderly, gently, said: "Why camest thou not to me? Wert thou waiting till I sent for thee?"

107. THE maiden said: "O king, who, however venturesome, would dare to approach you aware that you were frowning? This sadness of yours upsets even the lights of heaven. Let a man seek to solve the difficulty; this, I think, would be better than grieving."

108. HE answered: "O my child, however much this sad affair grieves me, thy sight and nearness cause me joy. My grief is dissipated as if I had taken an electuary. I believe that when thou knowest thou too wilt justify my sighing and groaning.

109. "I MET a certain beautiful, wondrous youth, his ray enlightened the firmament and the bounds of the earth. I could not find out why he was afflicted, nor for whom he wept. He came not to see me; I was irritated and quarrelled with him.

110. "WHEN he saw me, he mounted his horse and wiped the tears from his eyes. I cried out that he must be seized; he utterly destroyed my men; like an evil spirit, he was lost to me, he saluted me not like a man. Even now I know not whether he was real or a vision.

111. "I WONDER, what has happened? How was it and what have I seen? He has killed my warriors and shed torrents of blood. Can one believe him a human being when he has so completely disappeared! God was wont to protect me but now he has forsaken me.

112. "HIS tender mercies at length have become thus bitter to me; I have forgotten the past days of my joy. Every one will make me sad and comfort me no more. However long my days may be, I can no more rejoice."

113. THE maid replied: "Deign to hearken to my uttered words. O king, why repine at God or Fate! Why accuse of

bitterness the All-seeing, who is tender to all! And why should the Creator of good make evil!

114. "IF this knight was indeed a man of flesh wandering over the earth, others must have seen him; they will appear to instruct you. If not, it is a devil who has appeared to you to disturb your joys. Refrain from sadness. Why art thou become cheerless?

115. "THIS is my advice: Thou art king, ruler over kings; wide is your boundary, boundless is your power; send everywhere men with news of this story; soon shall you know whether this youth be a mortal or not."

116. HE commanded men and sent them forth even to the four corners of the heavens, saying: "Go, spare yourselves no pains; search, hunt for that youth, let nothing hinder you; send a letter whither ye cannot go nor attain."

117. THE men went, they wandered about for a year; they looked, they sought that youth, they inquired again and again. They could find none of God's creatures who had seen him. Wearied in vain, they returned.

118. THE slaves said: "O king, we have wandered over the lands, yet could we not find that youth, so we could not rejoice; we could meet no living man who had seen him; we have not been able to serve you, now devise some other plan."

119. THE king replied: "My daughter, my child, spoke truth.
I have seen a hideous, unclean spirit; he has been sent as
my foe, flying down from heaven. Grief is fled from me;
I care nothing for all that."

120. THUS he spoke, and sporting was increased with rejoicing
they called the minstrel and the acrobat wherever they
were found, many gifts were distributed, he summoned all
to the throne-room. What other did God create with
generosity like unto his!

IV

T'hinat'hin Sends Avt'handil to Find the Knight

121. AVT'HANDIL sat alone in his chamber, clad only in
    an undergarment; he was singing and making merry,
    before him stood a harp. To him came T'hinat'hin's black
    slave, and said: "She of the aloe form, the moon-faced one,
    sends for thee."

122. AVT'HANDIL was glad to hear this joyful news. He rose
    and donned his best and brightest coat. He rejoiced to meet
    the rose; they had never yet met alone. Pleasant is it to gaze
    on beauty, and be near one beloved.

123. PROUDLY and boldly Avt'handil came to her, he was
    ashamed of none. He will see her for whom the tear of woe
    full oft had flowed. The peerless one sat mournful, she shone
    like lightning, her rays eclipsed the moon.

124. HER fair form was clad in unlined ermine, she wore
    negligently veils whose price it were hard to tell; but her
    black, heart-piercing eyelashes and the thick, long tresses
    which embraced her white throat were her real adornments.

125. PENSIVE she sat in her red veil; she quietly greeted Avt'handil, and gently bade him be seated. The slave placed a seat; he sat down modestly and respectfully. Face to face he gazed on her, full of great joy.

126. AND the maiden answered: "I am frightened, I fear this misery, I should like to be silent, but have no strength and no patience, yet I know the cause that makes thee call me here, my face remains sad and my reason seems lost."

127. THE knight said: "How indeed can I speak to one so dread! If the moon meet the sun it is consumed, it fades away. I am no longer at leisure to think; I fear for myself. Tell me, then, why you are sad and what will relieve you."

128. THE maiden replied with elegant words, not ill-chosen, saying: "Since thou hast hitherto remained far from me, amazed at what has seemed impossible to thee, I must first tell thee of the malady which afflicts me, as a plague.

129. "DOST thou remember, when thou and Rostevan killed game in the plain, how ye saw a certain stranger youth who wiped his tears away? Since then I have been a prey to thoughts of him. I beg thee to search for him, to seek him within the bounds of the sky.

130. "ALTHOUGH I have been unable to hold converse with thee hitherto, yet from afar have I perceived thy love for me; I know that without pause the hail has fallen from thine eyes upon thy cheek. Thou art made prisoner by love; thy heart is taken captive.

131. "THIS service of mine which I bid thee do befits thee for these two reasons: First, thou art a knight, among all flesh there is none like unto thee; secondly, thou art in love with me, this is true and no slander. Go, seek that brother-in-arms, be he near or far.

132. "THEREBY shalt thou strengthen my love for thee; by delivering me from my sadness, thou shalt cripple the foul demon; plant the violet of hope in my heart, strew roses; then come, O lion, I shall meet thee like a sun; meet thou me.

133. "SEEK three years him whom thou hast to seek; if thou find him, come gaily telling thy victory. If thou find him not, I shall believe he was a vision. Thou shalt meet the rosebud unwithered, unfaded.

134. "I SWEAR if I wed any husband but thee, even should the sun become man, incarnate for my sake, may I be cut off for ever from Paradise, may I be swallowed up in Hell, love for thee would slay me, piercing my heart with a knife!"

135. THE knight replied: "O sun, who causest the jet to blink, what else can I answer, or what can I come to know? I awaited death; thou hast renewed my will to live. I shall certainly obey thee like a slave in service."

136. AGAIN he spoke: "O sun, since God has created thee a sun, so that the heavenly planets obey thee wherever they may be, I have heard from you that which has overwhelmed

me with grace; my rose shall not wither, thy ray shines generously upon it."

137. ONCE more they made an oath together, they promised each other, they confirmed it and discoursed much, with many a word; what grief they had borne until now became easy. Their white teeth flashed white lightning as if transparent.

138. THEY sat together, they made merry, they talked simply of a hundred things, they spoke with their crystal and ruby faces and jet eyes. The knight said: "Those who gaze upon thee become mad; my heart is burned to ashes by the fire that comes from thee."

139. THE youth went away, but he could not bear parting from her, he looked back, his eyes were dazed, crystal hails down and freezes the rose, his graceful form was trembling; he had heart for heart, he had lent his to love.

140. HE said to himself: "O sun, separation from thee is thus early manifested on the rose: my crystal and ruby have faded, I am become yellower than amber. What shall I do, then, when I cannot see thee for a long time? This shall be my law: death for the beloved is fitting."

141. HE lay down on his bed, he weeps, it is difficult for him to wipe away the tears, he shivered and swayed, like an aspen in the wind; when he fell into a slumber he dreamed his beloved was near; he starts, he cries out loud, his suffering increases twentyfold.

142. SEPARATION from his beloved made him jealous. Tears like pearls were shed upon the rose, making it tender. When day dawned he apparelled himself, fair to look upon; he mounted his horse, set out and came to court for an audience.

143. HE sent a chamberlain into the hall of audience with a message from him to the king, saying: "O king, I venture to tell you what I have thought: all the face of the earth is subjected to you by your sword; now, if it be better, I shall make known these tidings to all the vicinage.

144. "I WILL go, I shall travel, I shall wage war, I shall go to the rounds of the marches, I shall, by piercing the heart of your enemies, announce T'hinat'hin's accession; I shall cause the obedient to rejoice, the disobedient will I make to weep, I shall send you gifts incessantly, I shall not be sparing of greeting."

145. THE king expressed his great gratitude; he said: "O lion, stretching thine arm in battle irks thee not. Behold, this thy counsel is matched by thy valour. Thou mayst go, but what shall I do if it happen that thou tarry long?"

146. THE knight came in; he did homage, and spoke some words of thanks: "O monarch, I wonder that you should deign to praise me. Now God will perchance lighten for me the darkness of separation, and let me see again in joy your joyful face."

147. THE king hung upon his neck and kissed him like a son;
like unto them have none been, neither upbringer nor
upbrought. The knight rose and went away, to him their
day seemed separated; Rostevan, wise and soft-hearted,
wept for him.

148. AVT'HANDIL set out, a brave knight marching boldly;
twenty days he journeyed, many a day he made one with
the night. She is the joy of the world, she is treasure and
due; he puts not away the thought of T'hinat'hin, of her for
whom the flame burns.

149. WHENEVER he came there was rejoicing in the kingdom,
nobles met him, they gave generous gifts; the sun-faced had
not wasted time in his rapid journey. The drums of joy met
them that came into his presence.

150. HE had a strong city to strike terror in the marches;
outside was a rock, I tell thee, with an unmortared wall.
The knight spent there three days in the pleasant chase; he
invited his pupil, Shermadin, to sit in council with him.

151. THIS is the slave Shermadin, mentioned above, brought
up with Avt'handil, faithful and self-sacrificing to him.
He knew not hitherto of the fire which burned the knight;
now Avt'handil revealed the hopeful words of the sun.

152. HE said: "Lo, Shermadin, for this I am ashamed before
thee; thou knowest all my affairs and hast given heed to
them; but hitherto thou hast not known what tears I have
shed; in her from whom I had suffering I now find joy.

153. "I AM slain by love and longing for T'hinat'hin; from the narcissi hot tears moistened the frosted rose; I could not till now show my hidden woe, now has she bidden me hope, therefore thou seest me joyful.

154. "SHE said to me: 'Learn news of that lost knight, then come, I shall fulfil thy heart's desire; I want no husband save thee, even if a planted tree falls to my lot.' She gave me the balm of my heart until that moment burned.

155. "FIRST, I am a knight; I wish to go forth to serve my lady. Faithfulness to kings is fitting, vassal must act as vassal; then, she has extinguished the fire, my heart is no longer consumed to soot; a man must not bend before misfortune, but meet it like a man.

156. "OF all lords and vassals thou and I are most friendly; therefore I entreat thee to hear this from mine own mouth; in my stead I appoint thee lord and chief over mine armies, I could not entrust this matter to others.

157. "LEAD forth the soldiers to battle, rule the nobles, send messengers to court telling the state of affairs, write letters in my stead, present priceless gifts; why should it be known that I am not here?

158. "REPRESENT me in military duties and in the hunting-field, wait here for me three years, keep my secret; perchance indeed I shall return, my aloe-tree shall not fade; but if I come not back, mourn me, weep for me, utter sighs.

159. "TELL the king forthwith—it is not a desirable deed—announce my death to him, be as if thou art drunk; say to him: 'For him is come to pass the thing which none escape.' Give to the poor my treasure—gold, silver and copper.

160. "THUS shalt thou help me after the best fashion, by this thou shalt aid me most; do not forget me soon, think of me often, take good thought of provision for me, pray for my soul. Remember my childhood; let thy heart be motherly towards me."

161. WHEN the slave heard this he wondered, he was alarmed, from his eyes the hot tears poured like pearls. He said: "How can the heart deprived of thee rejoice? I know thou wilt not stay; so I cannot hinder thee in this matter.

162. "WHY didst thou say thou wouldst appoint me in thy stead? How can I undertake the lordship, how can I imitate thee or resemble thee? It were better that the earth cradled me too than that I should have to think that thou art alone; rather let us both steal forth, I will accompany thee, take me with thee."

163. THE knight replied: "Hearken unto me, I tell thee truth without any falsehood: when a lover would roam the fields alone he must wander; a pearl falls to the lot of none without buying and bargaining. An evil and treacherous man should be pierced with a lance.

164. "TO whom could I tell my secret? Save thee, none is worthy. To whom can I entrust the lordship save thee, who else can do it well? Fortify the marches that the enemy may not encamp near. Perchance I shall return, if God make me not to be wholly lost.

165. "HAZARD kills equally be it one or a hundred. Loneliness can matter nought if the group of the heavenly powers protect me. If I come not hither in three years, then will it beseem thee to mourn and wear funeral garb. I will give thee a letter, whoever is my courtier must obey thee."

V

Avt'handil's Letter to His Vassals

166. HE wrote as follows: "My vassals, my instructors and some my pupils, faithful, trusty and tried, attentive to my behests like shadows, hearken to my letter all assembled!

167. "GIVE ear! I, Avt'handil, earth beneath your feet, write this unto you; with mine own hand have I written this epistle. For a little while I have preferred roaming to drink and song; for bread and meat I shall trust to my bow and thumb.

168. "I HAVE in hand a certain matter which makes me journey to a far country; I depart alone, and this year shall I travel. I ask you only this: I beseech you let me find the realm unshaken by the foe.

169. "I HAVE appointed Shermadin to be lord in my stead; until he learn of my life or death he will shine upon you all like the sun; he will make the rose to be frosted and not fade, he will cause all misdoers to melt away like wax.

170. "YOU know, too, how he has grown up with me like a brother and like a son; you must obey him as if he were Avt'handil; let him make to sound the trumpet, do everything as I have hitherto done; if I come not at the time appointed, mourning and not laughter will be seemly to you."

171. THE eloquent and nice-worded one ended this letter, he tied gold round his waist, habited himself to travel alone; he said: "I shall mount in the plain." The soldiers formed in line, then they came forth; he tarried no time indoors.

172. HE said: "Let all go hence; herein I need none as a partisan." He sent the slaves away also, he remained by himself, alone he withdrew himself, he hastened through the rushes. His slayer, T'hinat'hin, is always in his thoughts

173. HE galloped over that plain; he was lost to the soldiers' sight. What human being might have seen him and pursued him, his sword could not harm him; his arm was hampered. He was heavy laden with a burden of grief for her sake.

174. WHEN the soldiers hunted and sought their lord, and could no longer find the sun-faced, their countenances paled, their great joy turned into heaviness, they ran everywhere to seek him, whoever had a swift horse.

175. "O LION, whom can God put in thy place!" They ran and brought out other messengers from elsewhere; they could learn nothing of him; he passed from that place. His disheartened hosts shed hot tears.

176. SHERMADIN assembled together the courtiers and nobles he showed them the letter in which Avt'handil had told them his tidings. When they heard it, all remained heart-pierced, they beat themselves, there was not a tearless heart, not an unbruised breast.

177. ALL said: "Though our state without him is irksome to us, to whom save thee could he give his seat and throne? Of a truth we shall obey thee, whatever thou commandest any of us." They made that vassal lord; all did him homage.

VI

Avt'handil Sets Forth in Quest of the Knight

178. DIONISI[1] the wise, Ezros[2] bear me witness in this:
It is pitiable when the rose wherewith the ruby of
Badakhshan is not to be compared, and whereto a reedstem
serves as form, becomes covered with rime and frostbitten;
wherever he wanders abroad he is wearied of abodes.

179. AVT'HANDIL travelled over that plain at a flying pace,
he left the bounds of the Arabs, he journeyed in foreign
lands; but separation from his sun had taken away part of
his life. He said: "If I were near her now I should not shed
hot tears."

180. FRESH snow had fallen, and, freezing on the rose,
blasted it. He wished to strike his heart; sometimes he
uplifted his knife. He said: "The world has increased my
grief ninety, a hundredfold. I have gone away from all
rejoicing, from harp, lyre and pipe."

---

[1] Dionysius, the Areopagite.
[2] Ezra.

181. THE rose separated from its sun faded more and more. He said to his heart: "Be patient!" Thus he fainted not wholly. He journeyed through passing strange places on his quest, he asked tidings of wayfarers, he was friendly with them.

182. AVT'HANDIL, shedding tears which flowed to increase the sea, seeks him everywhere. The land seems to him a couch, his arm his pillow. He says to himself: "O beloved, I am far from thee, my heart stays with thee; I lament, for thy sake death would be joy to me."

183. HE journeyed over all the face of the earth, he went thoroughly over it, so that beneath heaven was no place left where he had not been; but he met none who had heard tidings of him he sought; meanwhile three years save three months had passed.

184. HE arrived in a certain dreadful country, exceeding rough; for a month he saw no man, no son of Adam. Neither Vis nor Ramin[1] saw such woe like unto his. By day and by night he thought of her, his beloved.

185. HE reached as a resting-place the slope of a great high mountain; thence appeared a plain which it would take

---

[1] The story of the love of Vis and Ramin, of which the scene is laid in Merv, is the oldest novel in the world. It is by the Persian poet Fakhrud-din Gurgani.

seven days to cross. At the foot of the mountain flowed
a river that could not be bridged; both sides were covered
down to the water's edge with forests.

186. HE goes up, turns round and counts the time, the remaining
days—he has two months left. He sighs at this, he rejoices
not. "Alas! if the thing were revealed!" Again he is timid
in heart by reason of this. No man can turn evil to good;
none can be born again of himself.

187. HE became thoughtful; he stood to consider the matter.
He said to himself: "If I return thus, why have I spent so
much time in the field? What can I dare say to my star,
how I have spent the days? I have learned not even
gossip regarding him I seek.

188. "IF I return not, I must spend yet more time in the quest,
if I can learn no tidings of him I seek; when the time
agreed upon with Shermadin is past, his cheeks will be
bathed in tears; he will go and tell the king whatsoever
things are fitting.

189. "HE will tell him of my death, as I myself bade him.
Then would there be mourning, weeping; bitter would the
matter be for them. Thereafter should I return after
travelling everywhere." On this he thinks, weeping,
distressed in mind.

190. HE said: "O God, why make Thy judgments crooked
because of me? Why, alas! should I have made such a
journey in vain? Thou hast rooted up joys from my heart;
Thou hast given griefs a nest there. All my days my tears
will never cease."

191. THEN he said, "Patience is better," and communed thus
with himself: "Let me not die a day too soon, cast not
down my heart; without God I can do nothing, my tears
flow in vain. No one can change that which is decreed; that
which is not to be will not be."

192. HE said to himself: "Die, for thee it is better than
shameful life. Thou wilt go back; T'hinat'hin, who
brightens the sunny day, will meet thee; she will ask thee
for tidings of that sun; what does groaning avail?" Thus
thinking, he forthwith sets out for the reedy, watery edge
of the wood.

193. "SURELY have I passed by in turn all beings under the
sun, but regarding that man nought can I learn anywhere.
Doubtless they who called him a Kadj[1] spoke truth. Now
tears avail me not; why should I weep in vain?"

194. AVT'HANDIL descended the mountain, he crossed river
and woods, he put his steed to a gallop towards the plain;
the murmur of the water and trees annoys him; the power
of his arms and his pride were spent; the crystal field with
the jetty growth was beautiful.

195. HE resolved to return, he sighed and groaned; he turned
towards the plain; he traced out the road with his eyes; for
a month he has seen no human being anywhere; there were
terrible wild beasts, but he hunted them not.

---

[1] Kadj—a sorcerer

196. THOUGH Avt'handil was become wild with heartgroaning and sighing, yet he wished to eat, after the wont of Adam's race; he killed game with his arrow, with arm longer than Rostom's[1]; he alighted on the edge of the reedy ground and kindled a fire with a steel.

197. HE let his horse pasture while he roasted the meat. He saw six horsemen coming towards him. He said: "They look like brigands; else what good is to be found? No other human being has ever been here."

198. HE took his bow and arrow in his hand, and went gaily towards them. Two bearded men were leading their beardless brother; his head was wounded, his heart had swooned from loss of blood; they wept and grieved; alas! his spirit was almost fled.

199. HE called out: "Brothers, who are ye? I took you for brigands." They replied: "Be calm, help us and put out the fire; if thou canst not help us, add grief to our grief, and make it complete; weep with us who need pity, scratch thy cheeks too."

200. AVT'HANDIL approached; he spoke to the men with the grieved hearts. They told him their story, speaking with tears: "We are three brothers, for this we shed bitter tears; we have a large fortified town in the region of Khataet'hi.[2]

---

[1] A character in *The Book of Kings (Shah-Nameh)*, by Firdausi, a Persian poet of the tenth century.

[2] Cathay.

201. "WE heard of good hunting ground, we went forth to the chase, countless soldiers accompanied us, we dismounted on the bank of a stream; the hunting pleased us, for a month we went not away; we killed wild beasts without measure in the plain, on the mountain and on the ridge.

202. "WE three brothers shamed the archers with us, so we three vied still one with another; 'I kill best, I am better than thou,' thus each pushed his claim with words; we could not manifest the truth, we wrangled, we strove with one another.

203. "TO-DAY we sent away the soldiers loaded with stags' hides. We said among ourselves: 'Let us judge truly who of us is mightier with his arm.' We remained alone, we were private, we killed in our own sight, we shot not before onlookers.

204. "WE had three armour-bearers with us; we ordered the soldiers to go away, mistrusting nought; we hunted over plain, through wood and den, we slaughtered the wild beast, and not even a bird flew up.

205. "SUDDENLY there appeared a knight, morose and gloomy of visage, seated on a black horse, black as Merani; his head and form were clad in a tiger's skin with the fur outside, and beauty such as his has ne'er been seen by man before.

206. "WE gazed upon his rays, we scarce could support the brightness, we said: 'He is a sun on the earth; we cannot

say in heaven.' We wished to seize him, we were venturesome and tried; this is the cause of our sighs, moans, weeping.

207. "I, THE eldest man, earnestly begged my younger brothers to give me this man to fight, my next brother praised his horse, this one only asked leave to conquer him. We granted him this as his due. As we went towards him he came forward unchanged, calmly and in beauty.

208. "RUBY mingled with crystal beautified the pale roses of his cheeks. His tender thoughts towards us turned to wrath, he explained nothing, neither did he let us go, he showed not any consideration for us at all, with his whip he ripened us who had spoken tartly to him.

209. "WE gave him over to our youngest brother, we elders kept back, he seized upon him: 'Stand!' Thus he spake to him with his tongue. The knight held no sword in his hand, so we moved away; he struck him on the head with his whip, we saw the blood flow indeed.

210. "WITH a stroke of his whip he cleft his head thus, like a corpse he became lifeless, like earth he was brought to earth; thus he humbled, levelled with the ground, him who had been audacious to him. Before our eyes he went away, bold, severe and haughty.

211. "HE turned not back again; he went away quietly and without haste. Lo! There he rides—look! Like the sun and moon." The weeping ones joylessly showed him far off to Avt'handil; there only appeared his black steed carrying along that sun.

212. BEHOLD, it befell Avt'handil that his cheeks need no longer be covered with snow from tears, since he had not passed so much time abroad in vain; when a man attains the thing wished for, when he must find what he sought, then need he no longer remember past woes.

213. HE said: "Brothers, I am a wanderer without a place. To seek that knight I have gone far from the home of my upbringing. Now from you I have learned what it was by no means easy to discover. May God never again give you cause to grieve.

214. "AS I meet my wish, my heart's desire, so even may God not let your brother suffer." He showed them his resting-place. "Go at your ease," said he, "give him repose in the shade, rest your weary selves."

215. THUS he spoke and went his way, he spurred on his horse, he flew like a hawk not hindered by the string, or like the moon meeting the sun, the sun apparelled in cloth of gold, for this cause he has extinguished his burning fires.

216. HE drew nearer, he bethought himself how he might contrive the meeting: "Senseless converse yet more enrages a madman. If a wise man would compass a difficult deed, he must not lose his presence of mind and tranquillity.

217. "SINCE your man is so unreasoning and dazed that he suffers not any to speak with him or look on him, if I go up we shall meet only to slaughter each other, either he will kill me or I shall kill him; he will be still more hidden."

218. AVT'HANDIL said: "Why should I suffer so many woes in vain? Whatever he is, it cannot be that he has no nest; let him go whithersoever he will, whatever walls encompass him there shall I seek him if my powers fail not."

219. TWO days and nights they fared, one behind, one before, wearied by day and by night, eating no food; nowhere they paused, not one moment of time, from their eyes tears flowed, moistening the plains.

220. ONE day they travelled, and at eventide high rocks appeared. In the rocks were caves, in front a stream flowed down, it was not possible to say how many rushes were at the water's edge, tall trees whose tops eye could not reach rose high against the rock.

221. THE knight made for the cave; he passed the streams and rocks. Avt'handil alighted from his horse, he betook himself to the great trees, he climbed up to look, at the foot he tethered his horse, thence he watched; that knight went shedding tears.

222. WHEN the knight, the tiger-skin-clad, passed the woods, a maiden dressed in a black mantle came forth to the door of the cave, she wept aloud, her tears uniting with the sea; the knight dismounted, with his arms he embraced her neck

223. THE knight said: "Sister Asmat'h, our bridges are fallen into the sea; we shall never, timely, come upon the track of her for whom fires burn us." Thus he spoke and beat his

hands upon his breast; the tears rained down. The maiden swooned, he embraced her; they wiped each other's tears of blood.

224. THE forest became thicker from the tearing of their hair; each embraced the other, the youth the maid, and the maid the youth; they wailed, they lamented, the rocks reechoed their voices; Avt'handil gazed in wonder on their behaviour.

225. THAT maid composed her soul, she endured the wound of her heart, she led the steed into the cave, she took off its trappings, she unbuckled the knight, she ungirded his armour. They went in. That day they did not come out again.

226. AVT'HANDIL was surprised. "How am I to know this story?" said he. Day dawned. The maiden came forth clad in the same colour; she put the bridle on the black horse, she furbished it with the end of her veil; she saddled the horse, she carried the armour quietly, with no clattering.

227. IT was the custom, it seems, with that knight never to tarry longer. The maiden wept and beat her breast, she tore her thick hair; they embraced each other, he kissed her and mounted his horse. Asmat'h, already gloomy, became more gloomy still.

228. AVT'HANDIL once more saw near him the face of that man, his moustaches had hardly grown, he was without a beard. "Is it not the sun of heaven?" said he. He smelt the

smell of the aloe wafted on the wind. For him the killing of a lion was just as easy as for a lion to kill a goat.

229. HE rode out the same road he had come in by the day before, he passed the rushes, he went beyond, far into the plain. Avt'handil gazed in wonder; secretly he was hidden in the tree. He said: "God has managed this matter exceeding well for me.

230. "HOW could God have done better for me than this? I will seize the maid, I will make her tell me the story of that knight; I shall also tell her all mine, I shall make her know the truth. I shall not smite the knight with the sword, nor shall I have to be pierced by him."

VII

Avt'handil's Tale as Told to Asmat'h in the Cave

231. HE came down and loosed his horse, which he had tied to the tree, he mounted and rode up; the door of the cave was open, the heart-shaken, tear-flooded maiden ran out thence; she thought the rose-faced, crystal-haloed one was come back.

232. SHE knew not the face, it was not like the face of that knight; swiftly she turned, with a cry she made for rock and tree; the knight leaped from his horse, seized her like a partridge in a net; the rocks resounded with the maid's monotonous cry.

233. SHE yielded not to that knight; even the sight of him was hateful. Like a partridge under an eagle she fluttered hither and thither; she called on a certain Tariel for help, but he succoured her not. Avt'handil threw himself on his knees; he entreated her with his fingers.

234. HE said: "Hush! what ill can I do thee? I am a man of Adam's race. I have seen those roses and violets grown pale. Tell me something of him. Who is the cypress-formed, the halo-faced? I shall do nought else to thee, be comforted, cry not thus loudly."

235. THE weeping girl said—and her speech was more like discussion than complaint.—"If thou be not mad, let me go; if thou art mad, return to reason. Now thou lightly askest me to tell thee a very hard matter; try not in vain, look not to me to tell his story."

236. AGAIN she said: "O knight, what wilt thou, or what dost thou request of me? This thing cannot be even written with the pen. Once thou shalt say 'Tell me!' a hundred times I shall tell thee 'No!' As smiling is better than weeping, so I prefer mourning to song."

237. "MAIDEN, thou knowest not whence I come, what woes I have endured! For as long as I have sought tidings, from none have I heard them. I have found thee; however much my words may annoy thee, I cannot let thee go till thou tell me. Be not bashful with me."

238. THE maiden said: "Why have I fallen in with thee? Who am I? Or who art thou? The sun is not near me, this thou knewest, O hoarfrost, therefore thou thus annoyest me; long discourse is tedious, so I shall speak shortly to thee; on no account shall I tell thee aught, do whatsoever thou wilt."

239. YET again he adjured her, he threw himself on his knees before her, but nought could he win from her; he wearied of entreaty, his indignation mounted to his face, blood flowed to his eyes, he arose, he drew her by the hair, he put a knife to her throat.

240. THUS he spoke: "How can I forgive thee so much ill-will?
If I weep, shall the tear be in vain. It is better for thee
to tell me, I shall trouble thee no more; if not, may God
slay mine enemy as I slay thee!"

241. THE maid replied: "Thou hast done exceeding ill to
think of using force. If thou kill me not I shall not die;
I am hale and alive. Why shall I tell thee anything until
the time when I shall no longer see woes, and if thou kill
me I shall have no head to converse with thee."

242. AGAIN she said: "Oh, why didst thou find me! Who art
thou that speakest with me? Who? I cannot be made to tell
this story with living tongue. I will make thee kill me at
mine own wish; like a despised letter, easily shalt thou
tear me.

243. "THINK not that death would be suffering to me, for it
would free me from weeping; it is the drier-up of the ford of
tears; the whole world seems to me as straw, even so do I
weigh it; I know not who thou art, that I should tell thee
trusty words."

244. THE knight said to himself: "Thus shall I not make her
speak, I must think of some other way; it is better to ponder
the matter." He let her go, and sat down apart; he wept, he
began to shed tears. He said to the maiden: "I have angered
thee; now I know not, alas! how I shall survive."

245. THE maiden sat morose, she is sulky, she is not yet sweetened. Avt'handil sits below weeping; no longer does he speak. In the rose-garden the pool of tears is dammed up. The maiden, too, weeps over yonder, her heart softening towards him.

246. She pitied the weeping knight, therefore her hot tears flowed, but she sat, strange to the stranger, she spake not. The knight perceived that her hasty thoughts towards him were calmed; with flowing tears he entreated her; he arose and bent his knee before her.

247. HE said: "I know that now I am by no means to hope from thee; I have angered thee; I remain a stranger to thee and thus lonely; yet even now I have hope for myself from thee, for it is said that sin shall be forgiven unto seven times.

248. "THOUGH my beginning in service has pleased thee ill, it is fitting to pity the lover; understand thou this: from any other, whomsoever, I can have no aid, none is my strength. I yield thee my life for my heart's sake. What more can I do?"

249. WHEN the maid heard from the knight of his love, with heart sobs she began to shed tears a hundredfold more; again she raised her voice in wailing, she smiled not. God gave Avt'handil his wish, his heart's comfort.

250. HE said to himself: "These words have changed her colour; doubtless her tears flow faster for that she is mad for someone." He spoke once more: "O sister, a lover is pitied even by his foes; thou, too, knowest that he himself seeks death, he shuns it not.

251. "I AM a lover, a madman to whom life is unbearable. My sun sent me to seek that knight. Even a cloud not reach me where I have been on that quest. I have found thy heart; his to thee, thine to him.

252. "HIS face I have imprinted on my heart like a holy picture. For him mad, cut off, have I given up all my joy. One of two things do thou to me: make me a prisoner or set me free, give me life or slay me, adding grief to grief."

253. THE maiden spoke to the knight a word more pleasant than her first: "What thou hast now thought of is much better; just now thou didst sow enmity in my heart, now thou hast found in me a friend more sisterly than a sister.

254. "THEN, since thou hast thought of love as thine aid, henceforth it will not be that I shall not be thy servant; if I devote not myself to thee, I shall make thee mad, I shall make thee sad; I shall die for thy sake if I find not some means to help thee.

255. "NOW, whatever I tell thee, if thou wilt be obedient to me therein thou shalt meet whatever thou seekest, thou

shalt certainly not fail; if thou hearkenest not to me thou
shalt not find, let thy tears flow as will; discontent
with the world shall come upon thee, thou shalt die, thou
shalt be put to shame."

256. THE knight replied: "This only resembles one thing: Two
men were journeying somewhere along some road; the one
who was behind saw the one in front fall into a well. He
came up, called down, weeps and cries 'Woe!'

257. "THUS he spoke: 'Comrade, stay there, wait for me, I
go to bring ropes, I want to pull thee out.' The man who
was beneath laughed, he marvelled greatly, he shouted up:
'Unless I wait, whither can I flee from thee, whither can
I go?'

258. "NOW, sister, thou holdest the rope about my neck;
without thee I can undertake nothing; whatever thou doest
to me rests with thee, thou art balm to the mad. Otherwise
who would bind his sound head with hay-ropes?"

259. THE maid replied: "Thy discourse, O knight, pleases me.
Doubtless thou art some good knight, worthy of the praise
of the wise. Since thou hast heretofore suffered such griefs,
hearken to what I tell thee, and thou hast found what thou
seekest.

260. "NOWHERE can news of that knight be found. If he
himself tell thee not it will not be told; none other shouldst
thou believe. If thou canst wait so long, wait until he come.

Be calm; freeze not the rose, let not be snowed up in
tears.

261. "I WILL tell thee our names if thou wishest to know
them: Tariel is the name of that distracted knight; I am
called Asmat'h, whom the hot fire burns, sigh upon sigh,
not once alone, but many times.

262. "MORE words about him than these I cannot tell thee. The
elegant, slender-formed roams the plain. I eat, alas! alone
of the meat brought by him from the chase. He may come
anon, I know not, or he may tarry a long time.

263. "I ENTREAT thee to wait; go not elsewhere. When he
comes I shall plead with him; it may be I shall be able to
do something. I shall make you known to each other; I shall
make him love thee. He himself will tell thee his story; thou
shalt make thy beloved to rejoice."

264. THE knight listened to the maid, he was obedient, he
submitted. Thereupon they looked round, they heard a
splash from the glen, they saw the moon come forth from
the water, its rays beaming. They hastened back: they
made no long tarrying there.

265. THE maid said: "O knight, God give thee soon what thou
desirest; but make thyself unseen, hide thyself inside. No
human being is disobedient to that knight; perchance I
may so contrive that the sight of thee anger him not."

266. THE maiden hastily hid Avt'handil secretly in the cave.
That knight alighted from his horse; his quiver and sword
adorn him. They wept aloud, their tears flowing even to the
sea. Avt'handil gazed forth, himself hidden from view.

267. THE bath of tears turned the crystal to the colour of
jasper. A long time the knight and that black-robed maiden
wept. She unbuckled his armour and took it in; she also led
in the horse. They were silent; the black knife of jet cut
off the tears.

268. AVT'HANDIL watched, a prisoner but now freed from
his dungeon. The maid laid down the tiger's skin, the
knight sat upon it, he sighs with added grief; the jetty
eyelashes are plaited by tears of blood.

269. THAT maiden betook herself to the lighting of a gentle
fire with a steel; she thought he would eat meat roasted,
whole; she gave it to him, he bit off a piece, it was difficult
for him to eat, he had not strength; he began to spit it
out unchewed.

270. HE lay down a little, he fell asleep, but only for a short
time; he was afraid, he screamed aloud, he leaped up as
if dazed, he cried and incessantly beat his breast with a
stone and his head with a stick; the maiden sits apart
looking at him, and scratches her face.

271. "WHY hast thou returned?" she asked. "Tell me what has
happened to thee." He answered: "I came upon a certain
king hunting; he had countless soldiers, heavy weighed their

baggage, he hunted in that plain where beaters were scattered.

272. "IT was melancholy for me to see men, the fire flamed up still more; I came not near to meet him; I pitied myself. I returned pale from them. I hid in the wood. I thought: 'If he pursues me no more, I shall go away at daybreak tomorrow.'"

273. THE maiden's tears sprang forth a hundredfold, ten thousandfold more. She said: "Thou roamest alone with wild beasts in the deep forest, thou approachest no man for converse and entertainment; thou canst not help her thus; why dost thou waste thy days in vain?

274. "THOU hast fared over the whole face of the earth; how couldst thou not find one man in whom to take pleasure, and who could be with thee without making thee mad, though it would not lessen thy grief? If thou diest and she perisheth, what doth this profit thee?"

275. HE said: "O sister, this is like thy heart, but for this wound there is no balm upon earth. Who can find such a man as hath not yet come into the world? My joy is death, the severance of flesh and soul.

276. "WHERE, why should God cause a man to be born under the same planet as I, even if I desired his companionship and converse? Who could bear my woes, or even attempt it? Save thee, sister, I have no human being anywhere."

277. THE maid said: "Be not angry with me, I fear and entreat thee; since God has appointed me thy vizier, I cannot conceal the best that I know in the matter: to go to extremes is of no use; thou hast overstepped the bounds."

278. THE knight replied: "I know not what thou askest of me; tell me clearly. How can I create a man for my service without God? God needs me to be unhappy; what can I do? Of a truth I am become as a wild beast, to this pass have I brought myself."

279. THE maid again spoke: "I have harassed thee with overmuch advice, but if I could find a man who would come to thee of his own free will, who would stay near thee, who would rejoice thee by his acquaintance, wilt thou swear not to kill him nor do him any hurt?"

280. HE answered: "If thou wilt show him to me, greatly shall I rejoice at sight of him. I swear by the love of her for whose sake I wander mad in the fields, I shall do nought unpleasing, I shall never cause any bitterness to him; I shall be pleasant and love him, and do all I can to be amiable."

VIII

The Meeting of Tariel and Avt'handil

281. THE maid rose and went to bring that knight. "He is not angry," quoth she, to encourage him. She took him by the hand and led him forth, like the full moon. When Tariel saw him he thought him like the sun.

282. TARIEL met him. They were both fit to be ranked as suns, or as the moon in heaven, cloudless, spreading her rays on the plain beneath. Compared with them the aloe-tree was of no worth; they were like the seven planets; to what else shall I liken them?

283. THEY kissed each other, they were not bashful at being strangers; they opened the rose, from their lips their white teeth shone transparent. They embraced each other's neck, together they wept; their jacinth, which was worth rubies, they turned into amber.

284. THE knight turned, he grasped Avt'handil's hand in his hand; they sat down together, and wept long with hot tears Asmat'h calmed them with wonderful words: "Slay not yourselves; darken not the sun with your eclipse."

285. TARIEL'S rose was only covered with a light frost, not frozen. He said to Avt'handil: "Haste, tell me thy secret. Who art thou? Whence art thou come? Where is thy home? As for me, death has forgotten me; even by it am I abandoned."

286. AVT'HANDIL gave answer; beautiful are his words: "O lion and hero Tariel, thou who behavest gently, I am an Arabian, from the court of Arabia; I am consumed by love, unquenchable fire burns me.

287. "I LOVE the daughter of my lord; her lusty-armed servants now view her as their queen. Though thou knowest me not, I have seen thee, if thou wilt call it to mind. Dost thou remember when thou slewest the strong-armed slaves?

288. "WE saw thee roaming in the plain, and we came upon thee. My lord was angry with thee, and we quarrelled fiercely with thee. We called thee, thou camest not, we pursued thee with soldiers; thou didst dye the fields crimson with the blood thou madest to flow.

289. "THOU didst cut the heads of all with a whip, without a sword. The king mounted, thou wert lost to us, we could not cut off thy track; like a Kadj thou wert hidden, the slaves were terrified. This enraged us still more; we were completely stunned.

290. "THE king became gloomy; you know that a monarch also has humours. They looked for thee, they sought thee everywhere, they traced a map. They could find none who had seen thee, neither young nor old. Now she has sent me, she to whom neither sun nor ether is to be compared.

291. "SHE said to me: 'Learn for me news of that vanished sun; then will I do that which thou desirest.' She told me that for three years the stream of tears was to flow without her; dost thou not marvel that I could bear the lack of the sight of her smile?

292. "UNTIL now I have seen no man who saw thee. I saw Kurds who spoke rudely with joy; thou didst strike them with thy whip; one thou madest like a corpse; they whose brother was dying told me."

293. TARIEL recalled their bygone fight. He said: "I remember the affair, though it happened long ago. I saw thee and thy master together at the chase. I was weeping because I was thinking, alas! of my destroyer.

294. "WHAT did you want with me? What did you desire? What had we in common? You, mighty, were sporting; we bathed our cheeks in tears. When you set the slaves upon me you dared to take me; now, methinks, instead of capturing me you bare away corpses.

295. "I LOOKED round when I saw thy lord approach me, I had pity on his kingship; therefore I laid not my hands upon him, I fled before your eyes, I said nothing. My horse looks an invisible spirit, to what else can I compare him?

296. "BEFORE a man can blink or wink the eye, I can flee that which I know to be unpleasant. Those Kurds, on the other hand, I did not consider myself unjust to them; their overbearance and my prowess ill became them.

297. "NOW thou art come with good intent, the sight of thy face rejoices me, O cypress-tormed, sunlike-faced, brave as a hero; but thou hast toiled, thou art not untried by trouble; hard is it to find a man abandoned by God in heaven."

298. AVT'HANDIL said: "How dost thou praise me, thou worthy of the praise of the tongue of the wise? What am I to deserve such praise from thee? Thou art the image of the one sun, the light of heaven above, for the misery of the flowing of so many tears cannot change thee.

299. "THIS day has made me forget her who darkened my heart I renounce her service; as for that, it shall be as thou wishest. Thus, though a jacinth is better, still a thousand times more do I desire enamel. I shall stay near thee till death, more than this I desire not."

300. TARIEL said: "Thy heart now is warm to me. I am amazed. What service worthy of thine attachment have I done for thee? But such is the law: lover pities lover. Thou art parted from thy beloved; what can recompense thee for this?

301. "THOU art come forth to seek me in thy lady's service. God has made thee find me. Thou also hast endeavoured manfully. But how shall I tell thee why I am thus wandering? If I speak of it, hot fire will fire me; I shall become a flame, a smoke."

302. UPON this Tariel was silent, burned and enflamed. He said to Asmat'h: "Since thou hast been near me all the

time, how dost thou not know that this bruised bruise is incurable? Anew this weeping knight burns me; I am his debtor for tears.

303. "HOW can man find that which has not been created by God? Therefore has my heart been born in the embers of a glowing furnace. My path has been cut off, I am bound in a net, caught in a snare. Of my feasts—only straw for my bed and my nabadi[1] remain.

304. "BUT merciful God, whom the sun has made known to us, has accorded me two blessings to-day: the first is that two lovers will be reunited by me, and the second that mayhap the flaming fire will be unable to consume me."

305. HE said to the knight: "Whatever man takes to himself a brother—ay, or a sister—must have not care of death and trouble for their sake. How should God save the one if He cause not the other to perish? Listen, and I shall tell thee whatever befall me."

306. HE said to Asmat'h: "Come, sit down here, bring water with thee, sprinkle me when fainting, bathe my breast. If thou seest me a corpse, weep for me, sob ceaselessly, dig a grave for me, here let the earth cradle me."

307. HE sat down unbuttoned to tell his tale; he laid bare his shoulders. Like the sun clad in clouds he sat; a long time

---

[1] *Nabadi*—a shaggy cloak of goat-skin.

he shed no ray. He could not open his lips to speak; he clenched them. Then he drew his breath, cried out, hot tears gushed forth.

308. HE sobbed: "O beloved, mine own, lost to me! My hope and life, my thought, my soul, my heart! Who cut thee off I know not, O heart a hundred times kindled!"

IX

The Telling of His Tale by Tariel When He First Told It to Avt'handil

309. "HEARKEN, give heed to the hearing of my tidings, discourses and deeds such that I can scarce utter them! She who maddens me, for whom I am overpowered by melancholy, for whom flow streams of blood, from her I never expect comfort.

310. "THOU knowest, as every man knows, of India's seven kings. P'harsadan possessed six kingdoms; he was sovereign generous, rich, bold, ruler over kings, in form a lion, in face a sun, a conqueror in battle, a leader of squadrons.

311. "MY father sat on the seventh throne, king, terror of adversaries; Saridan was his name; not underhanded in the destruction of enemies, none dared offend him either openly or secretly; he hunted and made merry, careless of Fate.

312. "HE hated solitude; it created hosts of cares in his heart. He said to himself: 'By conquest I have taken from foes the vicinage of the marches, I have chased them forth

everywhere, I am seated in power, I have pomp and might';
he said: 'I will go and enjoy the favour of King P'harsadan.'

313. "HE resolved to despatch an envoy to P'harsadan; he
sent a message saying: 'Thou hast the rule of all India; now
I also wish to exhibit before you the power of my heart;
may the glory of my faithful service remain!'

314. "P'HARSADAN, on hearing those tidings, made great
jubilation. He sent a message: 'I, ruler of the lands, give
thanks to God, because thou, a king like me enthroned in
India, hast done this; now come, I shall honour thee like
a brother and parent.'

315. "HE bestowed on him one kingdom well worthy of a good
knight, also the dignity of Amirbar–the Amirbar in India is
also Amirspasalari; when he sat as king, he was not absolute:
he only lacked the overlordship, in all else he was sovereign
lord.

316. "THE king considered my father equal with himself; he
said: 'I wager that no man has an Amirbar like mine.'
They waged war and they hunted; they forced their enemies
to make peace. I am not like him, as no other man is like me.

317. "THE king and the sun-like queen had no child, for this
they were sad; a time came when the armies were seized
with alarm thereat. Woe befall that cursed day when I was
given to the Amirbar! The king said: 'I shall rear him as my
son; he is even of mine own race.'

318. "THE king and queen took me as their child, they brought me up as lord of all the soldiers and countries, they gave me wise men to instruct me in the behaviour and deportment of kings. I grew up, I became like the sun to look upon, like a lion in mien.

319. "ASMAT'H, tell me whatever thou knowest to be false in my story! When I was five years old I was like an opened rosebud; to me it appeared no labour to slay a lion—it was like a sparrow. P'harsadan cared not that he had no son.

320. "ASMAT'H, thou art witness of my pallor! I was fairer in beauty than the sun, as the hour of dawn than darkness. Those who saw me said: 'He is like a nursling of Eden.' My person now is but a shadow of what it was then.

321. "I WAS five years old when the queen became with child." When he had said this the youth sighed, and weeping said: "She bare a daughter." He was like to faint; Asmat'h sprinkled water on his breast. He said: "She for whom these flames now burn me was like the sun even then.

322. "THE tongue with which I now speak cannot utter the praise of her. P'harsadan sat down to announce the good news with jubilation and pomp. From everywhere came kings bringing many kinds of gifts. They gave away treasure; they filled the soldiers with presents.

323. "MISSIVE followed missive when the queen was confined.
Many messengers came, all India was informed. The moon
and the sun rejoiced, the sky sparkled with joy, every
human being was happy and frolicked in merriment.

324. "THE guests at the birth festivities separated. They began
to rear me and the maiden; even then she was like the
sun's rays augmented threefold; the king and queen loved
us and looked on us alike. Now shall I utter the name of her
for whom my heart is consumed by flame."

325. THE knight swooned when he sought to mention her name.
Avt'handil also wept; his fire made his heart like soot. The
maiden revived Tariel; she sprinkled water on his breast.
He said: "Hearken! but this truly is the day of my death.

326. "THAT maiden was called by the name Nestan-Daredjan.
When she was seven years old she was a gentle and wise maid
moon-like, not equalled by the sun in beauty; from her how
can the heart bear separation, even if it were adamant or
forged steel?

327. "SO she grew up, and I was able to go to battle. Since
the king looked upon the maid as the heir to the kingship,
he gave me back into the hands of my father. When I was
of that age I played at ball, I hunted, I killed a lion like a
cat.

328. "THE king built a house, and in it a dwelling for the
maid; for stone he used bezoar, cut jacinths and rubies; in

front was a little garden and a fountain of rose-water for bathing; there abode she for whose sake a furnace of flame consumes me.

329. "DAY and night cut aloes poured forth their incense from censers. Sometimes she sits in the tower; sometimes she descends to the garden when it is shaded. Davar was the king's sister, a widow who had been wedded in Kadjet'hi; to her the king gave his child to be taught wisdom.

330. "THE palace was curtained with cloth of gold and costly brocades; none of us saw her how she became crystal and rose of face; Asmat'h and two slaves she had, they played backgammon. There her shape was formed; she grew up like a tree in Gabaon.

331. "I WAS fifteen years old. The king brought me up as a son; by day I was before him, and he did not even give me leave to sleep at home. In power a lion, to the eye a sun, in form I was like one reared in Eden; they lauded the feats done by me in archery and in the lists.

332. "THE arrow I shot slew beasts and game; returned from the plain, I played at ball in the moedan[1]; then I went home, I used to make a feast, accustomed continually to rejoice. Now Fate has sundered me from the crystal-ruby-faced!

---

[1] *Moedan*—public square.

333. "MY father died; the day of his death was come. This
event brought to nought all sign of merriment for
P'harsadan; it rejoiced those whom terror or fear of him
as a foe exhausted; the loyal began to mourn and his
enemies began to rejoice.

334. "I SAT in the dark for a year, annihilated by Fate; by
day and by night I groaned, calmed by none; then courtiers
came to draw me from the dark, they told me the king's
command; he said: 'Son Tariel, wear mourning no longer!

335. "'WE are even more grieved than thou at the loss of our
peer.' He gave a hundred treasures, and commanded that
I should put off my black raiment. He gave me all the
lordship that had belonged to my father. 'Thou shalt be
Amirbar; fulfil the duties of thy father.'

336. "I WAS inflamed; inextinguishable furnaces burned me
for my father's sake. The courtiers standing before me
led me out from the dark; the monarchs of India made
jubilation at my coming forth; they met me afar off, they
kissed me with regard like parents.

337. "THEY seated me near their thrones, they honoured me
like their son, they both told me gently of my obligation
of duty; I was recalcitrant, and to behave as my father had
done seemed a horror to me. They would take no denial: I
submitted, and did homage to them as Amirbar.

338. "MANY years have passed, I know not how to tell you, it is so difficult to relate. Variable, inconstant, the world always does evil. The sparks from its anvil burn me incessantly."

X

Tariel Tells the Tale of His Falling in Love
When He First Fell in Love

339. WHEN he had wept for some time he again began to tell his tale: "One day the king and I had come home from the chase, and he said: 'Let us see my daughter!' He took me by the hand.... Does it not surprise thee that I live when I remember that time?

340. "I SAW the garden fairer indeed than all places of delight: the voice of birds was heard, sweeter than a siren's, there were many fountains of rose-water for baths, over the door were hung curtains of cloth of gold.

341. "SLIM cypress encircled the emerald wall of the courtyard The king dismounted and drew near to the bezoar-stone tower. He entered; the great palace was hung with rugs. My soul, how can you endure the piercing lances of those days?

342. "THE king ordered me to take some durajis[1] and carry them to the maiden. I took them and went to burn myself

---

[1] *Durajis*–francolins.

at a flame. Then I began to pay the debt of Fate. It needs a lance of adamant to pierce a heart of rock.

343. "I KNEW he wished none to see his sun-like one; I stood outside, and the king went in through the curtain of the door; I could see nothing, I only heard the sound of talk; he commanded Asmat'h to take the durajis from the Amirbar.

344. "ASMAT'H drew aside the curtain; I stood outside the curtain. I saw the maiden; a lance pierced my mind and heart. Asmat'h came, I gave her the durajis, she took them from me who was burned with fire. Ah me! since then in eternal fires I burn!"

345. NOW failed that light which despises even the sun; he could tell no more, he fainted, groaning bitterly. Avt'handil and Asmat'h wept; the vicinage re-echoed their voices. They said gloomily: "The arms that brought to nought heroes are become useless, alas!"

346. ASMAT'H sprinkled water upon him, Tariel came back to consciousness; for a long time he could not speak, melancholy bound and overcame his heart; he sat down and moaned bitterly, his tears were mingled with the earth; he said: "Woe is me! what a great agitation is her memory to me!

347. "TRUSTERS in this ephemeral world have their pick of her gifts, they are lucky, but at last are not spared her treachery; I praise the prudence of those sages who oppose her. Hearken to my tidings if life remain in me!

348. "THEY took in the durajis, I could make no way for myself. I fell, I fainted, force was fled from mine arms and shoulder. When I came back to life I heard the voice of weeping and woe; the household surrounded me like one who is embarking on a ship.

349. "I LAY in a fair bed in a great chamber; the king and queen wept over me with undrying tears, they scratched their faces with their hands, tearing their cheeks; mullahs sat round, they called my sickness bewitchment of Beelzebub.

350. "WHEN the king saw mine eyes open he embraced my neck; he said to me with tears: 'My son, my son, dost thou indeed live? Speak one word!' I could give no answer; like a madman I was greatly affrighted. Again I fell into a faint blood rushed into my heart.

351. "ALL the muqris[1] and mullahs watched round me, in their hands they held the Koran, all of them read; they thought I was struck by the Adversary of mankind, I know not of what they raved. For three days I was lifeless; inextinguishable fires burned me.

352. "THE doctors also marvelled, saying: 'What manner of sickness is this ? Nothing medicable afflicts him; some

---

[1] *Muqris*–an Arabian word meaning learned expounders of the Mussulman doctrine.

melancholy has laid hold of him.' Sometimes I leaped up like a madman, I uttered idle words. The queen poured forth tears enough to make a sea.

353. "FOR three days was I in the palace neither alive nor dead; then understanding came back to me, I remembered what had befallen me; I said: 'Alas! in what a plight am I, despairing of life!' I prayed the Creator for patience; I ventured to make a discourse of entreaty.

354. "I SAID: 'O God! abandon me not, hearken to my supplication, give me strength to endure that I may rise a little; to stay here will reveal my secret; let me reach home! He did so ànd I mended; I steeled my wounded heart.

355. "I SAT up.... Many men were come from the king, they carried back the good news: 'He sits up!' The queen ran in, the king came running bareheaded, he knew not what he did, he glorified God, all others were silent.

356. "THEY sat down on either side of me; I sipped some soup, I said: 'My lord, now my heart is stronger. I long to mount a horse, to see river and field.' They brought me a horse, I mounted, the king went with me.

357. "WE went forth; we passed by the moedan and the riverbank. I went home, I sent back the king, who accompanied me to the threshold of the house. I went in; I felt worse, woe was added to woe; I said to myself: 'I would die! What more can Fate do to me!'

358. "THE bath of tears changed the crystal to saffron colour;
ten thousand knives cut my heart still more. The doorkeeper
of the bedchamber entered, he called out the treasurer;
I said to myself: 'What news does he know, either this one
or that one?'

359. "'IT is Asmat'h's slave.' 'What knows he?' I called.
'Ask!' He came in. He gave me a love-letter. I read it.
I was surprised that I could diminish the burning of my
heart; I had no suspicion of her, my heart burned with
melancholy for this.

360. "I WAS surprised wherefore I was loved, or how Asmat'h
dared to declare it to me. But, thought I, disobedience
avails not, she will denounce me for silence, she will lose
hope of me, then will she reproach me. I wrote what answer
was fitting to enamourment.

361. "DAYS passed, and heart burned me still more with
flame. I no longer watched the soldiers going to the plain
to sport. I could not go to court. Many physicians began to
come. Then I began to pay the joys and debts of the world.

362. "THE physicians could do nothing for me; the twilight
of darkness fell upon my heart. No one else discovered the
burning of the hot fire. They blamed my blood. The king
ordered them to bleed my arm; I let it be done, so as to
hide my sufferings, to let none suspect.

363. "AFTER my arm was bled I lay melancholy alone in my
bed. My slave came in; I glanced at him to ask what he

wanted. 'It is Asmath's slave,' said he. I told him to bring him in. I thought in my heart: 'What has she found in me, or who is she?'

364. "THE slave gave me a letter; I read it slowly. I learned from the letter that she wished to come quickly to me. I wrote in reply: 'It is time. Thou art right to be surprised. I shall come if thou wantest me; suspect me not of tardiness in coming.'

365. "I SAID to my heart: 'Why do such lances make thee thus melancholy? I am Amirbar, king: all the Indians are subject to me. If it come to their knowledge they will weight the deed a thousand times; if they find it out they will not let me travel in their regions.'

366. "A MAN came from the king saying he wished to hear the news. I ordered him in; the king commanded me to be bled. I said: 'My arm has been bled; I have begun to mend. I come to your presence; it is fitting for me to rejoice the more for this again.'

367. "I WENT to court. The king said: 'Now, do this no more!' He seated me quiverless on a horse; he girded not my loins. He mounted, he let fly the falcons, the durajis shrank with fear, the archers formed in ranks said: 'Bravo! Bravo!'

368. "WE made a feast at home that day for those who had been in the plain; the singers and minstrels were not dumb; the king gave away many precious stones praised as unique; none of those present were left dissatisfied that day.

369. "I STROVE, but could not keep myself from melancholy;
I thought on her, the fire burned into a larger flame in my
heart. I took my comrades with me, I sat down; they called
me an aloe-tree; I drank and feasted to hide my misery
and grief.

370. "MY treasurer of the household whispered in mine ear:
'A certain woman asks if she can see the Amirbar; veils
cover her face, worthy of the praise of the wise.' I replied:
'Take her to my chamber; she is invited by me.'

371. "I ROSE up; those sitting at the banquet prepared to
depart. 'By your leave,' said I, 'do not rise; I shall not
tarry long.' I went forth and entered the chamber, a slave
stood on guard at the door, I nerved my heart to suffer
shame.

372. "I HALTED at the door; the woman came forward to
meet me and did me homage. She said to me: 'Blessed is he
whoever is worthy to come before thee!' I marvelled;
whoever saluted a lover? I thought: 'She knows not how
to make love; and she knew she would sit quiet.'

373. "I ENTERED, sat down on the sofa, she came to the edge
of the carpet, not daring to sit near me for she did not
judge herself worthy. I said: 'Why do you remain there
when you are seeking for my love?' The maiden answered
nothing, she was calculating her words.

374. "SHE said to me: 'This day makes my heart to burn with
a flame of shame. Thou thinkest I came hither to thee for

that purpose, but I find cause for hope in the fact that I have not waited long for thee; I cannot say if I am worthy of this, God's mercy fails me.'

375. "SHE rose; she said to me: 'I am bashful of thee, my reason is perplexed. Suspect me not of what has been said by command of my mistress; such great boldness is in order to please her heart. This letter will tell thee for whom I speak.'"

XI

First Letter Written by Nestan-Daredjan to Her Lover

376. "I SAW the letter; it was from her for whom fire consumes
my heart. The sunbeam wrote: 'O lion! let not thy wound
appear. I am thine. Die not, but I hate vain fainting. Now
Asmat'h tells thee all that is spoken by me.

377. "'PITIFUL fainting and dying, what love dost thou think
this! It is better to exhibit to the beloved deeds of heroism.
All dwellers in Khataet'hi are our tributaries; now their
ill-will towards us cannot be borne by us.

378. "'I WAS desirous to wed thee even before, but hitherto
I have not found opportunity to speak. The other day
I saw thee deprived of reason sitting in the litter; then I
heard all that had befallen thee.

379. "'I WILL tell thee truth; hearken to this that I say to
thee: Go, do battle with the Khatavians, exhibit thyself to

me in a goodly manner, this is better for thee. Weep idly no more; why moisten more the rose! What more can the sun do to thee! Behold, I have turned thy darkness to dawn.'"

XII

First Letter Written by Tariel to His Beloved

380. "ASMAT'H spoke to me boldly, she was not timid.
What can I tell of myself, who I was, how can I estimate my
joy? My heart was beating, it trembled, it failed me, my
face became crystal again, rubies flamed in my cheeks.

381. "WITH mine eyes I gazed upon the letter written by her.
I wrote in answer: 'O moon, how indeed can the sun surpass
thee! May God not give me that which is not like thee! I
feel as in a dream; I cannot believe in my survival.'

382. "I SAID to Asmat'h: 'I cannot devise more answer than
this. Say thus to her: "O sun! since thou art arisen as a
light for me, behold thou hast revived me who was dead;
I shall faint no more henceforth, whatever be the service
I am a liar if I shun it.'"

383. "ASMAT'H said to me: 'She told me: "Let us do thus,
thus were it better: Whoever sees thee will discover nothing
of my discourse with him; he will come to see me as if he
were making love to thee." She entreated me to tell the
Amirbar so to behave.'

384. "THIS counsel pleased me, the wisdom of the heart of her whom even the sun took care not to gaze on; she had given to me to hear the refined conversation of her in whose rays daylight was like darkness.

385. "I GAVE Asmat'h choice jewels with a golden cup. She said to me: 'No, I do not want them; I have these to satiety.' She took one ring weighing a drachma: 'This is enough for a token; I am full of other bracelets.'

386. "THE maid arose and went forth. The spears spared my heart, joy lightened my darkness, the fire which had burned me was extinguished. I went in and sat down at the banquet where my comrades were drinking; joyful, I distributed gifts, the jubilation increased."

XIII

Tariel Writes a Letter and Sends a Man to the Khatavians

387. "I SENT a man to Khataet'hi and a letter from me; I wrote: 'The king of the Indians is of a truth powerful from God; every hungry soul of those faithful to him is sated; whosoever is disobedient will have himself to blame.

388. "'BROTHER and lord, by you we will not be embittered. When you see this command wend hither; if you come not we shall come; we will not steal upon you. It is better you should come to us, spill not your own blood.'

389. "I SENT the man, I gave my heart up yet more to rejoicing, I made merry at court; the fire unbearable in its burning was extinguished. Then the world, Fate, gave me lavishly what I desired; now I am mad, so that I annoy even the wild beasts if I approach them.

390. "AT first the plan of roaming, then reason soothed me. I feasted with my comrades, but the greatness of desires hindered me from joy; sometimes they filled me with melancholy, I uttered curses against Fate."

XIV

Nestan Summons Tariel to Her

391. "ONE day, on my return from the king's palace, I came to my chamber. I sat down and thought of her, slumber fell not upon mine eyes, I had the letter of hope, therefore was I merry. The doorkeeper called the slave; he told him a secret matter.

392. "'IT is Asmat'h's slave,' quoth he. I ordered him to be brought into the chamber. She wrote to me that she whose knife had pierced my heart commanded me to come. Joy lightened my darkness; she loosened my chains. I went, I took the slave, I spoke not at all with him.

393. "I ENTERED the garden; I met none to speak to me. The maid met me merry, smiling; she said: 'I have bravely extracted the thorn from thy heart, it is no longer therein; come and see thy rose unfaded, unwithered.'

394. "THE maid with an effort raised the heavy curtain; there stood a palankeen adorned with choice rubies where sat she whose face was like the sun flashing; her eyes, like inky lakes, looked beautifully at me.

395. "A LONG time I stood, and she spoke no word to me whom
she yearned for; she only looked at me sweetly as at an
intimate. She called Asmat'h, they spoke together; the maid
came and whispered in my ear: 'Now go; she cannot say
anything to thee.' Again the flame reduced me to soot.

396. "ASMAT'H led me forth, I went out, I passed the curtain.
I said: 'O Fate, who not long ago didst heal my heart, thou
gavest me hope then; why hast thou scattered my joy? My
heart is still more devastated again by the pain of parting.'

397. "ASMAT'H promised me comfort. We walked through the
garden; she said to me: 'Let not the brand be thus seen
upon thy heart because of thy going; shut the terrace of
sorrows, open the door of joy. She is ashamed to speak;
therefore she behaves with dignity.'

398. "I SAID: 'O sister, I think this heart-balm is from thee.
I adjure thee, part me not from life, extinguish this
flame with tidings, cut me not off from letters, send them
ceaselessly; if thou learnest something for me I think thou
wilt not keep it hidden from me.'

399. "I MOUNTED my horse, I went thence, a stream flowed
from the channel of tears. I went to bed; maddened, I had
no power to sleep. I, the crystal and ruby, became bluest
indigo. I preferred night; I wished not for the dawn of day.

400. "THE men that had been sent returned from Khataet'hi—it was time for them to come—they brought a proud and insolent message: 'We are no cowards, neither are our keeps unfortified. Who is your monarch? What lord is he over me?'

XV

The Letter Written by the King of the Khatavians in Answer to Tariel

401. "HE wrote: 'I, Ramaz the king, write a letter to thee, Tariel. I marvelled at what was written in the letter penned by thee. How dost thou summon thither me who am lord over many peoples! I will look at no other letter which comes from thee.'

402. "I COMMANDED the soldiers to be summoned; I sent forth the Lord of the Marches. They gathered together the armies of India more numerous than the stars, from near and far all hastened towards me, plain, rock and waste were altogether filled with soldiers.

403. "THEY came swiftly; they made no tarrying at home. I held a review; the good order of the troops pleased me—their alertness and valour, beautifully drawn up in squadrons, the speed of their steeds, their Khvarazmian[1] armour.

404. "I RAISED the royal standard with flag of red and black. I commanded the countless troops to set out in the morning.

---

[1] Khvarazmia, the Khanate of Khiva.

I myself wept, I mourned exceedingly my evil fate: 'If I see not the sun I know not how I can ever depart.'

405. "I WENT in. The sadness of my pensive heart was increased unto me; burning tears welled forth from mine eyes like a pool. 'My luckless fate,' said I, 'has never yet ruled. Why did my hand lay hold of the rose since thus it could not cull it!'"

XVI

The Meeting of Tariel and Nestan

406. "A SLAVE entered; a wondrous thing befell me. He gave
to me in my exceeding grief a letter from Asmat'h; she
wrote: 'Thy sun for whom thou longest calls thee. Come!
This better than to weep there and moan at the deed of
Fate.'

407. "SO much did I rejoice as was fitting. It was twilight,
I went forth, I entered the garden gate; where Asmat'h had
first met me, there she appeared standing; she said with a
smile: 'Enter; the moon awaits thee, the lion.'

408. "I ENTERED the house reared beautiful with terrace
upon terrace, the moon shone forth surrounded with rays
of light at the full; within the curtain she sat clad in green
raiment, majestic and rare, wondrous of face and form.

409. "I WENT in and stood on the edge of the carpet; the fire
in me began to be quenched, the darkness of my heart was
lightened, joy rose up like a column. She rested upon a
cushion–she was far fairer than the sun's rays–she hid her
face from me, she looked up a moment to see me.

410. "SHE commanded: 'Asmat'h, beg the Amirbar to be
seated!' She placed a cushion opposite her to be praised
as the sun; I sat down, I gave up to joy my heart abused
by Fate. I marvel that my life stays in me while I speak the
words she said.

411. "SHE said to me: 'Last time thou wert ill-pleased that
thou wert sent away without being spoken to. I, at parting,
as the sun, withered thee up like a flower of the field. Thou
wert doomed to shed tears from the narcissus-pool; but
for me, bashfulness and reserve are necessary towards the
Amirbar.

412. "'THOUGH great modesty befits a woman towards a man,
yet is it much worse not to speak and to hide woes; if
I smile outwardly I felt inwardly secret grief; last time
I sent the maid I gave her a true message.

413. "'WHAT we two have hitherto known of each other, even
now know me thine by these firm promises; I assure thee of
this by great vows and oaths; if I deceive thee may God
make me earth, may I not sit in the nine heavens!

414. "'GO, attack the Khatavians, fight and make raids; may
God grant that thou be victorious, come back to me of
good cheer. But what shall I do until it falls to my lot to
look upon thee again! Give me thy heart undivided forever:
take mine for thyself.'

415. "'NOW that of which thou hast deemed me worthy no
human being deserves; this grace is unexpected, from God

this does not surprise me; thy rays have flooded my dark heart and made it translucent; thine shall I be till the earth cover my face.'

416. "UPON the book of oaths I swore and she swore to me; thus she confirmed her love to me: 'If any save thee give pleasure to my heart may God slay me, henceforth thus will I speak to myself, thus will I train myself.'

417. "I STAYED some time before her, we spoke sweet words, we ate some pleasant fruit, talking one to the other; then weeping and shedding tears I rose to depart, the beauties of her rays were spread like light in my heart.

418. "IT irked me to go far from her crystal and ruby and enamel. The world was renewed to me, I had an abundance of joy; that light appearing in ether as sun seemed to be mine; now I am surprised that being separated from her I have still a heart like a steep rock."

XVII

Tariel's Departure for Khataet'hi and Great Battles

419. "IN the morning I mounted, I commanded the trumpet and bugle to be sounded; I cannot tell thee of all the armies nor of their readiness to mount; I, a lion, set forth for Khataet'hi, none can accuse me of cowardice; the soldiers marched without a road, they followed no track.

420. "I CROSSED the boundaries of India, I went on a considerable time; a man met me from Ramaz, the khan over Khataet'hi; he repeated to me a message conciliatory to the heart: 'Your Indian goats are able to eat even our wolves.'

421. "HE presented me with astounding treasures as a gift from Ramaz; he said: "'He entreats thee, destroy us not, it is not a thing thou shouldst do; put us on our oath, thereby are our necks bound with twigs, without devastation we shall deliver over to thee ourselves our children and possessions.

422. "'FORGIVE us in that we have sinned against thee, we ourselves repent; by God, if thou wouldst have mercy on

us, bring not thine armies hither, destroy not our land, let not the heavens fall upon us in wrath; we give thee our castles and cities, let a few knights come with thee.'

423. "I PLACED my viziers at my side, we discussed and counselled; they said: 'Thou art young, therefore we sages venture to say to thee, alas! they are exceeding treacherous; we have seen it indeed once already; may they not slay thee treacherously, may they not bring on us woe!

424. "'WE counsel thus: Let us go forth with brave heroes only, let the soldiers follow close behind us, let them be apprised of the tidings by a man; if they be true-hearted, trust them, make them swear by God and heaven; if they submit not to thee, pour forth thy wrath and moreover the wrath of heaven upon them.'

425. "THIS advice counselled by the viziers pleased me; I returned a message: 'O King Ramaz, I know thy decisions; life is better than death to thee. We shall not be stopped by stone walls. I will leave the soldiers, I will come with a few, towards thee will I march.'

426. "I TOOK with me three hundred of the soldiers, good brave knights, I went forth and left all the army; I said: 'Wherever I shall go, march over the same fields, follow me closely, help me, I shall call you if I need help.'

427. "I TRAVELLED three days; another man of the same khan met me, again he presented me with many beautiful robes; he said: 'The khan wishes thee to be near him, proud and mighty one; when he meets thee then shalt thou know many such gifts.'

428. "YET more he said: 'What I have told thee is true. I myself come forward to meet thee, I haste to see thee.' I said, 'Tell the khan: Certainly, by God, I shall do your commandment, tenderly shall we meet each other, we shall be like father and son.'

429. "DEPARTED thence I alighted on the bounds of a certain deep forest; again messengers came, they were not shy to salute me, they brought fair steeds as a present to me, they said: 'Of a truth the king would desire to see thee.'

430. "THEY said to me: 'The king informs thee: I myself also come towards thee; having left my house, early to-morrow I shall meet thee.' I kept the messengers, I put up a felt tent not a rich one; I received them very amiably, they lay down together like groomsmen.

431. "NO good deed done to a man can pass away thus. A certain man returned; he came to me and said secretly: 'I owe you a great debt hard for me to pay; I cannot forsake and forget thee.

432. "'I WAS to some extent brought up by your father. I heard the treachery planned for you; I ran to let you know of it. It would grieve me to see the elegant-formed, the rose-faced, a corpse. I will tell thee all; hearken to me, be calm.

433. "'THAT thou be not vainly deceived, these men are traitors to thee; in one place are hidden for thee one hundred thousand troops, then in another place are thirty thousand; that is why they call upon thee to hasten; if thou take not measures at once mischance will come upon thee.

434. "'THE king will come a little way to meet thee whose admirers can never cease; secretly they will be clad in armour; thou trusting them while they cajole thee the soldiers will make smoke, on all sides they will surround, as it is when ten thousand strike one so must they overwhelm thee.'

435. "I SPOKE pleasantly to the man and gave him thanks: 'If I am not slain I shall repay thee for this according to thee desires. Now let not thy comrades suspect; go, be with them. If I forget thee may I be surely lost.'

436. "I TOLD no human being; I kept it secret like gossip. What is to be will be; all advice is equal. But I sent men towards the armies though the way was long; I gave the message: 'Come quickly, hasten over mountain and hill.'

437. "IN the morning I gave a sweet message to the messengers. They were to tell King Ramaz: 'I am coming to meet thee; come, I also come soon.' Another half-day I journeyed on; I took no heed of trouble; there is a providence, if I am to be killed to-day where below can I hide myself!

438. "I MOUNTED a certain peak; I saw dust in the plain. I said to myself: 'King Ramaz is coming; though he has spread a net for me, my sharp sword, my straight lance, will pierce their flesh.' Then I spoke to my troops; I set forth a great plan.

439. "I SAID: 'Brothers, these men are traitors to us; why should the power of your arms be weakened on that account? Those who die for their kings, upwards their spirits fly!

Now let us engage the Khatavians. Why should we gird on
the sword in vain!'

440. "PROUDLY, with fierce words, I commanded them to don
armour; we clad ourselves for fight in chain coats of mail
with shoulder-pieces; I formed squadrons, I set out, I went
in great haste; that day my sword cut in pieces mine
adversary.

441. "WE approached. They perceived that our forms were
clad in armour. A man came with a message from the
king; he said: 'We look upon your treachery as untimely,
now we see your armour, this causes us displeasure.'

442. "I SENT back a message: 'I too know what thou hast
contrived for me; you have made certain plans, but they
will not come to pass; give orders, come and fight me as is
the law and custom, I have taken my sword in my hand
to slay you.'

443. "WHEN the messenger came, why did they send yet
another? They made smoke for the soldiers, they made plain
what was hid, they came forth from ambush, they advanced
from both sides, they formed into many ranks, though,
thank God, they could not harm me.

444. "I TOOK a lance, I applied my hand to helming myself,
I was eager for the fray to break them, I extended a
stadium's length, I made ranks and advanced in a long line.
They drew up innumerable cohorts, they stood calm and
undisturbed.

144

445. "WHEN I came near they looked at me: 'He is a madman,' said they. I, strong-armed, made my way thither where the main body of the army stood; I pierced a man with my lance, his horse I overturned, they both departed from the sun, the lance broke, my hand seized the sword; I praise. O sword, him who whetted thee.

446. "I SWOOPED in like a falcon among a covey of grey partridges, I threw man upon man, I made a hill of men and horses; the man thrown down by me spins like a dragon-fly; I completely destroyed at one onslaught the two front squadrons.

447. "CROWDING they surrounded me, about me was a great fight; when once I struck none could stand, I made blood spurt forth as from a fountain, he whom I clove hung on his horse like a saddle-bag, wherever I was they fled from me, they were wary of me.

448. "AT the evening hour their watchman cried forth from the summit: 'Stand no longer, let us go, heaven looks again on us in wrath, a terrible dust is coming, we should beware of this, let not their countless tens of thousands of soldiers completely destroy us.'

449. "MY soldiers whom I had not brought with me, when they heard of it, set out, they travelled day and night without stopping, neither plain nor mountain could contain them; they appeared, they beat the kettledrum, the trumpet sounded aloud.

145

450. "THE enemy saw them, they started to flee, we raised a shout, we pursued over the fields in which we had fought our battle. I unhorsed King Ramaz; we found each other with swords. We captured all his armies; we slew them not.

451. "THOSE who fled were overtaken by the rearguard, they began to seize them, to throw down the terrified, the vanquished; Tariel's troops had a reward for their sleeplessness and night-watching; the prisoners, even those that were unwounded, ceased not to wail like sick men.

452. "WE dismounted to rest on the battle-field. I had wounded my arm with the sword; it seemed to me a mere scratch. My armies came to see me and praise me, they could not speak, they knew not how to express their admiration.

453. "THE glories which they thrust upon me were sufficient for one man; some blessed me from afar, some tried to kiss me; those nobles who had trained me wept over me, they saw that which had been cut by my sword, they marvelled exceedingly.

454. "I SENT soldiers everywhere to bring in booty; they came together loaded. I was proud of myself; I had dyed the plain with the blood of those who had sought to slay me. I did not fight at the gate of the cities; I seized them without a battle.

455. "I SAID to Ramaz: 'I have learned of thy treacherous deed; now that thou art captured justify thyself; fortify not strongholds, count them all into my hand; else, why should I overlook thy guilt towards me?'

456. "RAMAZ said to me: 'I have no more power left; give me one of my lords over whom I may have lordship; I will send him to the guardians of the castles; let me speak with them; I will give all into thine hands, since I make it thy property.'

457. "I GAVE him a lord, I sent knights with him, I caused all the governors of fortresses to be brought before me, they gave the strongholds into my hands; thus I made them repent the war. With what can I compare the abundance of treasure!

458. "THEN I went in to travel through and inspect Khataet'hi; publicly they presented me with the keys of the treasuries; I settled the country, I commanded: 'Be ye without fear, the sun shall not burn you, be assured you will be left unburned.'

459. "I EXAMINED the treasuries one by one from end to end; I should be weary if I mentioned all the wondrous kinds of treasures. I saw together a short cloak and veil; if thou didst see it thou wouldst desire to know its name.

460. "I COULD not learn what stuff it was nor what kind of work; everyone to whom I showed it marvelled and said

149

it was a divine miracle; neither was the basis of the tissue like that of brocade nor carpet, its strength was as if it had been wrought like iron—I might say tempered in fire.

461. "I PUT them aside as a present for her whose ray enlightened me; I chose as a gift for the king whatever was best: a thousand mules and camels, all strong-limbed, I sent them loaded; he also learned the good news."

XVIII

Letter of Tariel to the King of the Indians When He Triumphed Over the Khatavians

462. "I WROTE a letter: 'O king, great is your good fortune! The Khatavians plotted treachery to me, though it fell on them to their hurt; therefore am I tardy in telling you my true tidings. I have captured the king; I come to thee with spoil and prisoners.'

463. "WHEN I had put everything in order I set out from Khataet'hi. I took the treasures, I despoiled the kingdom, I could not get enough camels, I loaded bullocks with the burdens; I had found glory and honour, for what I had desired that had I obtained.

464. "I LED away captive the King of Khataet'hi. I came to India, sweet was the meeting with my foster-father; what eulogy he uttered to me cannot be repeated, for me to tell it were unseemly; he undid mine arm, he bound it with a soft bandage.

465. "FAIR tents stood pitched in the moedan for him who desired to speak with and gaze upon me. That day the king

who rested there spread a banquet, he caressed me, sitting near me he gazed at me.

466. "THAT night we spent in feasting; pleasantly we made merry there. In the morning we left the moedan; we entered the city. The king commanded: 'Call the soldiers, assemble them, show me this day the Khatavians, lead in the prisoners.'

467. "I LED in King Ramaz captive before him. The king looked sweetly on him as on a son whom he had cradled. It made the deceitful and treacherous one seem deserving, and this is the excess of heroism in a brave man.

468. "HE entertained the King of the Khatavians, he caressed him, he conversed with him for a long time in a fitting manner; at dawn I was called, he spoke to me a compassionate word: 'Shall I pardon the Khatavian, my former enemy?'

469. "I VENTURED to reply: 'Since God forgives the sinner, be you also merciful to him whose might is brought to nought.' He said to Ramaz: 'Know that I send thee hence forgiven, but show not thyself before me again disgraced.'

470. "HE levied a tribute of a hundred times a hundred drachmas, all in Khatavian money, also brocades and satins; then he clad him and all his courtiers, and sent them away with pardon in place of wrath.

471. "THE Khatavian thanked him, bent, paid lowly homage; he said: 'By God, I repent my treachery towards you; if ever I sin against you again then kill me.' He departed and took all his folk with him.

472. "A MAN of the king's came; it was dawn, and the morning grey was past; he brought a message: 'For three months have I been separated from thee, I have eaten no game killed by arrow in the field; if thou be not tired come forth, though it be time to be tired.'

473. "I APPARELLED myself, I went into the hall of audience; a pack of harriers met me, all the space round the hall was full of falcons. The king sat decked in beauty like the sun; he rejoiced at the coming of me, the lovely and fair.

474. "HE said secretly to his wife, but unknown to me: 'To gaze on Tariel returned from war is desirable, he brings light to the onlooker's heart, however dark it may be; whatever I ask thee to do, do it without delay.

475. "NOW, without consulting thee I have thought of a plan; but thou too must know it: Since the maid is to be queen, and has been so nominated by us ourselves, whoever shall see her, now let him who is like a tree in Eden see her—lo! even to-day; seat her by thy side, both of you meet us in the palace, I shall come joyful.'

476. "WE hunted over plain, mountain-foot and hill; there was a multitude of hounds, falcons and hawks. We returned early without having gone a stage from the long road. They did not play at ball; they broke up two games.

477. "FOLK eager to gaze on me filled the city, the bazaar and the roofs; tasselled robes adorned me who had finished the war; I was fair as a pale-hued rose bathed in tears, he who looked on me swooned; true is this, and no falsehood.

478. "THE veils I had found in the city of the Khatavians I bound round me, they became me, I maddened still more the heart of the mad. The king dismounted; we entered the apartments of my foster-parents. I saw the flash of her cheeks like sunlight, I trembled.

479. "THE form of that sun was clad in robes of orange; behind her was a host of eunuchs in cohorts and lines; with light she quite filled house, street and quarter; there, amid the roses, shone in beauty coral-pearl twins.

480. "I WHO had fought and been wounded had mine arm hung from my neck in a sling. The queen rose from her throne and came forward to meet me. She kissed me hard like a son, she made my rose cheek blue; she said to me: 'Henceforth expect not the foe to engage thee.'

481. "NEAR at hand they made place for me, there where it pleased me; opposite sat the sun for whom my heart was dying. Stealthily I looked at her, she looked at me; no other converse was there; when I tore away mine eyes from her, thereby was life made hateful to me.

482. "THERE was drinking and feasting on a scale fitting to
their might, such another rejoicing eye has not seen,
goblet and cup were all of turquoise and ruby; the king
gave order that no drunk man be suffered to depart.[1]

483. "BEING there I gave myself up to an excess of joy; when
she gazed at me and I at her, my fire began to be
extinguished. I called upon my wild, mad heart to have a
care of me. How exceedingly pleasant it is to look face
to face on the beloved!

484. "THE minstrels ceased to sing. 'Be silent!' They bent
their heads. The king said to me: 'Son Tariel, how can we
tell thee how we rejoice! We are in bliss, therefore our
adversaries are woeful; right are thine admirers, not idly
do they vaunt.

485. "'NOW, though it is fitting that we should clothe thee
who art mighty in glory, we clothe thee not, we doff not
those robes beauteously adorning thee. Now thou whose
rays are spread abroad hast a hundred treasures from us,
thou thyself canst have sewn what thou desirest, be not
bashful before us.'

486. "THEY gave me all the treasures with the hundred keys
that locked them. I blessed them for those treasures and
paid them my respects. Rising, they kissed me, shining
like two suns. How can I describe the gifts they presented to
the army?

---

[1] They were to be tended in the palace.

487. "HE sat down again joyful, drinking and singing increased, again the feast went on, the lyre and tinkling of harps. The queen retired when day met twilight and until evening joy was not joy.

488. "WE broke up; we could no more endure the drinking of double goblets. I went into my chamber, my perception became like that of one dazed; I had no power in me, made prisoner as I was, to extinguish that fire. I remembered, and the memory of being gazed on by her rejoiced me."

489. "A SLAVE came; he told me true tidings: 'A veiled woman asks tidings of you.' Then I knew at once, I leaped up in all haste, with trembling heart; she came in, I saw Asmat'h, who was coming towards me.

490. "FOR the sake of her for whom I am dying I was pleased to see Asmat'h, as if I saw herself. I hindered her from doing me homage, I kissed her, I took her hand and seated her near me on my couch, and greeted her: 'Blessed art thou, come as a shoot from the aloe-tree!

491. "'TELL me news of her; speak to me of nought else.' She said to me: 'I will tell thee truth; now from me thou shalt not hear words uttered merely to give pleasure. To-day ye saw each other, and tenderly were pleased; now again she commands to make known news of her through me.'

XIX

Letter of Nestan-Daredjan Written to Her Beloved

492. "SHE gave me a letter, I gazed on it; it was from the light of the face of the lands. She wrote: 'I have seen the loveliness of thy gem-like brilliancy; fair wert thou returned from battle, after urging on thy horse; not ill seems to me the cause of the flow of my tears.

493. "'IF God hath given me my tongue it befits me to use it for thy praise; dead for thy sake I can by no means speak, for lacking thee I die. The sun made a little garden of rose and jet, as a garden for the lion; by thy sun, my self pertains to none save thee.

494. "'THOUGH thou hast shed a stream of tears yet have they not flowed in vain; henceforth weep no more, put away grief from thee. Those who look upon thee curse unrestrained those who look upon me. Veil me with that which but now was bound round thee.

495. "'GIVE me the veils that sometime adorned thee; when thou seest me, thou also shalt be pleased that that which is thine adorns me. Bind on thine arm this bracelet if thou honourest what is mine, and such another night thou shalt not pass as long as thou livest.'"

XX

Tariel's Weeping and Fainting

496. HERE Tariel become like a wild beast, weeps, his grief
    increases a thousandfold; he said: "I have the armlet which
    she formerly bound on her arm!" He undid it, took it off,
    man cannot estimate its worth, he pressed it to his lips, he
    swooned and fell like a corpse.

497. He lay more lifeless than a corpse at the door of the tomb.
    On both sides are seen bruises from his fist which he had
    struck on his breast. A stream of blood flows from
    Asmat'h's scratched cheeks; she poured water on him
    again, she succoured him, the sound of gurgling water is
    heard there.

498. AVT'HANDIL, too, sighed bitterly; he gazed on the
    unconscious form. Asmat'h multiplied her groans; her tears
    hollowed out the stones. Then she restored him to
    consciousness, his fires she quenched with water; he said:
    "I live; this passing world even now is drinking my blood."

499. PALE he sat up, he stared with his eyes like one dazed:
    the rose was become quite saffron and wan; a long time he

neither spoke nor looked at them; he was mightily oppressed that he remained alive and died not.

500. HE said to Avt'handil: "Hearken! Though I have the mind of a madman, I will tell thee my tale and that of her who has buried me. It seems to me a joy to meet the friend thou hast not met. It surprises me that I am alive, that I survive hale.

501. "THE sight of Asmat'h, in whom I trusted as in a sister, pleased me. When I had seen the letter, she gave me this armlet, I bound it on mine arm at once, I doffed from my head that strange and rare thing of some strong, black stuff, the veil."

XXI

Tariel's Letter
in Answer to his Beloved

502. "I WROTE: 'O sun! thy ray beaming forth from thee
struck my heart; my alertness and boldness are brought
to nought; mad for thee, I have perceived thy beauty and
loveliness; with what service can I pay thee in exchange for
life?

503. "'THEN when thou didst make me to survive and sufferedst
me not to be wholly sundered from life, now this time I
compare with that time. I have received thine armlet; I
have bound it round mine arm. How can I show my joy as
much as is fitting?

504. "'OF a truth I offer thee, lo! the veil which thou
demandest; also a cloak, of the same stuff, the like of which
thou wilt not find. Leave me not to swoon, help me, succour
me, come! Whom can I submit to in this world save thee?'

505. "THE maid arose and forsook me. I lay down and fell pleasantly asleep, but I shivered, I saw my beloved in my sleep; I awoke, I had her no more, life was a burden to me thus I passed the night, I heard not her voice."

XXII

Counsel About Nestan-Daredjan's Marriage

506. "EARLY in the morning they summoned me to the palace when day was yet at the dawn. I rose; I learned their tidings and went at the same moment. I saw them both sitting with three viziers. When I entered they bade me be seated; I sat down before them on a chair.

507. "THEY said to me: 'God has brought old age upon us so that we are exhausted, the time of age approaches us, youth has passed from us. We have no son, but we have a daughter whose rays fail us not; we care not for the lack of a son, we are reconciled to that.

508. "'NOW we want a husband for our daughter. Where shall we find him to whom we may give our throne, whom we may form in our image, make him ruler of the kingdom, guardian of the realm, that we be not destroyed, that we may not let our enemies whet their swords for us?'

509. "I SAID: 'How can your heart not feel the want of a son! But she who is like the sun suffices for our hope.

Whomsoever you choose as son-in-law, he will rejoice greatly. What more can I say? You yourselves know what will be fitting.'

510. "WE began to take counsel on the matter. I tried to keep my heart firm though it was weakened; I said to myself: 'I shall say nothing and can do nothing to hinder this.' The king said: 'There is Khvarazmsha, King of the Khvarazmians, if he would give us his child for ours there is none like him.'

511. "IT was clear that they had settled it beforehand; they glanced at each other, their words also were guarded; it was not for me to venture to say anything to hinder them, only I became as earth and cinders; my heart quivered to and fro.

512. "THE queen said: 'Khvarazmsha is a king reigning with power. Who could be better than his son for our son-in-law!' How could I dare to dispute since they themselves desired it! I added assent. The day of the overthrow of my soul was fixed.

513. "THEY sent a man to Khvarazmsha asking for his son. Their message was: 'Our whole realm is without an heir, there is one daughter fit for childbearing, not to be wedded abroad; if thou wilt give us thy son for her, wait not for aught further.'

514. "THE man arrived loaded with short cloaks and veils.
Khvarazmsha rejoiced with great joy; he said: 'From God
has befallen us that which we desired; what other child
like unto her could we take to our arms?'

515. "AGAIN they sent other men to bring the bridegroom;
they entreated him: 'Tarry not, come at our demand.'
I was wearied after exercise at ball-playing, and went to my
chamber to rest; sadness entered into my heart, I began to
endure woes."

XXIII

Counsel Between Tariel and Nestan-Daredjan
and Its Results

516. "EXCESSIVE melancholy approached my heart as if to
strike with a knife, but when Asmat'h's slave entered I sat
proud and strong. He gave me a letter; in it was written:
'She who is like an aloe-tree in form commands thee to
come hither soon without putting off time.'

517. "I MOUNTED, went forth, entered the little garden, as
thou canst imagine, with a full measure of joy; I passed
through the little garden and arrived at the tower; I saw
Asmat'h standing at the foot; I looked and saw that she
had been weeping, tear stains could be seen on her cheeks;
I was sad, and did not ask; she was troubled by desire for
my coming.

518. "I SAW her frowning; this oppressed me exceedingly. She
no longer smiled on me as she had formerly smiled; she
said no word to me, only her tears showered down; thereby
she wounded me the more, she healed not my wounds.

519. "SHE carried my thoughts very far away. She led me into the tower and raised the curtain. I went in, I saw that moon every woe forsook me, the ray fell on my heart, but my heart was not melted.

520. "THE light falling upon the curtain was not light; her face was carelessly covered by the golden veil I had given her; the peerless one, apparelled in that same green garment was seated in a reclining position on the couch; a shower of tears fell on her face flashing with radiance.

521. "SHE crouched, like a tiger on the edge of a rock, her face flashing fury; no longer was she like the sun, the moon, an aloe-tree planted in Eden. Asmat'h seated me far off; my heart was struck as by a lance. Then she sat erect with frowning brows, angry, enraged.

522. "SHE said to me: 'I marvel why thou art come, thou breaker of thy binding oath, fickle and faithless, thou forsworn; but high Heaven will give thee guerdon and answer for this!' I said: 'How can I reply to what I know not?'

523. "I SAID: 'I cannot answer thee if I know not the truth. Wherein have I sinned, what have I done, I senseless and pale?' Again she said to me: 'What shall I say to thee, false and treacherous one! Why did I let myself be deceived, woman-like! For this I burn with flame.

524. "'KNOWEST thou not of the bringing of Khvarazmsha to wed me? Thou wert sitting as counsellor, thy consent to

this was given, thou hast broken thine oath to me, the firmness and bindingness thereof. Would to God I might bring thy cunning to nought!

525. "'REMEMBEREST thou when thou didst sigh "Ah! Ah!" when thy tears bathed the fields, and the physicians and surgeons brought thee medicines? What else is there that resembles a man's falsehood? Since thou hast denied me, I, too, will renounce thee. Let us see who will be the more hurt.

526. "'I TELL thee this: Whosoever shall rule India I have the rule also, whether they go trackless or by the road! It may not be thus! Now thou hast fallen into error. Thine opinions are like thee—even so untrue!

527. "'WHILE I live, by God, thou shalt no more dwell in India. If thou seekest to tarry, the soul shall be parted from thy body! None other shalt thou find like me, even though thou stretch thy hand unto heaven!'" When the knight had ended these words he wept, moaned, and said: "Ah me!"

528. HE said: "When I heard this from her, hope revived in me exceedingly; once more mine eyes had power to look upon her light; now I have lost it, why art thou not surprised that dazed I live? Woe to thee, fleeting world! Why seekest thou to drain my blood?

529. "I LOOKED, and saw on the lectern the Koran lying open;
I raised it, I stood up, and, praising God and afterwards
her, said: 'O sun, thou burnedst me, and in truth my sun
is set; since thou slayest me not, I will venture to make
thee some answer:

530. "'IF what I tell thee, these words, be falsely cunning,
may Heaven itself be wrathful with me, may all the sun's
rays be turned against me! If thou considerest me worthy
to be judged, I have done no ill.' She said: 'What thou
knowest, speak!' She nodded to me.

531. "THEN again I ventured to say: 'If I, O sun, have broken
my vow to thee, may God now forthwith show His anger by
hurling a thunderbolt from heaven upon me! Who save
thee has for me a face like a sun, a form like a tree? So how
can I remain alive if a lance strike my heart!

532. "'THE sovereigns summoned me to court, they held a
solemn council, beforehand they had appointed that youth
as thy husband; even if I had opposed it I could not prevent
it, I should have been a fool for my pains; I said to myself:
"Agree with them for the nonce; it is better for thee to
fortify thy heart."

533. "'HOW could I dare to forbid it, since P'harsadan
understands not, knows not that India shall not remain
masterless! It is I alone who am India's owner; none other
has any right. I know not him whom he will bring hither,
nor who is mistaken in this matter.

534. "'I SAID: "I can do nothing in this; I shall contrive some other means." I said: "Be not assailed by a multitude of thoughts." My heart was like a wild beast; a thousand times I was ready to fly to the fields. To whom can I give thee? Why shouldst thou not take me?'

535. 'I SOLD soul for heart's sake; thus the tower became for me a market.' That rain which at first had frozen the rose became milder; I saw pearl in the coral, round about the pearl the coral was tenderly enfolded; she said: 'Why do I, too, judge this to be right?

536. "'I DO not believe thee to be treacherous and faithless, a denier of God, not thankful to Him; entreat of him myself and lordship in gladness over India; I and thou shall be sovereigns—that is the best of all matches!'

537. "THE wrathful, enraged one became tender to me; either the sun was on earth or the full-faced moon; she set me near her, she caressed me, hitherto unworthy of this, she conversed with me; thus she extinguished the fire kindled in me.

538. "SHE said to me: 'The prudent should never hasten, he will contrive whatever is best, he will be calm under the passing world. If thou suffer not the suitor to come in to India, woe if the king be wroth with thee, thou and he will quarrel, India will be laid waste.

539. "'ON the other hand, if thou allow the bridegroom to come in, if he wed me, if it so fall out, we shall be

sundered each from other, our gay garb will be turned to mourning, they will be happy and glorious, our sufferings will be magnified a hundredfold. This shall not be said, that the Persians[1] hold sway in our court.'

540. "I SAID: 'May God avert the wedding of thee by that youth! When they come into India and I discover their quality, I shall show forth to them my strong-heartedness and prowess; I shall so slay them that they become of no account!'

541. "SHE spoke to me saying: 'A woman should act in a womanly way as befits her sex; I cannot have thee shed much blood, I cannot become a wall of division. When they come, slay the bridegroom without killing his armies. To do true justice makes even a dry tree green.

542. "'THUS do, my lion, most excellent of all heroes; slay the bridegroom stealthily, take not soldiers, slaughter not his armies like cattle or asses; how can a man bear the burden of much innocent blood!

543. "'WHEN thou hast killed him, tell thy lord, my father, say to him "I could never let India be food for the Persians; it is mine own heritage, never will I give up even a drachm of it; if thou wilt not leave me in peace I will make a wilderness of thy city!"'

---

[1] Khvarazma was a province of Persia.

544. "'SAY not that thou wantest my love or desirest me, so will the righteousness of thy deed seem the greater; the king will then entreat thee in the most desperate and abject manner; I shall give myself into thy hands, reigning together will suit us.'

545. "THIS counsel and advice pleased me exceedingly; I boasted that I would wield my sword for the slaying of my foes. Then I rose to depart. She began to entreat me to sit down; I longed to do so, but could not bring myself to clasp and embrace her.

546. "I TARRIED some time, then I left her, but I became like one mad, Asmat'h went in front of me; I shed hot tears; my grief increased a thousandfold, my joy was reduced to one; then I went unwillingly away, and so I went slowly."

XXIV

The Coming to India of Khvarazmsha's Son and His Slaying by Tariel

547. "A MAN came. 'The bridegroom cometh,' announced he; but, wretched man! he knew not what God was preparing for him. The king looked pleased, he spoke no woeful words he bade me sit near him; 'Come,' said he, and inclined his head.

548. "HE said to me: 'For me this is a day of joy and merriment Let us celebrate the wedding in a palace as befits our sister Nestan; let us send a man, let us have all the treasures brought from every part, generously let us distribute, let us fill them with treasure; avarice is clownishness.'

549. "I SENT in all directions men carrying treasure. The bridegroom also came, they were no laggards; our men met them from inside, from outside came the Khvarazmians; the sum of their soldiers could not be contained even by the fields.

173

550. "THE king commanded: 'Prepare the moedan with tents, let the bridegroom rest, let him tarry there a little while; the other armies can go thither without thee to see him, thou shalt see him here, go not, the knights will be sufficient to see him.'

551. "I RAISED on the moedan tents of red satin. The bridegroom arrived, he dismounted; it seemed not like Easter Eve; those inside began to go out, there was a host of courtiers there, the soldiers began to form in ranks according to their regions.

552. "I WAS wearied, as is the wont of one who has done duty; tired, I turned homeward, and wished to sleep. A slave came and gave me a letter from Asmat'h the sweet: 'Come quickly! She who is like a full-grown aloe commands thee.'

553. "I DISMOUNTED not; I went quickly obedient. Asmat'h had been weeping; I asked her: 'Why flow thy tears?' She said to me: 'Being engaged in thy defence, how can I avoid weeping? How can I justify thee unceasingly, whatever kind of advocate I may have become!'

554. "WE went in, we saw her seated on a cushion, her brows puckered; the sun could not more illume the vicinage than she. I stood before her. She said to me: 'Why standest thou there? The day of battle comes—or, wert thou forsaking me, wert thou false to me and deceiving me again?'

555. "I WAS angered, I said nothing, hastily I went out again; I called back: 'Now shall it be seen if I did not wish it!

Am I become so cowardly that a woman urges me to fight?'
I went home, I concerted his slaughter, I was not idle.

556. "I COMMANDED a hundred servants: 'Prepare for battle!'
We mounted, we passed through the city without letting
anyone perceive us. I went into the tent. It is a horror to
tell with the tongue how the bridegroom was lying; I
killed that youth without shedding of blood, though it was
necessary for blood to flow.

557. "I CUT the tangled edge of the tent, I tore it, I seized
the youth by his legs and struck his head on the tent-pole.
Those lying at the door cried; their lamentation was
marvellous. I mounted my horse, departed, my coat of
chain-mail protected me.

558. "AN alarm was raised against me; there was cry to pursue
me. I went on, they began to follow, I slew my pursuers.
I had a strong city, impregnable to the foe; I reached it
safely, pleasantly, unhurt.

559. "I SENT a man, I made known to all the soldiers: 'Let
all who will aid me come hither!' My pursuers did not weary
of coming in the depth of dark night; when they
recognised me they kept their heads whole.

560. "I AROSE at daybreak; I apparelled myself when night
dawned into morn. I saw three lords sent by the king; he
sent a message, saying: 'God knows I have fostered thee
like my son; why hast thou thus changed my rejoicing
into heaviness?

561. "'WHY didst thou make Khvarazmsha's innocent blood to fall on our house! If thou didst desire my daughter, why didst thou not tell me so? Thou hast made life distasteful to me, thine aged foster-father; thou thyself hast brought it about that thou remainest not with me till the day of my death.'

562. "IN answer I sent a message: 'O king, I am stronger than copper, and this alone hinders me from being destroyed by the fire and flame of death; but, as you know, a king should be a doer of justice; by your sun! I am far from desiring your daughter.

563. "'THOU knowest how many palaces and thrones are in India; I am the sole heir left, all has fallen into your hands, all their heirs have died out, their heritage remains to you; by right the throne belongs to none but me.

564. "'I SWEAR by your virtue, I cannot flatter you, now this is not just: God gave thee no son; thou hast an only daughter. If thou appointedst Khvarazmsha king, what would have been left for me in exchange? Can another king be seated on the throne of India while I wear my sword?

565. "'I WANT not thy daughter, marry her, rid her of me. India is mine, to no man else will I give it; whoever contests my right, him will I cause to be uprooted from the earth; kill me! if I need any foreign helpers.'

XXV

Tariel Hears Tidings of the Loss of Nestan-Daredjan

566. "I SENT those men. I was mad in mind; since I could learn nought of her I grew more inflamed with grief. I went to look from a wall I had built overlooking the plain. I learned a dreadful thing, though I lost not my head.

567. "TWO pedestrians appeared, I went to meet them; it was a woman with a slave; I recognized who was coming, it was Asmat'h, with dishevelled head, blood flowing from her face; no more did she call to me smiling, nor did she greet me with a smile.

568. "WHEN I saw her I became perturbed; my mind was maddened. I cried from afar: 'What has befallen us, why does the fire consume us?' She wept pitifully, she could hardly utter words, she said to me: 'God had engirt the sphere of the heavens in wrath for us!'

569. "I CAME near, I enquired again: 'What has happened to us? Tell me the truth.' Again she wept aloud piteously, again the flame burned her; for a long time she could

speak no word to me, not the tenth part of her griefs; her breast was dyed crimson with the blood trickling from her cheeks.

570. "THEN she said to me: 'I will tell thee, why should I hide it from thee? But inasmuch as I shall make thee to rejoice, so have mercy upon me, suffer me not to live, let me not survive, I entreat thee, have pity on me, save me from the passing world, fulfil thy duty to thy God.'

571. "SHE said to me: 'When thou slewest the bridegroom and the alarm was raised, the king heard it, he leaped up, he was sore stricken thereat; he called for thee, he ordered thee to be summoned, in a loud voice he cried; they sought thee, they could not find thee at home, and thereat the king complained.

572. "'THEY told him: "He is not here; he has somewhere passed the gates." The king said: "I know, I know, too well I understand; he loved my daughter, he shed blood in the fields, and when they saw each other they could not refrain from gazing.

573. "'"NOW, by my head! I will slay her who is called my sister; I told her God's will, she has caught her in the devil's net; what have those wicked lovers given or promised her? If I allow her to remain alive I renounce God; this is ready for her punishment."

574. "'SELDOM was it the king's wont to swear by his head, and when he thus swore he brake not his oath, forthwith he fulfilled it. Someone—who knows who?—who heard this

wrath of the king told it to Davar the Kadj, who knows even heaven by her sorcery.

575. "'SOME enemy of God told Davar, the king's sister: "The brother hath sworn by his head, he will not leave thee alive, the people know it." She spoke thus: "The good God knows that I am innocent, and let that same people know who it is that slays me and for whose sake I am slain."

576. "'MY mistress was the same as when thou didst leave her, head was still wrapped in thy veils, beautifully they became her. Davar spoke words such as I had never heard: "Harlot, thou harlot, why didst thou slay me? I think thou too shalt not rejoice.

577. "'"WANTON, harlot woman, why didst thou cause thy bridegroom to be slain, or why dost thou make me pay for his blood with mine? My brother shall not slay me in vain for what I have done, what I have made thee do! Now God grant thou mayst never meet him whom thou didst incite to hinder this!"

578. "'SHE seized her, dragged her along, tore her long hair, wounded her, bruised her, fiercely she frowned; Nestan could make no answer, but only sighed and moaned, a black woman was of no avail, she could not heal her wounds.

579. "'WHEN Davar was sated with beating and bruising, two slaves with Kadj-like faces came forth; they brought an ark

they spoke rudely to her, they put that sun inside, thus
was she made prisoner.

580. "'SHE said to them: "Go and lose her in the middle
of the great seas. Do not show her frozen water, let not
this water be slippery." Gleefully they began to laugh,
screaming with joy. All this I saw, nor did I die of it;
stronger than rock am I.

581. "'THEY passed the windows towards the sea, immediately
she was out of sight. Davar said: "Who would not stone me
for doing this? Who? Before P'harsadan slay me, I shall die.
Life is wearisome to me!" She struck herself with a knife,
died, fell in a stream of blood.

582. "'WHY marvel'st thou not to see me alive, unpierced by
a lance! Now do to me what befits a bringer of such
tidings; by the Most High, deliver from this unbearable
life me who have not yet ceased to breathe.' Her tears fell
piteously, undiminished, undrying.

583. "I SAID: 'Sister, why should I kill thee, or what is thy
fault? What shall I do in return for the debt I owe her?
Now I devote myself to seek her wherever rock and water
are found.' I became quite petrified; my heart grew like
hard rock.

584. "EXCESSIVE horror maddened me; fever and trembling
came upon me. I said to myself: 'Die not! To lie idle is of
no avail; better is it to roam forth to seek her, to run and
wander in the fields. Has come the time for thee, who wishest
to go with me!'

585. "I WENT in, I arrayed myself quickly, accoutred I mounted my horse. A hundred and sixty good knights serving me a long time joined me, we passed forth from the gates in order of battle. I went to the seashore, I saw a ship, the master of the ship saw me apparelled.

586. "I ENTERED the ship, I went out to sea, I cruised amidst the sea. I let no ship from any quarter pass unseen. I waited, but I heard nothing. Mad as I was I became still more maddened; God hated me so that He forsook me wholly.

587. "THUS I spent a year—twelve months which were to me like twenty—but I found no man, even in a dream, who had seen her. All those who were attendant upon me were dead and perished. I said: 'I cannot defy God; what He wills even that will I do.'

588. "I WAS weary of tossing on the seas, so I came ashore. My heart had become altogether like a beast's, I hearkened to no counsel; all those who were left to me in my misfortune have been scattered from me, but God abandons not a man thus forsaken by Fortune.

589. "ONLY this Asmat'h and two slaves remained with me as my comforters and counsellors. I could learn no news of Nestan, not even the weight of a drachm. Weeping seemed to me as joy, and streams of tears flowed down."

XXVI

The Story of Nuradin-P'hridon When Tariel Met Him on the Seashore

590. "I LANDED by night; I came ashore where gardens were
seen. It seemed as if there were a city; we came near, on
one side the rocks were hollowed out. The sight of men gave
me no pleasure; brands were imprinted on my heart. I
dismounted to rest at a spot where there were lofty trees.

591. "I FELL asleep at the foot of the trees; the slaves brake
bread. Then I woke sad, the soot of sorrow made night in
my heart; in so long a time I had learned nought, neither
gossip nor sooth; my tears pressed from mine eyes wet
the fields.

592. "I HEARD a shout. I looked round, a knight cried out
haughtily, he was galloping along the seashore, he was hurt
by a wound, his sword was broken and soiled, blood flowed
down; he threatened his foes, was wrathful, cursed,
complained.

593. "HE sat upon a black steed, the same which I now possess;
like the wind he swept along, enraged, wrathful. I sent
a slave to tell him I was desirous to meet him; I bade him
say: 'Stand! Declare unto me who angers thee, O lion!'

594. "HE spoke not to the slave, nor did he hear a word. Hastily I mounted, I went along to meet him; I overtook him, I came before him, I said: 'Stay, hearken to me! I too wish to know thine affair.' He looked at me, I pleased him, he checked his course.

595. "HE looked me over, and said to God: 'How hast Thou made such a tree!' Then he said to me: 'Now will I tell thee what thou askest me: Those enemies whom I had hitherto esteemed as goats have proved lions to me; they fell upon me traitorously when I was unready, I could not don mine armour.'

596. "I SAID: 'Stand, be calm, let us dismount at the foot of the trees! A goodly knight withdraws not when cuts are given with the sword.' I led him with me; we went away fonder than father and son. I marvelled at the tender beauty of the knight.

597. "ONE of my slaves was a surgeon, he bound up the wounds, he drew out the arrowheads so that the wounds hurt not. Then I asked: 'Who art thou, and by whom was thine arm hurt?' He set himself to tell me his story; he bewailed himself.

598. "FIRST he said to me: 'I know not what thou art, nor to what I can liken thee. What has thus consumed thee, or who first made thee full? What has turned thee sallow who wert planted rose and jet? Why has God put out the candle lighted by Himself?

599. "'NEAR by is the city of Mulghazanzar, which belongs to me. My name is Nuradin P'hridon, I am the king ruling there; here where ye are stationed is my boundary. I have little, but in all its parts it is of excellent quality.

600. "'MY grandfather shared his territory between my father and uncle. In the sea is an island, this he said was my share, it had fallen into the hands of that uncle whose sons have now wounded me; the hunting remained to them, they quarrelled with me.

601. "'TO-DAY I went forth to the chase, I hunted on the seashore, I wished to hunt with falcons, so I took not many beaters; I told the troops: "Wait for me till return." I kept no more than five falconers.

602. "'I WENT by ship; from the sea came forth a creek. I considered as nothing those divided from me; I said to myself: "Why should I take precautions against mine own folk?" They seemed timid to me; their multitude appeared not. I hunted and hallooed; I withheld not my voice.

603. "'OF a truth, they were wroth to think I scorned them thus; they secretly surrounded me with soldiers, they blocked the roads to the ship; mine own uncle's sons rode at their head, waving their arms they rushed on my soldiers to fight.

604. "'I HEARD them; I perceived the outcry and the flashing of swords. I begged a boat of the boatmen; but once I called out "Woe is me!" I went into the sea, warriors met

me like wavers, they would have overwhelmed me, but could not compass it.

605. "'YET more great hosts approached me from behind, from this side and that they came upon me, from one side they could not overpower me. When those in front could not come near me, from the back they shot at me; I trusted in my sword–it broke, my arrow were exhausted.

606. "'THEY engirt me; I could do no more. I made my horse leap over from the boat, I crossed the sea by swimming, those who beheld me were amazed; they slew all who were with me, I left them there; whoever pursued me could not confront me, when I turned I made them turn.

607. "'NOW that will be whatever is God's will. I think my blood will not be unavenged. May I have the power to bring my boast to fulfilment! I will make their existence a lamentation evening and morning. I will call the crows and ravens and make a banquet of them!'

608. "THAT youth won me to like him; my heart went out toward him. I said to him: 'There is no need at all for thee to hasten; I too will go with thee, there will they be slain; we two warriors shall surely not be afraid of them!'

609. "THIS also I said: 'Thou hast not heard my tale; I shall tell it to thee more fully when we have time.' He said to me

'What joy can weigh against this to me! To the day of my death my life will be devoted to thy service!'

610. "WE went to his fair, though small, city. The troops met him; for him they covered their heads with dust, they scratched their faces and threw away the fragments like splinters; they embraced him, they kissed his sword, its hilt and ring.

611. "AGAIN I pleased; I his new friend seemed fair to him. They spoke my praises: 'O sun, thou art a bringer of fine weather to us!' We went and saw his fair, rich city. Every form was clad in broad brocade."

XXVII

Tariel's Aid to P'hridon, and Their Victory Over Their Foes

612. "HE was healed, and able to fight and use horse and armour. We prepared galleys and the number of a host of troops; it needed a man to pray to God for some aid for those who gazed upon them.–Now will I tell thee of that knight's battle, the punisher of his adversaries.

613. "I PERCEIVED their design, and saw them donning their headgear. Ships met me, I know not if there were eight in all; swiftly I threw myself upon them; they began to row; I struck one of the ships with my heel and upset it; like women they bewailed themselves.

614. "I BETOOK myself to yet another, and seized the prow of the ship with my hand; I drowned them in the sea, I slew them; they had no opportunity for battle. The rest fled from me, they made for their harbour; all who saw me marvelled, they praised me, they hated me not.

615. "WE crossed the sea, we landed. Mounted they threw themselves on us. Again we engaged; there began the vicissitudes of battle. P'hridon's bravery and agility pleased me then; in warfare a lion, in face a sun, that aloe-tree fought.

616. "WITH his sword he cast down both his cousins, he cut their hands clean off; thus he crippled them; he led them away bound by the arms; the one did not abandon the two. He made their knights to weep, his knights to vaunt themselves.

617. "THEIR soldiers fled from us, we threw ourselves upon them, we scattered them; swiftly we seized the city, we wasted not time; we broke their legs with stones, we tanned their skin to leather. Kill me, if it was possible to empty the treasure both by lading and stowing!

618. "P'HRIDON inspected the treasures and put his seals upon them; he himself led away his two vanquished cousins; he shed their blood in exchange for his, and poured it out on the fields. Of me he said: 'Thanks to God who has planted aloe-trees!'

619. "WE went back to P'hridon's. The triumph exhibited by the citizens was heard; jugglers there laid hold on the heart of beholders. All uttered praise to me and Nuradin, in a panegyric; they said to us: 'Through the strength of your right arms their blood still flows!'

620. "THE soldiers acclaimed P'hridon as king and me as king of kings, themselves as subjects and me as sovereign of them all. I was gloomy, they could never find me culling roses; they knew not my story, there it was not lightly spoken of."

XXVIII

P'hridon Tells Tariel Tidings of Nestan-Daredjan

621. "ONE day the king and I went forth to the chase; we
climbed upon a cape jutting out into the sea. P'hridon
said to me: 'I will tell thee how, when we were out riding
for sport, I once saw a wonderful thing from this cape.'

622. "I BADE him speak, and P'hridon told me even this tale:
'One day I wished to hunt, I mounted this steed of mine. In
the sea it seemed a duck and on the land a falcon; I stood
here and watched the flight of the hawk thitherward.

623. "'NOW and then as I climbed uphill I gazed out to sea.
I perceived a small thing far away on the sea, going so
swiftly that nothing of its kind could equal it; I could not
make it out; in my mind I marvelled at these two things.

624. "'I SAID to myself: "What is it? To what can I liken it?
Is it bird or beast?" It was a boat tented over with many-
folded stuff; a steersman guided it. I fixed mine eyes upon
it, and there in an ark sat the moon; I would have given
her the seventh heaven as habitation.

625. "'TWO slaves as black as pitch crept out, they put ashore a maiden, I saw her thick-tressed hair, the lightning that flashed from her—to what colours can it be likened?—would illumine the earth and make the sunbeams of no account.

626. "'JOY made me hasten, quiver, stagger. I loved that rose who is not frozen by the snow. I resolved to engage them, I said: "Let me go towards them; what creatures can fly away from my black steed?"

627. "'I PRESSED my horse with my heel. There was a noise and rustling among the rushes. I could not reach her, however much I used the spur; they were gone. I came to the seashore and looked round, she appeared only as a last ray of the setting sun, she went farther away, she was gone from me, therefore was I consumed by flame.'

628. "This I heard from P'hridon; heat was added to my fire. I threw myself down from my horse, I wholly abased myself; with mine own blood shed from my cheeks I anointed myself. Kill me! That anyone but I should have seen that tree!

629. "THIS behaviour of mine astonished P'hridon, it seemed passing strange to him; but he was exceedingly pitiful to me, by weeping he placated me, like a son he soothed me, he pled with me, treated me with deference, and, pearl-like, hot tears sprang from his eyes.

630. "'ALAS! What have I, misguided, madly told thee?' I said: 'It matters not, grieve not for that! She was my moon for her the fire consumes me hotly. Now will I tell thee my tale, since thou thyself wishest to have me as comrade.'

631. "I TOLD P'hridon all that had befallen me. He said to me: 'What have I, mistaken, shamed, said to thee? Thou mighty king of the Indians, wherefore art thou come to me? A royal seat and throne become thee, a whole palace.'

632. "AGAIN he said to me: 'To whom God gives for form a young cypress, from him He withdraws the spear, though at first He lacerates his heart therewith. He will grant us His mercy, He will thunder it from heaven, He will turn our sorrow to joy, He will never grieve us.'

633. "WE went back tearful; we sat down alone together in the palace. I said to P'hridon: 'Save thee, none is mine aid. God has not sent thy like to earth, and since I know thee what more do I want?

634. "'THOU hadst no friend until the time when thou didst meet me; use now thy tongue and mind to counsel me in this: What can I do? What is the best thing to bring joy to her and me? If I can do nought I shall not survive a moment.'

635. "HE said to me: 'What better fate could I have from God than this? Thou art come to be gracious to me, king, sovereign of India. Needs it that after this I should desire any gratitude? I stand before thee as a slave to obey thee slavishly.

636. "'THIS city is the highway for ships coming from all parts, an emporium of much foreign news of all kinds. Here shall we hear of the balm to assuage the fire which

198

burns thee. God grant that these woes and pains pass away!

637. "'WE will send out sailors who have fared on the sea before let them find for us that moon for whose sake grief is not lacking to us; until then be patient, so that thy mind torture thee not; grief will not last for aye, shall not joy overcome it!'

638. "THAT very instant we called men, we settled the business: we commanded them: 'Go with ships, sail over the sea, seek her out for us, fulfil the desire of her lover; undergo a thousand hardships for this, not merely seven or eight.'

639. "HE appointed men wherever there were havens for ships; he gave orders: 'Seek out everywhere, wheresoever you hear of her.' Waiting seemed to me a consolation, my pains became lightened; absent from her I felt joy, and for the sake of that day I am ashamed.

640. "P'HRIDON set up a throne for me in the place for the overlord. He said to me: 'Hitherto have I erred, I could not comprehend what I should have understood; thou art the great king of the Indians; who can please thee? Wherewithal? How? Who is the man who would not be thy subject!'

641. "WHY should I lengthen the story? From all sides came the seekers of news, empty, and wearied of empty places; they had learned nothing at all, they knew not any news. As for me, afresh the undrying tear flowed still more from mine eyes.

642. "I SAID to P'hridon: 'How this day seems horrible to me,
I have God for my witness thereto; to speak thereof is hard
for me; without thee night and day alike seem eventide to
me; I am loosed from all joy, my heart is bound with grief.

643. "'NOW since I may no longer expect any news of her,
I can no longer stay; give me leave, I seek thy permission.'
When P'hridon heard this he wept, he watered the field with
blood, and said: 'Brother, from this day vain is all my joy!'

644. "THOUGH they tried very hard, they could not hold me
back; his armies came before me on bended knees, they
embraced me, kissed me, wept and made me weep. 'Go not
away; let us be your slaves so long as life is ours.'

645. "I SPOKE thus: 'Parting from you is very hard for me also,
but it is hardly possible for me to have joy without her.
I cannot forsake my captive Nestan, whom you yourselves
pity greatly; let none of you hinder me, I will not stay nor
be held back by any.'

646. "THEN P'hridon brought and gave me this horse of mine;
he said: 'Behold! this steed is given to you, the sun-faced,
the cypress; more I know thou desirest not, who could
despise such a gift? This will please thee by its breaking-in
and its swiftness.'

647. "P'HRIDON escorted me; as we went we both shed tears;
there we kissed each other, with cries we parted, all the host
lamented for me, truly, in their hearts, not with the tongue;
our severing was like that of foster-parent and child.

648. "DEPARTED from P'hridon, I went on the quest, again
I fared so that I missed nought on land or out at sea; but
I met no man who had seen her, and my heart became
wholly maddened, I was like a wild beast.

649. "I SAID to myself: 'No longer shall I rove and sail in vain;
perchance the company of beasts may make my heart forget
grief.' I said seven or eight words to my slaves and to this
Asmat'h: 'I know I have brought grief upon you; you have
good reason to murmur against me.

650. "'NOW go and leave me, provide for yourselves, look no
longer on the hot tears flowing from mine eyes.' When they
heard such discourse they said to me: 'Alas! Alas! let not
our ears hear what thou sayest!

651. "'LET us not see any master or lord apart from thee, may
God not sunder us from your horse's footprints! We would
gaze upon you, a fair and adorable spectacle.' Fate,
forsooth, makes a man listless, however valiant he may be.

652. "I COULD not send them away; I hearkened to the words
of my slaves, but I forsook the haunts of human tribes, the
retreats of goats and stags seemed a fitting abode for me;
I roamed, I trod every plain below and hill above.

653. "I FOUND these manless caves, hollowed out by Devis.
I combated them, I destroyed them, they could by no
means prevail against me; they killed my slaves, ill had they
buckled on their coats of mail. The passing world made me
gloomy; its showers again bespattered me.

654. "BEHOLD, brother! since that day am I here, and here I die. Mad I roam the fields; sometimes I weep and sometimes I faint. This maid will not abandon me; she too is burned by fire for Nestan's sake. I have no other resource to try but death.

655. "SINCE a beautiful tiger is portrayed to me as her image, for this I love its skin, I keep it as a coat for myself; this woman sews it, sometimes she sighs, sometimes she groans. Since I cannot kill myself, in vain is my sword whetted.

656. "THE tongues of all the sages could not forth-tell her praise. Enduring life, I think upon my lost one. Since then I have consorted with the beasts, calling myself one of them; I am suitor for death, nought else I entreat of God."

657. HE beat his face, he rent it, he tore his cheeks of rose; the ruby turned to amber, the crystal was shattered. Avt'handil's tears flowed too; one by one they dripped from his lashes. Then the maid soothed Tariel; on bended knee she besought him.

658. TARIEL, calmed by Asmat'h, said to Avt'handil: "I have made everything pleasant for thee, I who never found pleasure for myself. I have told thee the tale of mine irksome life; now go and see thy sun, thou whose time for meeting is nigh."

659. AVT'HANDIL said: "I cannot bear to part from thee; if I separate from thee tears indeed will flow from mine eyes. Verily I tell thee—be not wroth at this boldness—she for whose sake thou diest will not be comforted thereby.

660. "WHEN a physician–however praiseworthy he be–falls sick, he calls in another leech, another skilled in the pulse; him he tells what illness inflaming him with fire afflicts him. Another knows better what is useful advice for one.

661. "LISTEN to what I say to thee; I speak to thee as a sage and not as a madman; a hundred times must thou give heed, once sufficeth not. A man so furious of heart can do nought well. Now I desire to see her for whose sake hot fire consumes me.

662. "I SHALL see her, I shall confirm her love for me, I shall tell her what I have learned; nought else have I to do. I beseech thee to assure me, for God and heaven's sake, let us not abandon one another, make me swear and make thou an oath to me.

663. "IF thou promise me that thou wilt not go hence, I shall assure thee by an oath that for nought shall I forsake thee; I shall come again to see thee, I shall die for thee, for thee shall I rove. If God will, I shall make thee cease to weep thus for her for whom thou diest!"

664. HE answered: "How is it that thou, a stranger, so lovest me, a stranger? It is as hard for thee to part from me as for the nightingale from the rose. How can I forget thee, how can I cease to remember thee! God grant that I may again see thee, full-grown young aloe-tree.

665. "IF thy form remain a tree, and thy face turn round to see me, my heart will not flee into the fields, it will become neither a deer's nor a goat's. If I lie to thee or cheat thee,

may God judge me in wrath! Thy presence will charm away my sadness and dissolve it!"

666. HEREUPON they swore, the frank friends, those jacinths of amber hue, wise-worded but mad-minded. They loved each other; forever would affection's flame burn their hearts. That night the fair comrades spent together.

667. AVT'HANDIL wept with him; fast fell the tears. When day dawned he went forth, kissed him and parted from him. Tariel was so grieved that he knew not what to do. Avt'handil wept, too, as he rode through the rushes.

668. ASMAT'H went down with Avt'handil, she conjured him with an oath, she kneeled, she wept, she bent her fingers in entreaty, she besought him to come back soon; as a violet, so she faded. He replied: "O sister, of what can I think save you!

669. "SOON shall I come; I shall not forsake thee nor waste time at home. But let him not go elsewhere; let not that fair form wander. If I come not hither in two months I shall be doing a shameful thing; be assured that I am fallen into unceasing grief."

XXIX

The Story of Avt'handil's Return to Arabia After He Had Found and Parted From Tariel

670. WHEN he was gone thence sadness was surely slaying him: he scratched his face, he froze the rose of his cheeks, his hand became thorny; all the beasts licked up the blood that flowed from him. His swift pace shortened the long course.

671. HE came there where he had parted from his armies. They saw him, they knew him, they rejoiced in such manner as was fitting. They told the good tidings to Shermadin too; men quickly ran to him: "He is come for whose sake hitherto joy has been embittered to us."

672. HE went to meet him, he embraced him, he put his mouth on Avt'handil's hand, pouring forth tears he joyfully kissed the shedder of tears in the field. Thus he spoke: "O God, do I see really or darkly? How am I worthy of this, that mine eyes should gaze upon thee safe and sound!"

673. THE knight saluted him low, he put face upon face, he said "I thank God that no grief afflicts thee!" The lords did homage, whoever was worthy kissed him; there was great jubilation, great and small alike rejoiced.

674. THEY came where a dwelling-house had been built; all the city was assembled to see him; forthwith he sat down to feast, gay, proud, merry; an assemblage of tongues could not fully describe the joy of that day.

675. HE told Shermadin, he narrated to him all he had seen—how he had found that knight whom he likened to the sun. Avt'handil was hampered by tears; he said with half-closed eyes: "Without him it seems to me alike to dwell in palace or hut."

676. SHERMADIN told him all the home news: "None knows of thy departure; whatever thou toldst me so have I done." He went not thence that day, he feasted and rested; at dawn he mounted, he set out when the sun enlightened the day.

677. HE sat no more at feasting, nor stayed he again private; Shermadin, the bearer of good tidings, went to announce Avt'handil's arrival; swiftly he fared, in three days he made a ten days' journey. That lion Avt'handil rejoiced that he was to see the sun's rival.

678. HE sent a message: "O king, proud art thou in might and majesty! I venture to tell thee this thing with fear, respect and precaution: I esteemed myself worthless in that I had learned nought of that knight, now I know and will tell thee all; I come in joy and safety."

679. ROSTEVAN is a king, proud, puissant, imperious, so Shermadin delivered all his message in person: "Avt'handil comes to the royal presence having found that knight." The king said: "Now I know that which I entreated and prayed for from God."

680. SHERMADIN made report to T'hinat'hin, that nightless light: "Avt'handil comes to thy presence; he brings thee pleasing news." Thereat, light flashed forth from her, even braver than the sun's. She gave him a gift, and robes to all his people.

681. THE king mounted and went to meet the knight who was coming thither, for this honour the sun-faced one incurred a great debt of gratitude; joyous and warm-hearted they met, and some of the multitude of lords seemed as if drunken.

682. WHEN he approached, the knight alighted and did homage to the king. Rostevan, possessed by excess of joy, kissed him. Glad-hearted and merry they entered the royal hall; all there assembled rejoice at the arrival of the knight.

683. AVT'HANDIL, the lion of lions, did homage to her, the sun of suns; there the crystal, rose and jet were beautified by tenderness; her face was brighter than heaven's light; a dwelling-house was no fit abode for them, the sky itself was their proper palace.

684. THAT day they made a feast; drinking and eating they made abundant. The king gazes on the knight, as a tender father on a son. They were both beautified by a snowfall of fresh snow, a dew on the rose; generously they gave gifts, pearls like small coin.

685. THE drinking was done, the drinkers separated each to his own home; they suffered not the lords to go, they set the knight near before them. The king inquires, and he relates what trials he had undergone, and then what he had seen and heard concerning the stranger.

686. "WHEN I speak of him, be not astonished if I ceaselessly lament, saying: 'Ah me!' To the sun alone can I liken him, or the face of him, the extinguisher of the mind of all who see him; a wilted rose among thorns, alas! he is far away!

687. "WHEN the unendurable world makes a man suffer grief, the reed becomes like a thorn, the enamel turns to saffron colour." While Avt'handil was telling this his cheeks were bedewed with tears. He told in detail the story he had heard from Tariel.

688. "HAVING captured the caves in battle, he has for his house the abode of the Devis. He has the damsel of his beloved as his attendant. He is clad in tiger's skin; he despises brocade and cloth of gold. No more sees he the world; an ever-new fire consumes him."

689. WHEN he had finished the story—the matter of his grief—the sight of the light of that sun, not ugly to look upon, gladdened him. They praised his rose-like hand which had been firmly held. "This prowess is sufficient for thee since thou art the undoer of grief."

690. T'HINAT'HIN rejoiced at the hearing of this news. That day she was merry at the drinking, and eating was not wearisome to her. Avt'handil met in his bedchamber T'hinat'hin's slave who spoke wisely. She ordered him to come to her. Tongue cannot tell how pleased he was.

691. THE knight went joyful, tender, not ill content, the lion who had roamed the fields with the lions of the field and had lost his colour, a knight of the world, in quality a gem and

a beautiful ruby of first water, but for heart's sake he had exchanged heart for heart.

692. BOLD sits the sun upon her throne, majestic, unconstrained, a fair aloe planted in Eden, generously watered by Euphrates' stream; the jetty hair and the eyebrow thickets adorned the crystal and ruby. Who am I that I should praise her? It needs the myriad tongues of Athenian sages to praise her fitly.

693. SHE set the joyful knight before her with his chair, they both sat full of gladness to converse as befitted them; they spoke with dignity and fluency, not with unpolished words. She said: "Thou hast found him in whose quest thou hast seen misfortunes?"

694. HE answered: "When the world gives a man his heart's desire, it befits not to recall grief which is as a day that is past. I found the tree, an aloe in form, watered by the stream of the world; there I found the face which was like the rose, but now is wan.

695. "THERE saw I the cypress, the rose-like, whose power was spent; he says: 'I have lost the crystal, and that where the crystal unites with enamel.' I burn for him because, like me unendurable fire consumes him." Then again he told the story he had heard from Tariel.

696. HE recounted all his misfortunes and sorrows by the road during the quest. Then he told her how God had thought him worthy to find what he desired. "World, life, man, all seems to him as to a beast; alone he roams mad with the brutes, he weeps in the field.

697. "ASK me not what praise can I speak, how couldst thou understand from me! Nothing can please one who has seen him; the eyes of the beholders are weakened as by the brilliance of the sun; the rose is become saffron, now the violet is gathered in nosegays."

698. HE told her in detail what he knew, what he had seen, heard: "Like a tiger he has a trail, and for house and abode a cave; a damsel is there ready to cherish him, to maintain his life and bear his sorrows. Alas! The world makes all dwellers in the world to shed tears!"

699. WHEN the maiden heard this story she had attained the fulfilment of her will; her moon-like face shone as 'twere with radiance at the full. She said: "What answer can I make to give comfort to him, and pleasure, and what is the balm for the healing of his wound?"

700. THE knight replied: "Who has confidence in a rash man? He for my sake sacrifices himself to be burned, he who must not be burned. I have appointed the time of my return; I have promised him to sacrifice myself for him. I swear it by my sun whom I contemplate as a sun!

701. "A FRIEND should spare himself no trouble for his friend's sake, he should give heart for heart, love as a road and a bridge. Then, again, the grief of his beloved should be a great grief to a lover. Lo! without him joy is nought to me, and myself I hold of none account."

702. THE sun-like one said: "All my heart's desire is fulfilled: first thou art come in safety having found that which was

lost, then the love implanted by me in thee has grown, I have found balm for my heart hitherto burned.

703. "THE passing world treats every man like the weather, sometimes there is sunshine and sometimes the sky thunders forth in wrath; hitherto grief has been upon me, now this gladness is my lot; since the world has joy in it why should any be sad!

704. "THOU dost well not to break the oath thou didst swear; it is necessary to fulfil strong love for a friend, to seek for his cure, to know the unknown. But tell me, what shall I, luckless, do if the sun of my heaven be hidden!"

705. THE knight replied: "By nearness to thee I have united to seven woes eight. Vain is it for one who is frozen to blow on water to warm himself therewith; vain is the love, the kiss from beneath, of the sun at its setting. If I be near thee, once is it woe, and if I go far from thee a thousandfold woe.

706. "WOE is me if I wander where, alas! the flame burns the roamer; my heart is the target of an arrow, a dart is shot to pierce it; the term of my life seems by this day to be shortened to one-third; I long for a refuge, but the time is past for seeking shelter against troubles.

707. "I HAVE heard your discourse, I have understood what you command; the thorn reveals the rose, why should I prick myself with prickles? But, O sun, become altogether a sun for me, and let me carry with me some hopeful token of life."

708. THE knight, sweetly and in sweet-sounding language giving good for good, spoke on this theme like a pleasant instructor to a pupil. The maiden gave him a pearl, she fulfilled his desire, and God grant that their present joy be perfected.

709. WHAT is better than for a man to approach the jet to the crystal and ruby, or to plant in the garden the aloe near the cypress, to water it and make a tree of it, to cause joy to the gazer and sorrow to him who cannot look thereon? Woe to the parted lover! He will be groaning, moaning, groaning.

710. THEY found all their joy in gazing at each other. The knight went away, sundered from her he went dazed in heart; the sun wept tears of blood more abundant than the sea, and said: "The world is insatiable, alas! in the drinking of my blood!"

711. THE knight went melancholy away, he beats his breast and so bruises it, for love makes a man weep and melts his heart. When a cloud hides the sun the earth is shadowed, so parting from his beloved makes twilight again, not morning.

712. BLOOD and tears mingled made channel upon channel on his cheeks. He said: "My sun is by no means satisfied with me because I sacrifice myself to her comfort. I marvel how the black eyelash brands the heart of diamond. Until I see her, O world, I wish for no joy from thee.

713. "HIM who yesterday was an aloe planted, watered and fully grown in Eden, him to-day the passing world thrusts through with her lance, pierces with her knife. To-day my

heart is caught in a net of unquenchable fire. Now know
I the way of the world; it is a tale and nonsense."

714. THUS speaking, the tears gush forth, he trembles and
shudders; with heart-sigh, with deep groan, his form bends
and sways. Converse with the beloved is embittered by
parting. Alas! O passing world! The end enshrouds and
swathes man.

715. THE knight went and sat in his chamber; sometimes he
weeps, sometimes he swoons, but in spirit he is near his
beloved, he is not cut off from her. Like verdure in hoarfrost
the hue of his face fades; see how soon lack of sun is
apparent on the rose!

716. ACCURSED is the heart of man, greedy, insatiable;
sometimes the heart desiring joys endures all griefs; blind
is the heart, perverse in seeing, not at all able to measure;
no king, nor even death itself, can master it.

717. WHILE he spoke to his heart hearty words, he took the
pearls, the love-token of his sun, which had engirt the arm
of his sun, and were comparable to her teeth; he put them
to his mouth, he kissed them, his tears flowed like byssus.

718. WHEN day dawned there came an inquirer calling him to
the court; the knight went forth, proud, gentle, not having
slept, unrefreshed by sleep. A host of spectators who had
hastened stood crowding one upon another. The king was
arrayed for the field; drum and clarion were prepared.

719. THE king mounted. How can the pomp of those times be
told now? By reason of the beating of the copper drums no
word was heard by the ears. The hawks darkened the sun;
hither and thither coursed the hounds; that day the fields
were dyed purple with the blood shed by them.

720. THEY hunted, they returned joyful, having traversed the
meadow; they took in with them lords, princes and all the
hosts. The king sat down; he found the couches and all the
pavilions adorned; harp harmonized with castanets, there
was a full choir.

721. THE knight sat near the king, one questioned, the other
replied; the crystal and ruby of their lips shone transparent
the lightning of their teeth flashed; those who were worthy
sat near, they listened; afar off the hosts were grouped;
none dared speak without mention of Tariel.

722. THE knight departed sad at heart, his tears flowed on the
fields; nought save his love passed before his eyes;
sometimes he rises, sometimes he lies down. How can one
sleep who is mad! Whose heart e'er hearkened to a prayer
for patience!

723. HE lies down; he says: "What can I imagine as any
consolation for my heart? I am sundered from thee, thou
tree, in form as a reed, reared in Eden, thou joy of thy
beholders, cause of woe to them that cannot gaze on thee.
Since I am unworthy to see thee manifestly, would that
I might behold thee in a dream."

724. THUS spake he, weeping, with flowing tears. Once more he addressed his heart: "Patience is like the fountain-head of wisdom. If we endure not what can we do? How can we adapt ourselves to anguish? If we desire happiness from God we must accept griefs also."

725. AGAIN he says: "O heart, however much thou hast the desire for death it is better to bear life, sacrificing self for her; but hide it, let not the flame of thy fire be seen again. It ill befits a lover to expose his love."

XXX

Avt'handil's Request to King Rostevan, and the Vizier

726. WHEN day dawned the knight arrayed himself and went forth early. He says: "I would that my love be not revealed that I may conceal it!" For patience he prays: "Contrive something for my heart!" The moon-like one mounted his horse; he went to the house of the vizier.

727. THE vizier heard of it, went to meet him: "The sun is risen upon my house; this day, meseems, a presentiment of joy announced to me this good news." He met Avt'handil, saluted him, respectfully addressed to the perfect one perfect praise. A welcome guest should have a cheerful host.

728. THIS host, not listless, ill-disposed or idle, helped the knight to dismount; they stretched on the floor under his feet a Cathayan rug. The knight illumined the house as the sun's beam the universe. They said: "To-day the western gale has wafted us the fragrant odour of roses."

729. HE sat; they that looked on him truly maddened their hearts. They who gazed on him accounted it an honour to swoon for his sake; many sighs were uttered, not once but a thousand times; they were ordered to depart, they went away, the household was thinned out.

730. WHEN the household was gone, the knight addressed the vizier; quoth he: "In the council chamber nought will ever be hidden from thee; in every matter of state the king does what thou desirest, and agrees with thee. Now hearken to my woes; cure me with what will heal me.

731. "THE fire of yon knight burns me, the flame that consumes him afflicts me; I am slain by longing and by not seeing the object of my desire; he would not grudge his life for me; what is due must be paid; one must love a generous ungrudging friend.

732. "THE sight of him caught my heart as in a net, therein it stays; my patience, too, remains with him; in that he burns those near him, God created him indeed a sun. Moreover, Asmat'h is become a sister to me, more than a born sister.

733. "WHEN I departed I swore with a fearful oath: 'I shall come again, I shall see thee not with a face despised of foes; thou art of darkened heart, I shall seek light for thee.' It is time for me to go, therefore am I burned with hot fire.

217

734. "ALL this I tell thee truly, not with braggart speech; he awaits me, and I cannot set forth. This it is that adds to the hot fires; I cannot break my vow, I mad cannot abandon him mad. When and where did ever a breaker of oaths prevail?

735. "GO to the palace, report on my behalf to King Rostevan what I have told thee. By his head I swear to thee, Vizier Ustasra, if he keep me not captive I shall not stay; if he keep me captive what can he make of me? Help me; let not the fire hurt and destroy my heart!'

736. "SAY from me: 'Let every mouth which is not speechless praise thee! Let God, the means of light, make known to thee how I fear thee. But that knight, an aloe-tree in form, burned me with fire; forthwith he took away my heart, in no wise could I keep it.

737. "'NOW, O king, for me existence lacking him is utterly impossible; he, the dauntless, has my heart. Of what avail am I here? If I can be of any service to him, to you first will the glory belong; if I fail to accomplish aught for him I shall set my heart at rest, mine oath will not have been broken.

738. "'LET not my going anger or grieve your heart. Let that befall my head whate'er God wills. May He grant you the victory, and send me your servant back to you; but if I return not may you still reign, may your foes be affrighted.'"

739. YET again the sun-faced one says to the vizier: "I have shortened my speech. Now speak thus to the king till others come in to inform him, pleasantly entreat for me my congee, summon up thy courage, and a hundred thousand red pieces shall be bestowed on thee as a bribe."

740. THE vizier said with a smile: "Keep thy bribe for thyself: for me it is sufficient favour from thee that thou hast found the road hither. How can I dare tell the king what I have now heard from you! I know of a truth he will fill me with favours, and gain is not disagreeable!

741. "BY his head! he will slay me straightway: I doubt whether he will delay even a moment. Thy gold will remain with thee, but for me, luckless, there will be earth for a grave. Slay me! What is of equal value with life to a man! The thing cannot be said and I cannot say it, however much anyone should reproach me.

742. "THIS road leads to no aim. How can I, luckless, lay down my life for thee? He will despoil me or kill me. He will say: 'How dost thou speak these words? Why didst thou not guess all there is to be done? Why art thou such a madman?' Life is better than loot; this I even now learn.

743. "EVEN if the king permit thee to depart, why should the hosts also be deceived? Why should they let thee go, why should they be hoodwinked, or why should they be removed far from their sun? If thou depart, our foes will become bold, will even themselves with us; but this must not be, as sparrows cannot change to hawks."

744. THE knight wept; with tears he spoke: "Must I strike a knife into my heart! O vizier, it is apparent in thee thou knowest not what love is, nor hast thou in others seen friendship or oath. Or if thou hast seen such, how canst thou prove that without him my joy is possible?

745. "THE sun has turned. I knew not what would make the sun turn. Now let us help him; it is better for us, in return he will warm our day. No one knows mine affairs like myself; what embitters me, what sweetens me. The discourse of idle men greatly grieves a man.

746. "OF what profit can I be to the king or his hosts since I am mad now, and my tears flow unceasingly! It is better that I go away; I will not break my word; oaths prove a man. What man has borne grief that Tariel has not?

747. "NOW, O vizier, how can thy cursed heart be calm in this juncture! Iron in my place would become wax and not hard rock; I cannot repay his tears, even if Gihon[1] flowed from mine eyes. Help me if thou wouldst desire help from me.

748. "IF he give me not leave I shall steal away, unknown shall I depart from him; as it entreats me so shall I deliver my heart to be consumed by fire. I know he will do nothing to thee because of me, if he be not disposed to exile thee. Promise me—whatever may happen to thee—'I shall sacrifice myself to be tortured!'"

---

[1] River in Messopotamia.

749. THE vizier said: "Thy fire consumes me also with fire. I can no longer look on thy tears, the world itself vanishes; sometimes speech is better than silence, sometimes by speaking we spoil things. I shall speak; if I die it matters not, my life will be sacrificed for thee."

750. WHEN the vizier had said this he arose and went to the palace. He saw the king arrayed; the sun-like face looked straight upon him. He was afraid, he dared not tell him unpleasing news; perplexed he stood, he thought not on war-like matters.

751. THE king saw the vizier struck dumb by sadness. He said: "What grieves thee? What knowest thou? Why art thou come sad?" He answered: "I know nothing at all, but I am indeed wretched. You will be justified in slaying me when you hear the astounding news.

752. "MY mourning neither adds to my grief nor surpasses it; I am afraid, though an envoy has no care for fear. Now Avt'handil bids thee farewell, he entreats, he wrangles not; he says that for him the world and life are nought without yon knight."

753. WITH timorous tongue he told him all he knew. He added thereafter: "How canst thou know by such words in what a plight I saw him and how his tears flowed? Though you should let your wrath fall forthwith on me, you are just."

754. WHEN the king had heard this he was wroth, he lost his senses, his colour waned and he became terrible, he would have terrified onlookers. He cried: "What has made a

madman of thee? Who else would have related this? It is the plight of a bad man to learn early what is evil.

755. "TRAITOR-LIKE, thou hast told me of this as if it were a merry matter; what more could anyone do to me save slay me faithlessly, treacherously? Madman, how couldst thou employ thy tongue to dare to speak thus to me now! Such a madman as thou art is unworthy to be vizier or aught else.

756. "SHOULD not a man spare his lord what is irksome, when he stupidly chatters stupid speech? Why were mine ears not deafened before hearing such a thing! If I kill thee, my neck must bear the responsibility for thy blood!"

757. AGAIN he spake: "If thou hadst not now been sent hither by him, by my head! I had cut off thy head, let there be no doubt of this! Go, withdraw! Look at the mad, stupid, desperate improper fellow! Brave word, brave man, brave the deed done by him!"

758. HE bent down, he threw chairs, he hit the wall and shattered them; he missed his aim, but for the vizier's sake he made the chairs like diamond, not willow-like. "How couldst thou tell me of the going of him who plaited the aloe-tree branches!" Hot tears hollowed out channels in the vizier's white cheeks.

759. THE wretched vizier hurried away; he dared say no more. He crept off crestfallen like a fox; his wounded heart pains

him. He comes in a courtier, he goes out gloomy, so much
does the tongue dishonour him. A foe cannot hurt a foe
as a man harms himself.

760. HE said: "What more will God show me like unto my
woes? Why was I deceived? Why was I darkened? Would
that someone might enlighten me! Whoever announces
anything so boldly to a sovereign, my evil days stand upon
him too; how can he ever enjoy peace!"

761. THE disgraced vizier went away in black luck. Gloomily,
sad-faced, he said to Avt'handil: "What thanks can I give
thee! Thanks to thee, what a courtier am I become! Alas!
I have lost my peerless self by mine own fault!"

762. HE begs the bribe and behaves sportively, albeit his tears
were not dry. I marvel why he spends his time in making
jokes, why he is not grieved in heart! Quoth he: "He who
gives not what he promised quarrels with the Mourav[1]. It is
said: 'A bribe settles matters even in hell.'

763. "HOW he took the matter, what he said to me, it is not to
be told by me. What evil, what stupidity, what idiocy, what
madness he attributed to me! I myself am no longer worthy
of the name of man; no longer have I sense. At this I
marvel—why he slew me not; God must have given him
patience.

---

[1] *Mourav*—the headman of a town.

764. "I KNEW too what I did; it happened not to me by mistake. I had pondered, I knew he would be wroth with me, therefore is my grief increased. None can avoid vengeance for a deed done by Providence. Still, for thy sake death seems joy to me; my woes are not in vain."

765. THE knight replied: "It is wholly impossible for me not to depart. When the rose withers the nightingale then dies; he must seek a dewdrop of water, for the sake of this he must rove everywhere, and if he cannot find it what will he do or wherewith shall he soothe his heart?

766. "WITHOUT him I cannot bear to sit or lie. I will choose to roam like the beasts, with them to run. Why does Rostevan desire me who am in such a state to fight his adversaries! It is better to have no man at all than to have a dissatisfied one.

767. "I WILL tell him once again; now, however angry the king may be, surely he can judge how my heart burns and flames. If he grant me not leave, I shall steal away when hope is gone. If I die, my portion and world will be uprooted."

768. WHEN they had conversed, the vizier made a banquet befitting them; he played the host, gave fair gifts to the fair guest, he enriched his attendants, both youths and greybeards. They parted; the knight went home as the sun was setting.

769. THE form of the sun-faced Avt'handil was like that of a cypress; he bound up a hundred thousand pieces of gold, three hundred pieces of gold brocade—he was generous and open-handed—sixty precious rubies and jacinths, the colour of which could not displease. He sent a man to carry these presents from him.

770. AVT'HANDIL sent a message to the king saying: "How can I give or bestow on thee that which befits thee? What return can I think of for the debts I owe thee? If I survive I shall die for thee; I shall make myself thy slave. I shall repay love with love, with a like weight."

771. HOW can I tell his peerlessness, valour, and praise him! He was a man fitting and worthy even of such a deed. Thus should service be, as much as lies in one's power. When a man is in trouble then needs he brother and kinsman.

XXXI

Avt'handil's Discourse With Shermadin When He Stole Away

772. THE sun-faced, dispenser of light, speaks to Shermadin and says: "This day is hope, the comforter of my heart, that thou wilt show what thou canst do for me." It needs a reader and a listener for the praise of this story of them.

773. HE says: "Rostevan did not grant me leave, he hearkened not even to a word from me; he knows not wherein one's being lies and how one's life is in another. Without Tariel in truth I live not, neither abroad nor at home. What unrighteous deed has God ever forgiven to anyone?

774. "THOUGH I resolved not to forsake him, and my decision is final—every liar and traitor insults God by his lies—the heart seeing not him weeps and sighs, moans and groans, it comes not near to any joy, it shudders, grows sullen, shuns all mankind!

775. "THREE are the ways of showing friendship by a friend: First, the wish for nearness, impatience of distance; then giving and not grudging, unweariedness in liberality; and attention and aid, roaming in the fields to help him.

776. "BUT why should I lengthen speech; it is time to shorten it
Now to steal away is the healing of this bruised heart.
Hearken to what I shall entreat so long as thou hast time in
my company, and fortify thyself in observance of what
I have already taught thee.

777. "NOW prepare as first leader to serve the sovereigns,
manifest thy valour and integrity in all things. Take care
of my household, command my troops, repeat anew the
service, the attention thou hast hitherto shown.

778. "KEEP my foes out of the marches, let not thy might fail
in aught, grudge no good to the loyal, may they that are
false-hearted towards thee be slain; if I return, well shall
thy due be repaid to thee by me; service to a master is
never lost."

779. WHEN he heard this, the hot tear flowed from Shermadin's
eyes. Quoth he: "Wherefore should I be affrighted by
sorrow in loneliness! But what shall I do without thee—
twilight will fall on my heart! Take me with thee to serve
thee; I will help thee however thou wishest.

780. "WHO has heard of so great wandering by one alone! Who
has heard of a knight holding back from his lord in trouble!
Thinking thee lost, what shall I, useless, do here?" The
knight answered: "I cannot take thee, however many tears
thou sheddest.

781. "HOW can I disbelieve thy love for me! But the thing
cannot be; thus time has taken up arms against me. To

whom can I entrust my house; save thee, who is fit? Calm
thy heart, believe me, I cannot take thee! I cannot!
I cannot!

782. "SINCE I am a lover I must run mad alone in the fields.
Should not one with blood-stained tears roam alone!
Errantry is the business of lovers; how can one wait till he
is grown old? This world is such, be thou assured thereof
and submit.

783. "WHEN I am far from thee, think of me, love me. I fear
not my foes; I shall take care of myself. A brave man must
be of good cheer, he must not mope in grief; I hate when a
man does not stop at a shameful deed.

784. "I AM such an one who considers this world as an old
cucumber, one to whom death for a friend seems a sport
and a play. I have left my sun, she grants me leave, why
should I linger! Then, if I leave my sun can I not leave my
home?

785. "NOW give thee my testament addressed to Rostevan.
I will confide thee to him, and entreat him to care for thee
as befits one brought up by me. Should I die, slay not
thyself; do not the deed of Satan; weep thereupon, fill the
channel of the eyes."

XXXII

The Testament of Avt'handil to King Rostevan When He Stole Away

786. HE sat down to write the will, thus piteously inditing:
"O king! I have stolen away in quest of him I must seek.
I cannot remain sundered from him, the kindler of my fires
Forgive me and be merciful to me like as God.

787. "I KNOW that in the end thou wilt not blame this my
resolve. A wise man cannot abandon his beloved friend.
I venture to remind thee of the teaching of a certain
discourse made by Plato: 'Falsehood and two-facedness
injure the body and the soul.'

788. "SINCE lying is the source of all misfortunes, why should
I abandon my friend, a brother by a stronger tie than born
brotherhood? I will not do it! What avails me the
knowledge of the philosophizing of the philosophers!
Therefore are we taught that we may be united with the
choir of the heavenly hosts.

789. "THOU hast read how the apostles write of love, how
they speak of it, how they praise it; know thou it and

229

harmonize thy knowledge: 'love exalteth us,' this is as it were the tinkling burden of their song; if thou conceive not this how can I convince ignorant men?

790. "HE who created me, even He gave me power to overcome foes; He who is the invisible Might, the Aid of every earthly being, who fixes the bounds of the finite, sits immortal God as God, He can in one moment change a hundred into one and one into a hundred.

791. "WHAT God wills not will not become fact. The violet fades, the rose withers, if they cannot gaze on the sunbeams every lovely thing is desirable for the eye to gaze on. How can I endure the lack of him, or how can life please me!

792. "HOWEVER angry thou art, forgive me that I have not kept your command; enthralled, I had no power to fulfil it. No! To go was the remedy for the flaming of my furnaces. Wherever I may be, what matters it to me if I have but my freewill?

793. "SADNESS avails thee not, nor useless flow of tears. The deed which is inevitably decreed above cannot be avoided. It is a law with men that they should struggle and suffer woes, and no creature of flesh hath power to thwart Providence.

794. "WHATEVER God has predestined to come to pass upon me let it be fulfilled, and when I return my heart will no longer remain ashes. May I see you also joyful in majesty

and manifold wealth. What I can do for him is my glory, and this is sufficient booty for me.

795. "O KING, this is my decision. Slay me! if anyone can disapprove! O king, can it be that my going grieves thee! I cannot be false, I cannot do a cowardly deed; he would shame me when we meet face to face in that eternity whereto we both shall come.

796. "MINDFULNESS of a friend ne'er doeth us harm. I despise the man who is shameless, false and treacherous. I cannot be false; I cannot do it for a mighty king. What is worse than a hesitant, tardy-going man!

797. "WHAT is worse than a man in the fight with a frowning face, shirking, affrighted and thinking of death! In what is a cowardly man better than a woman weaving a web! It is better to get glory than all goods!

798. "A NARROW road cannot keep back Death, nor a rocky one; by him all are levelled, weak and strong-hearted; in the end the earth unites in one place youth and greybeard. Better a glorious death than shameful life!

799. "AND now I fear, O king, to make this request to you: mistaken, mistaken is he who expects not death momentarily; it which unites us all comes alike by day and by night. If I see thee not living, life will be fleeting for me.

800. "IF the passing world, the destroyer of all, destroy me, an orphan I shall die travelling, unmourned by parent, nor

will those who brought me up, nor the friend whom I trust,
enshroud me; then indeed will your merciful, tender heart
have pity on me.

801. "I HAVE countless possessions weighed by none: Give the
treasure to the poor, free the slaves; enrich every orphan
without means; they will be grateful to me, remember me,
bless me; I shall be thought of.

802. "WHATEVER is not worthy of being kept in your
treasury, give part to build orphan homes, part to build
bridges; be not sparing in the spending of mine estate for
me; I have none save thee to quench the hot fires.

803. "HENCEFORTH thou shalt learn no more news from me,
herewith I commit my soul to thee; this letter tells thee so,
without flattering thee; the devil's deeds shall not seduce
my soul, it will prevail; forgive me and pray for me; what
can be exacted from me dead?

804. "I ENTREAT thee, O king, for Shermadin my chosen
servant. This year he hath an added day[1] of grief. Comfort
him with the favour I was wont to favour him withal; make
not the tears to flow from his eyes welling with blood.

805. "MY testament is ended, written by mine own hand.
Behold, mine upbringer, I have parted from thee; I am gone
away with maddened heart. Let not the sovereigns be

---

[1] In Georgian *naki*, the extra day in leap year.

grieved for my sake, be ye not clad in gloom, but be ye in your sovereignty feared by foes."

806. WHEN he had made an end of writing he gave the will to Shermadin. He said: "Convey this wisely to the king; none can excel thee in any service." He embraced him and wept over him bloody-hued tears.

XXXIII

Avt'handil's Prayer and His Flight

807. HE prayed and said: "Great God of earths and heavens, who sometimes punishest, sometimes art ready to reward, Unknowable and Unspeakable, Lord of lordships, give me to endure longings, O ruler of heart-utterances!

808. "GOD, God, I beseech Thee, who govern'st the deeps and heights; Thou didst create love, Thou hast decreed its law; the world has sundered me from mine excellent sun; uproot not the love sowed by her for me!

809. "GOD, God, merciful, I have none beside Thee; from Thee I beg aid on the road, however long I travel; shelter me from the mastery of foes, the turmoil of the seas, the evil one by night! If I survive, I shall serve Thee, I shall offer sacrifice to Thee."

810. WHEN he had prayed, he mounted his horse and privily passed through the gates; he sent back Shermadin, albeit he made great lamentations. The vassal weeps and beats his breast; his blood flowed over the rocks. What can rejoice the vassal deprived of the sight of his lord!

811. NOW will I begin another tale; I will attend the parting knight. There was no audience that day for the wrathful Rostevan. When day dawned he rose sullen; he was as if he poured flame from his face; he commanded the vizier to be called; thither they led him pale with fear.

812. WHEN he saw the vizier arrived with reverence in the hall of audience, Rostevan said: "I recall not what thou saidst yesterday; thou didst annoy and enrage me, for a long time I could not compose my soul, therefore did I scold thee, vizier, heart of hearts.

813. "I REMEMBER not what Avt'handil wanted, nor why I treated thee so ill! Truly say the sages: 'Spite is net of woes!' Never act in such a way! Consider the matter carefully. Now, tell me what thou saidst! Speak and repeat thy discourse!"

814. AGAIN the vizier submitted his speech of yesterday. When Rostevan heard it, he made no lengthy answer: "If I think thee not mad may I be the Jew Levi! Let me hear no more of this, else I wholly give thee up!"

815. WHEN the vizier went forth to seek, he could not find the enamel one, Avt'handil; only the slaves with flowing tears told of his flight. The vizier said: "I cannot go to court; I should remember former days. Whoever is daring let him dare; I repent what I have already said."

816. WHEN the vizier came not, the king again sent a man; the man learned the news and stood outside, none dared report the departure. Rostevan began to suspect, therefore grief increased tenfold. He said: "Doubtless he who alone overpowers hundreds has stolen away!"

817. WITH bent head he meditated; in his heart was great gloom. He sighed and looked up; he commanded a slave: "Go, let that villain come hither and tell me now; let him enter." When the vizier came back his colour paled and he was careful.

818. AGAIN the vizier entered the audience chamber, gloomily, not gaily. The king inquired: "Is the sun gone away, become inconstant like the moon?" The vizier told him all, how Avt'handil had gone away secretly: "The sun no longer shines on us; the weather is not bright!"

819. WHEN the king heard this, he cried out with an exceeding great cry, he lamented, he said: "Alas, my foster-son, my dazed eyes shall see thee no more!" He made the onlookers to marvel by scratching his face and tearing his beard. "Whither art thou gone, and where hast thou lost those pillars of light?

820. "IF thou hast thyself, none will think thee a wanderer; but as for me, what can I do, O foster-son? Now cells befit me as an abode; thou hast left me orphaned, me whose wretched heart longs for thee. Till I am reunited to thee, tongues cannot tell my sufferings!

821. "WHEN shall I see thee joyous returning from the chase? I shall no longer see thee after the game of ball, graceful in form, a faultless gem! No more shall I hear thine alluring voice. Now without thee, alas! what shall I do with the throne and the whole palace?

822. "I KNOW that hunger will not kill thee, however far thou roamest thy bow will provide thee, and thine arrowheads. Perchance God in His mercy will again lighten our woes; but if I die, O foster-son, by whom shall I be mourned!"

823. A NOISE was heard, a great host of men had assembled; there is a crowd of courtiers at the palace, seizing their beards with their hands; all rend and strike themselves, the sound of their slapping is heard. They said: "Darkness is upon us, accursed, since our sun is gone from the sky!"

824. WHEN the king saw his lords, he complained to them with tears and groaning. He said: "You see our sun has made his rays quite rare to us! In what have we annoyed him, wherein have we sinned, why has he parted from us, why forsaken us! How can any take for us the leadership of the hosts he maintained!"

825. ALL wept, lamented; then at length they grew calm. The king commanded: "Ask! is he alone, or with a squire?" The vassal Shermadin came fearfully, shamefacedly; he gave the testament, he wept, life seemed to him but loss.

826. HE said: "I found this written by him in his chamber; weeping slaves stood there, they tore hair and beard; he is

stolen away alone, neither youth nor greybeard is near him; if you slay me it will be just, an unseemly life irks me."

827. WHEN they read the testament, again they wept a long time. Then the king commanded: "Let not my troops don gay colours. Let us make the downtrodden, the orphans and widows, to pray; let us help them that God may give him paths of peace!"

XXXV

Avt'handil's Second Departure and Meeting with Tariel

828. WHEN the moon is far from the sun, distance makes her bright; when she is near, his ray consumes her—she is repelled, she cannot approach. But sunlessness dries up the rose and lessens its colour. Not seeing the beloved renews in us our old grief.

829. NOW will I begin the story of that knight's departure. He goes away and weeps with boiling heart; it cannot be said that his tears diminished. Every moment he turned back; he prayed that he might find his sun-like one in sun-like beauty. He gazed, he could not detach his eyes; if he tore them away he lost consciousness.

830. WHEN he was near fainting, he had no power to move his tongue, but tears run from his eyes, pouring forth as from a spring. Sometimes he turns; he looks for means to bear his pains. When he goes forward he knows not whither his horse has borne him.

831. HE said: "O mine own! Let him who is far from thee and yet silent be accursed; since my mind remains with thee,

let my heart also return to thee; the weeping eyes, too, wish and long to see thee. It is better that the lover should be subjected as much as may be to love!

832. "WHAT shall I do till I am united to thee, or in what thinkest thou I shall find joy! I would slay myself but that I doubt it would displease thee, but it would grieve thee to hear I was no longer living. Come then and let us living give our eyes to the shedding of tears."

833. HE wept and repeated: "Ten lances have pierced my heart! An army of Indians—the dense thicket of her eyelashes—has slain me. Her jet eyes lend her beauty. But why have they overcome me? Eyelashes, eyes, teeth, lips and black hair are the cause of my suffering."

834. HE said: "O sun, who art said to be the image of the sunny night of Him who is One in unity of being and Everlasting, whom the heavenly bodies obey to the jot of a second, turn not away my good fortune; hear my prayer till our meeting, mine and hers!

835. "THOU whom former philosophers addressed as the image of God, aid me, for I am become a captive, iron chains bind me! I, seeker of crystal and ruby, have lost coral and enamel; formerly I could not endure nearness, now I regret absence."

836. THUS he consumed himself; like a candle he melted. The fear of being too late made him hasten; he wandered on. When night fell, he found delight in the rising of the stars; he compared them to her, he rejoiced, he gazed on them, he held converse with them.

837. HE says to the moon: "I adjure thee in the name of thy God, thou art the giver of the plague of love to lovers; thou hast the balm of patience to make them bear it; hear my prayer to unite me with the face fair, through thee, like thine own."

838. NIGHT rejoiced him, day tortured him, he awaited the sunset. When he saw a stream he dismounted; he gazed on the rippling of the water, with it he united the rivulet of blood from the lake of tears; again he set out, he hasted onward on his road.

839. ALONE he lamented; he who was like the aloe-tree in form wept. He killed a goat in the plain where he came to a rocky place, roasted and ate of it and went on, sun-faced, martial in heart. He said: "I forsook roses, and behold me here woeful!"

840. I CANNOT now tell the words then spoken by that knight, or what he discoursed and lamented with such elegance. Sometimes his eyes reddened with their tears, the rose of his cheeks scratched by his nail. When he saw the caves he was glad; he went up to the door of the cave.

841. WHEN Asmat'h perceived him, she went to meet him, her tears fell fast; she rejoiced so greatly that she will never have such joy again. The knight dismounted, embraced her, kissed her, and conversed with her. When a man has waited for a man, the coming pleases him wondrously.

842. THE knight said to the damsel: "Where and how is thy lord?" The damsel wept with tears which might have fed

the sea. She said: "When thou wert gone, he roamed about, for it irked him to be in the cave; now I know nought of him, either by sight or tidings."

843. THE knight was pained as if some lance had struck him in the midst of his heart. He said to Asmat'h: "O sister, not thus should a man be! How could he break his oath! I deceived him not; how could he be false to me! If he could not keep it, why did he promise? If he promised me, why did he lie?

844. "SINCE save for him I counted not this world as grief, why did he forget me when I departed? Why could he not endure, what troubled him? How dared he break the oath he had sworn? But why should I marvel at evil from my Fate!"

845. AGAIN the maiden spoke: "Thou art justified in such sorrow; but when thou shalt judge aright–suspect me not of complaisance–is not heart needed to fulfil oath and promise? He, bereft of heart, awaits only the curtailment of his days.

846. "HEART, mind and thought depend one upon another. When heart goes the others also go and follow it. A man deprived of heart cannot play the man; he is chased forth from men. Thou sawest not, thou knowest not, what fires consumed him.

847. "THOU art right in murmuring that thou art separated from thy sworn brother, but how can it be told into what plight he fell, how can I tell thee the fact? Tongue will fail,

will be exhausted, the aching heart will ache still more. Thus think I, for I saw, I luckless born.

848. "HITHERTO none has heard in story of sufferings like unto his; such torture would affright not only men, but even stones; sufficient for a fountain are the tears that have flowed from his eyes. Whatever you say, you are right; one is wise in another's battle.

849. "WHEN he went forth, burned, consumed with fires, I asked him: 'Tell me, his adopted sister, what will Avt'handil do when he comes?' He replied: 'Let him come to seek me, me useless for his sake. I shall not leave this vicinage; I will not break my promise to him.

850. "'My vow I will not break, that oath will I not belie; I shall wait till the time appointed, however much the channels of tears may flow. If he find me dead, let him bury me, let him say Alas! and mourn. If I meet him living, let him marvel, for my life is doubtful.'

851. "HENCEFORTH the sundering of the sun and the mountain-top hath befallen me, only I must shed tears moistening the plains; maddened, I am tortured by the exceeding multiplication of groans; death has forgotten me, behold the deed of Fate!

852. "THIS true saying is written on a stone in China: 'Who seeks not a friend is his own foe!' Now that to which nor rose nor violet could be likened is become saffron. If thou seekest, then, seek him; do what befits thee."

853. THE knight said: "Thou art right in not justifying me in murmuring against him. But bethink thee what service I have done as one prisoner of love to another: I fled from my home, like a stag seeking water I seek him and think of him, I wander from field to field.

854. "THE crystal pearl-shells guard the ruby-hued pearl and apparel it; from her I have gone away, I could not stay near her, I could not make her happy, nor could I be happy; by my privy flight I have angered the equals of God, in return for their favours I have troubled their hearts.

855. "MY lord and upbringer, by the grace of God living in might, paternal, sweet, merciful, a sky snowing graciousness to him have I been faithless; I went away, verily I forgot all, and guilty toward him, I no longer await any good thing from God.

856. "ALL this afflicts me thus, O sister, for his sake. I have not deceived him, but am come a wayfarer by night and day. Now he is gone somewhere, he for whom I am consumed with fire, wearied in vain and weeping I sit with a sad face.

857. "SISTER, the hour and time give me no more leisure for converse. I repent not the past, early will I fulfil the word of the wise; I go, I will seek, either shall I find him or bring death early upon me; otherwise, since I am thus doomed by Fate, what can I embolden myself to say to God."

858. No more than this he said: he wept and went his way. He passed the caves, crossed the water, went through the reeds and came to the plain. The wind blowing over the fields froze the rose to a ruby hue. "Why givest thou me this plague?" He reproached Fate for this.

859. HE said: "O God, wherein have I sinned against thee, the Lord, the All-Seeing? Why hast Thou separated me from my friends? Why didst Thou lure me on to such a fate? One thinking of two, I am in a parlous plight; if I die I shall not pity myself, my blood be on my head!

860. "MY friend cast a bunch of roses on my heart, and so wounded it; that oath fulfilled by me he kept not. If, O passing world, thou partest me from him, my joy is past, to mine eyes another friend were reviled and shamed."

861. THEN he said: "I marvel at the spleen of a man of sense; when he is sad, of what avail is a rivulet from the terraced roof? It is better to choose, to ponder over the fitting deed. Now for me, too, it is better to seek that sun-like one, reed-like in form."

862. THE knight, weeping, besprinkled with tears, set himself to search; he seeks, he calls, he cries aloud, watching by night as by day; for three days he traversed many a mountain pass, reedy thicket, forest and field; he could not find him; sad he went, unable to learn any tidings.

863. HE said: "O God, wherein have I sinned against Thee? How have I displeased Thee so greatly? Why bring this fate upon me? What torture hast Thou sent upon me! Judge me, O Judge, hearken to my prayer; shorten my days, thus turn my woes to joy!"

XXXVI

Avt'handil Comes Upon the Unconscious Tariel

864. WEEPING and pale, the knight went his way and spoke;
he mounted a certain hill, the plain appeared in sunshine
and shadow. He saw a black horse standing with the bridle
on his neck on the edge of the rushes. He said:
"Undoubtedly it is he; of that there can be no doubt."

865. WHEN he saw, the heart of the knight leaped up and was
lightened; here to him, distressed, joy became not tenfold,
but a thousandfold; the rose of his cheeks brightened its
colour, the crystal of his face became crystal indeed, the
jet of his eyes grew jetty; like a whirlwind he galloped
down, he rested not from gazing at him.

866. WHEN he saw him, Tariel was indeed grieved; Tariel sat
with drawn face in state near unto death, his collar was
rent, his head was all torn, he could no longer feel, he had
stepped forth from the world.

867. ON one side lay a slain lion and a blood-smeared sword,
on the other a tiger stricken down a lifeless corpse. From

his eyes, as from a fountain, tears flowed fiercely forth: thus there a flaming fire burned his heart.

868. HE could not even open his eyes, he had wholly lost consciousness, he was come nigh to death, he was far removed from joy. The knight calls him by name, he tries to rouse him by speech; he cannot make him hear; he leaped towards him; the brother shows his brotherliness.

869. HE wipes away Tariel's tears with his hand, he cleansed his eyes with his sleeve; he sits down near by and only calls him by name; he says: "Know'st thou not me, Avt'handil, for thy sake wandering and mad?" But he heard little, staring with fixed eyes.

870. THIS is all thus, even as related by me. He wiped away the tears from his eyes, he somewhat recalled him to consciousness; then only he knew Avt'handil, kissed him, embraced him, treated him as a brother. I declare by the living God none like him was ever born.

871. HE said: "Brother, I was not false to thee, I have done what I swore to thee; unparted from my soul I have seen thee, thus have I kept my vow; now leave me; till death I shall weep and beat my head, but I entreat thee for burial, that I be not yielded to the beasts for food."

872. THE knight replied: "What ails thee? Why doest thou an evil deed? Who hath not been a lover, whom doth the furnace not consume? Who hath done like thee among the race of other men! Why art thou seized by Satan, why kill thyself by thine own will?

873. "IF thou art wise, all the sages agree with this principle: 'A man must be manly, it is better that he should weep as seldom as possible; in grief one should strengthen himself like a stone wall.' Through his own reason a man falls into trouble.

874. "THOU art wise, and yet knowest not to choose according to the sayings of the wise. Thou weepest in the plain and livest with the beasts; what desire canst thou thus fulfil? If thou renounce the world thou canst not attain her for whose sake thou diest. Why bindest thou a hale head, why openest thou the wound afresh?

875. "WHO hath not been a lover, whom hath the furnace not consumed? Who hath not seen pains, who faints not for somebody? Tell me, what has been unexampled! Why should thy spirits flee! Know'st thou not that none e'er plucked a thornless rose!

876. "THEY asked the rose: 'Who made thee so lovely in form and face? I marvel why thou art thorny, why finding thee is pain!' It said: 'Thou findest the sweet with the bitter; whatever costs dear is better; when the lovely is cheapened it is no longer worth even dried fruit.'

877. "SINCE the soulless, inanimate rose speaks thus, who then can harvest joy who hath not first travailed with woe? Who hath ever heard of aught harmless that was the work of devilry? Why dost thou murmur at Fate? What hath it done unexampled?

878. "HEARKEN to what I have said, mount, let us go at ease. Follow not after thine own counsel and judgement; do that thou desirest not, follow not the will of desires; were it not better thus I would not tell thee, mistrust not that I shall flatter thee in aught."

879. TARIEL said: "Brother, what shall I say to thee? Scarce have I control of my tongue; maddened, I have no strength to hearken to thy words. How easy to thee seems patience of the suffering of my torments! Now am I brought close to death; the time of my joy draws nigh.

880. "DYING, for her I pray; never shall I entreat her with my tongue. Lovers here parted, there indeed may we be united, there again see each other, again find some joy. Come, O friends, bury me, cast clods upon me!

881. "HOW shall the lover not see his love, how forsake her! Gladly I go to her; then will she wend to me. I shall meet her, she shall meet me; she shall weep for me and make me weep. Inquire of a hundred, do what pleaseth thine heart, in spite of what any may advise thee.

882. "BUT know thou this as my verdict, I speak to thee words of truth: Death draws nigh to me, leave me alone, I shall tarry but a little while; if I be not living, of what use am I to thee? If I survive, what canst thou make of me, mad? Mine elements are dissolved; they are joining the ranks of spirits.

883. "WHAT thou hast said and what thou speakest I understand not, nor have I leisure to listen to these things.

Death draws nigh me maddened; life is but for a moment. Now the world is grown distasteful to me–more than at any time heretofore. I, too, go thither to that earth whereon the moisture of my tears flows.

884. "WISE! Who is wise, what is wise, how can a madman act wisely? Had I my wits such discourse would be fitting. The rose cannot be without the sun; if it be so, it begins to fade. Thou weariest me, leave me, I have no time, I can endure no more."

885. AVT'HANDIL spoke again with words of many kinds. He said: "By my head! If thou diest what good will it do to her! Do it not! It is not the better deed. Be not thine own foe!" But he cannot lead him away; he can do nothing at all by speech.

886. THEN he said: "Well, since thou wilt by no means hearken to me, I will not weary thee; my tongue has hitherto spoken in vain. If death be better for thee, die! Let the rose wither–they all wither! One thing only I pray thee, grant me this"–for this his tears were flowing–

887. "WHERE the Indians[1] engird the crystal and rose with a hedge of jet–from this am I parted; hastily I went, not quietly. The king cannot keep me by his paternal converse. Thou wilt not unite with me, thou wilt renounce me; now how can I speak my joy!

---

[1] Black eyelashes.

888. "SEND me not heart-sore away, grant me one desire:
Mount once thy steed, let me see thee, ravisher of my soul,
on horseback: perchance then this present grief will flee
away, I shall go and leave thee, let thy will be done!"

889. HE entreated him: "Mount!" He begged and prayed him,
he entreated him eight times. He knew that riding would
chase away his sadness, that he would bend the reedy stem,
and make a tent of the jet eyelashes. He made Tariel
obedient; it pleased Avt'handil; Tariel sighed not nor
moaned.

890. HE said plainly: "I will mount; bring forward my horse."
Avt'handil brought the horse and gently helped him to
mount; he did not make him pant with haste; he took him
towards the plain, he made his graceful form to sway. Some
time they rode; going made him seem better.

891. AVT'HANDIL entertains him, and speaks fair words to
him; for Tariel's sake he moved his coral-coloured lips in
speech. To hear him would make young the aged ears of
a listener. He put away melancholy; he took unto himself
patience.

892. WHEN the elixir of grief perceived the improvement, joy
not to be depicted lightened his rose-like face—he,
Avt'handil, the physician of the reasonable, but despair of
the foolish, spoke words of reason to him who spoke
foolishly.

893. THEY began to converse; he spoke a frank word: "One
thing will I say to thee: Open to me what is secret. This

armlet of her by whom thou art wounded–how much dost thou love it? How dost thou prize it? Tell me, then let me die!"

894. HE said: "How can I tell thee the likeness of that incomparable picture! It is my life, the giver of my groans, better to me than all the world–water, earth and tree. To hearken to that to which one should not listen is more bitter than vinegar!"

895. AVT'HANDIL said: "I truly expected thee to say this. Now, since thou hast said it, I will answer thee, and think not I shall flatter thee; to lose Asmat'h were worse than the loss of that armlet. I commend not thy behaviour in choosing the worser.

896. "THIS armlet thou wearest is golden, molten by the goldsmith, inanimate, lifeless, speechless, unreasoning; thou no longer wantest Asmat'h! Behold a true judgement! First, she, luckless, was with Nestan; then she is thine own adopted sister.

897. "BETWEEN you and Nestan she formed a bond, by thee she has been called sister; she was the servant who contrived your meeting, while she herself was worthy of being summoned by thee; she, upbringer of her and brought up by her, she is mad for Nestan, and thou forsakest her, wretched woman, and wilt not see her? Bravo! a just judgement indeed!"

898. HE said: "What thou sayest is only too true. Pitiable is Asmat'h, who thinks of Nestan and sees me. I thought not to live; thou art come in time to quench the fires. Since I still survive, come, let us see, albeit I am still dazed."

899. HE obeyed. Avt'handil and the Amirbar set out. I cannot achieve the praise of their worth: teeth like pearls, lips cleft roses. The sweetly discoursing tongue lures forth the serpent from its lair.

900. THEREUPON Avt'handil says: "For thy sake will I sacrifice mind, soul, heart; but be not thus, open not thy wounds afresh. Learning avails thee not if thou do not what the wise have said; of what advantage to thee is a hidden treasure if thou wilt not use it?

901. "GRIEVING is of no use to thee; if thou art sorrowful what good will it do thee? Know'st thou not that no man dies save by the will of Providence? Awaiting the sunbeams the rose fades not in three days. Luck, endeavour and, if God will, victory shall be thy lot."

902. TARIEL replied: "This teaching is worth all the world to me. The intelligent loves the instructor; he pierces the heart of the senseless. But what shall I do, how can I endure when I am in excessive trouble? My griefs have hold of thee too. If, then, thou justify me not shall I not wonder?

903. "WAX hath an affinity with the heat of fire, and therefore is lighted; but water hath no such affinity if wax fall into water it is quenched. Whatever thing afflicts someone himself, in that will he hold for the sake of others too. Why know'st thou not once for all in what way my heart melts?"

XXXVII

Tariel Tells of the Killing of the Lion and the Tiger

904. "WITH my tongue will I relate to thee in detail all that hath befallen me; then indeed with wise heart judge the truth. I expected thee, awaiting thee was irksome to me, I could no longer endure the cave, I wished to ride in the plain.

905. "I CAME up that hill, I had traversed these reeds; a lion and a tiger met, they came together; they seemed to me to be enamoured, it rejoiced me to see them; but what they did to each other surprised me, horrified me.

906. "I CAME up the hill, the lion and tiger came walking together; they were to me like a picture of lovers, my burning fires were quenched. They came together and began to fight, embittered they struggled; the lion pursues the tiger flees. They were not commended by me.

907. "FIRST they sported gaily, then they quarrelled fiercely; each struck the other with its paw, they had no fear of death; the tiger lost heart, even as women do; the lion fiercely pursued, none could have calmed him.

908. "THE behaviour of the lion displeased me. I said: 'Thou art out of thy wits. Why annoy'st thou thy beloved? Fie on such bravery!' I rushed on him with my bared sword, I gave him to be pierced by the spear, I struck his head, I killed him, I freed him from this world's woe.

909. "I THREW away my sword, I leaped down, I caught the tiger with my hands, I wished to kiss it for the sake of her for whom hot fires burn me. It roared at me, and worried me with its blood-shedding paws. I could bear no more; with enraged heart I killed it too.

910. "HOWEVER much I soothed it, the tiger became not calm. I grew angry, I brandished it, dashed it on the ground, shattered it. I remembered how I had striven with my beloved. Yet my soul tore not itself altogether out of me. Why, then, art thou astonished that I shed tears!

911. "BEHOLD, brother! I have told the woes that grieved me. Life itself befits me not. Why didst thou wonder that I am thus fordone? I am sundered from life, death is become shy of me." So the knight ended his story, sighed, and wept aloud.

XXXVIII

Here is the Going of Tariel and Avt'handil
to the Cave, and Their Seeing of Asmat'h

912. AVT'HANDIL also wept with him and shed tears. He said:
"Be patient, die not, rend not altogether thy heart. God
will be merciful in this, though sorrow hath not shunned
thee; if He had willed to part you, He would not first have
united you.

913. "MISCHANCE pursues the lover, embitters life for him;
but to him who at first bears woe it yields joy at last. Love
is grievous, for it brings thee nigh unto death; it maddens
the instructed, it teaches the untaught."

914. THEY wept and went on; they wended their way to the
cave. When Asmat'h saw them she rejoiced indeed; she met
them, she wept, her tears wore channels in the rocks. They
kissed and wept aloud; each pressed the other to tell his
news again.

915. ASMAT'H said: "O God, Thou who canst not be expressed
by man's tongue! Thou art the fullness of all; Thou
fillest us with Thy sun-like radiance. If I praise Thee, how
can I praise Thee? What can I say in praise of Thee, who

art not to be praised by the intellect? Glory to Thee! Thou hast not slain me by the shedding of tears for them."

916. TARIEL said: "Ah, sister! for this have my tears flowed here. For that it erstwhile made us smile, the passing world makes us weep in turn; 'tis an old law of the world, not one newly to be heard of! Alas! were it not for pity of thee, death would be my joy.

917. "IF he be athirst, what sane, reasonable man would pour away water! I marvel why I am soaked in tears from mine eyes! Lack of water slays, water flows never dried. Alas! the opened rose, the beauteous pearl, is lost!"

918. AVT'HANDIL, too, was reminded of his sun and beloved. He said: "O mine own, how can I remain living without thee! Apart from thee my life is for me pitiable. Who can tell thee how I suffer, or how sore a fire burns me!

919. "HOW can the rose think, 'If the sun go away I shall not wither'? Or what, alas! will be our lot when the sun sets behind the hill? Heart, it is better for thee to harden thyself, petrify thyself wholly. Perchance it may happen to thee to see her; let not thy spirit be utterly spent!"

920. THEY calmed their souls, they were silent, fire burned both. Asmat'h followed, went in; like them, a furnace consumed her. She stretched out the tiger's skin he formerly used. They both sat down; they spoke of whatever pleased them.

921. THEY roasted meat and made a meal fitting the occasion; there the meal was breadless, and there was no multitude of vassals. They begged Tariel to eat; he had not power to eat; he chewed a morsel, spat it out, he hardly swallowed the weight of a drachm.

922. PLEASANT it is when man converses agreeably with man; he will listen to what is said, not let it pass in vain; thus the fire which burns so greatly is somewhat quenched; great comfort it is to speak of troubles when a man has the opportunity.

923. THAT night those lions, those heroes, were together, they conversed, and each revealed to the other his woes; when day dawned they began again many-worded conversations; they heard again from each other the oath formerly sworn.

924. TARIEL said: "Why speak many words? For that which thou hast done for me, God is surety for the debt. Oath for oath is enough; remembrance, friendship for a departing friend, are not the deed of a drunken man.

925. "NOW be merciful to me, make me not burn again in hottest fires; the flame which consumes me is not kindled by a steel; thou canst not extinguish it for me, thou thyself shalt be burned by the law of the creation of the world. Go, return, go back thither, to the place where thy sun is.

926. "To cure me seems hard even to Him who created me—understand ye who hear!—therefore I roam mad in the fields. Once I too was a doer of what befits the

reasonable; now the turn of madness has fallen to my
lot, and so I am mad."

927. AVT'HANDIL said: "What can I say in answer to this
thou hast said? Thou thyself hast spoken as a man sagely
instructed. How is it not possible for God again to cure
the wound! He is the upbringer of everything planted or
sown.

928. "WHY should God do this, create such as you and not
unite you, part you, madden thee with weeping? Mischance
pursues the lover. Look well into the matter, know it. If
you meet not each other again, then slay me!

929. "WHO else is a man save he that will endure what is
grievous? How can one let himself be bent by grief! What
subject of conversation is this! Fear not, God is generous
though the world be hard! Learn then what I teach thee;
I make bold to tell thee that he who will not learn is an
ass.

930. "HEED what thou hearest; let this suffice for teaching.
I asked leave of my sun to come away to you; I said to
her: 'Since he made cinders of my heart I am no longer
of use to thee, I will not stay; what else need I tell thee in
many words?'

931. "SHE said: 'I am content, thou art doing well and bravely,
the attention thou showest to him I accept as a service

to me.' At her request I came away. I am not drunk nor intoxicated! If I now return what shall I say? 'Why art thou come back like a coward?' will be her greeting.

932. "BETTER than such discourse is this, hearken to what I say: The man who is to do a difficult deed must be reasonable, the rose withered for lack of sun cannot make provision for itself; if thou art no longer of any use to thyself, be of use to me; brother must act brotherly to brother.

933. "WHEREVER thou wilt, stay there after thy rule: if thou wilt with wise heart, if thou wilt with maddened mind. With that loveliness of mien, that grace of form, do but strengthen thyself, die not, be not consumed by the flame!

934. "I BEG no more from thee: in a year's time meet me in this same cave, when I have gathered news from every ' quarter. As a token of that time I give thee the season when these roses shall again bloom abundantly; the sight of the roses will make thee start as at the bark of a dog.

935. "IF I exceed that time and come not hither to the cave, then know that I am not alive, undoubtedly I shall have died. It will be a sufficient token of this if thou shed tears for me. Then rejoice if thou wilt, or if thou wilt increase thy grief.

936. "NOW perchance wilt thou sorrow for the sake of what I have told thee? I go far from thee, and I know not whether horse or ship may fail me. No! lack of speech

avails not. I am not silent like a beast; I know not what God will do to me, nor the ever-revolving sky."

937. TARIEL said: "I will weary thee no more, nor say too much; thou wilt not listen to me however much I lengthen my discourse. If your beloved will not follow thee, follow thou him; do whatever he wills. In the end every hidden thing shall come to light.

938. "WHEN thou art convinced, then thou shalt know the difficulty of mine affairs; for me it is all one, roaming or not roaming; what thou hast told me that will I do, however much madness torture me. But if long days befall me in thine absence, what shall I do?"

939. THEY ended their discourse; they gave that promise to each other. They mounted, rode out, each killed game in the plain. They returned, their tearful hearts wept again; the thought of the parting on the morrow added grief to grief.

940. READERS of these verses, your eyes also are shedding tears! What, alas! shall heart do without heart, if heart part from heart! Absence and parting from a friend are the slayers of a man. Who, indeed, knows not, understands not, how hard is that day!

941. MORNING dawned; they mounted and said farewell to the maiden. From the eyes of Tariel, Asmat'h and Avt'handil tears flowed. The cheeks of all three hung out flags of crimson. Those lions ever made wild by grief went out to the beasts.

942. THEY descended from the caves and went away crying aloud with flowing tears. Asmat'h weeps and laments: "O lions! whose tongues can chant lamentations for you! The sun has burned and consumed you heavenly stars. Alas for my woes so great! Alas the sufferings of life!"

943. THOSE knights, departed thence, travelled that day together. They came to the seashore, there they tarried, they travelled not through dry land. That night they parted not; again they shared their fire. They wept for the absence from each other; they bewailed it.

944. AVT'HANDIL said to Tariel: "The channel of the flow of tears is dried! Why didst thou separate from P'hridon, the giver of this steed? Thence are tidings and means to be learnt regarding that beautiful sun. Now I go thither; teach me the way to thy sworn brother."

945. TARIEL teaches him by word the direction of the road to P'hridon's. He made him understand as well as he could by his power of speech: "Go towards the east; fare even unto the seashore. If thou seest him tell him of me; he will ask news of his brother."

946. THEY killed a goat and dragged it after them, they made a fire on the seashore, they sat down and ate such a meal as was fitting to their grief. That night they were together; they lay together at the root of a tree. I curse the treacherous passing world, sometimes generous, sometimes niggardly.

947. AT dawn they rose to part, they embraced each other.
The things said by them then would have melted anyone
who heard. They shed on the fields tears from the eyes like
waters from a spring. Long they stand in a close embrace,
breast was welded to breast.

948. WITH tears and face-scratching and tearing of hair
they parted; one goes up, the other goes down; roadless
they ride by bridle-paths through the rushes; as long as they
saw each other, with drawn faces they shouted; looking
upon their frowns the sun would frown too.

XXXIX

Of the Going of Avt'handil to P'hridon's When He Met Him at Mulghazanzar

949. ALAS! O world, what ails thee? Why dost thou whirl us round? What habit afflicts thee? All who trust in thee weep ceaselessly like me. Whence and whither carriest thou? Where and whence uprootest thou? But God abandons not the man forsaken by thee.

950. AVT'HANDIL, parted from Tariel, weeps; his voice reaches to the heavens. Quoth he: "The stream of blood which flowed anew flows once again. Now is parting as hard as union will be till we meet in heaven. Men are not all equal; there is a great difference between man and man."

951. THEN the beasts of the field drank their fill of the tears he shed there; he could not quench the furnace, he burned with frequent fire. Again the thought of T'hinat'hin fills him all the more with grief; the coral-rooted crystal shines on the rose of the lips.

952. THE rose is faded, it withers, the branch of the aloe-tree quivers, the cut crystal and ruby are changed into lapis-lazuli: He strengthened himself against death; against him it vaunted not itself. He said: "Why should I wonder at darkness since thou, O sun, hast abandoned me!"

953. HE said to the sun: "O sun, I compare thee to the cheeks
of T'hinat'hin, thou art like her and she is like thee, ye
light mountain and valley. The sight of thee rejoices me,
a madman, therefore unweariedly I gaze on thee; but why
have you both left my heart cold, unwarmed?

954. "THE absence of one sun for a month in winter freezes
us; I, alas! have parted from two; how, then, should my
heart not be harmed? Only a rock perceives not, is never
hurt! A knife cannot cure a wound; it cuts or causes a
swelling."

955. WENDING his way he laments to the sky, he speaks; to
the sun he says: "O sun, to thee I pray, thou mighty of
the mightiest mights, who exaltest the humble, givest
sovereignty, happiness; part me not from my beloved, turn
not my day to night!

956. "COME, O Zual[1], add tear to tear, woe to woe; dye my
heart black, give me to thick gloom, heap upon me a heavy
load of grief as on an ass; but say to her: 'Forsake him not!
Thine he is, and for thee he weeps.'

957. "O MUSHT'HAR[2], I entreat thee, thou just, perfect
judge, come and do justice, heart takes counsel with heart;
twist not justice, destroy not thus thy soul. I am righteous,
judge me, why wouldst thou wound afresh me wounded
for her!

---

[1] Zual–Saturn, planet of woe.

[2] Musht'har–Jupiter, planet of justice.

958. "COME, O Marikh[1], mercilessly pierce me with thy
spear, dye me and stain me red with the flow of blood; tell
her my sufferings, let her hear them with the tongue; thou
knowest what I am become, no longer my heart hath joy.

959. "COME, Aspiroz[2], aid me somewhat; she has consumed me
with the flame of fires, she who encircles the pearl with
lip of coral; thou beautifiest the fair with such charm as
thine; one like me thou abandonest and maddenst.

960. "OTARID[3]! save thee none other's fate is like to mine.
The sun whirls me, lets me not go, unites with me and
gives me over to burning. Sit down to write my woes! For
ink I give thee a lake of tears, for pen I cut for thee a trim
form, slim as a hair.

961. "COME, O Moon, take pity on me; I wane and am wasted
like thee; the sun fills me, the sun, too, empties me;
sometimes I am full-bodied, sometimes I am spare. Tell her
my tortures, what afflicts me, how I faint. Go, say: 'Forsake
him not!' I am hers, and for her sake I die.

962. "BEHOLD, the stars bear witness, even the seven confirm
my words: the sun, Otarid, Musht'har and Zual faint for
my sake; moon, Aspiroz, Marikh, come and bear me
witness; make her hear what fires consume me
unquenchable."

---

[1] Marikh–Mars, planet of vengeance.

[2] Aspiroz–Venus, planet of healing.

[3] Otarid–Mercury, planet of learning.

963. NOW he says to his heart: "As the tear still flows, and is not dried, what avails it to slay thyself! It is clear thou hast fraternized with the devil as a brother. I myself know that she who maddened me has for hair the tail of a raven; but if thou bearest not grief what is the enduring of joy?

964. "IF I remain, this is better for me"–he speaks of the uncertainty of life–"perchance it will be my lot to see the sun, I shall not forever cry Alas!" He sang with sweet voice; he checked not the channel of tears. Compared to his voice even the voice of the nightingale was like an owl's.

965. WHEN the knight's song was heard, the beasts came to listen; by reason of the sweetness of his voice even the stones came forth from the water, they hearkened, they marvelled, when he wept they wept; he sings sad songs, tears flow like a fount.

966. ALL living creatures on earth came to applaud: game from the rocks, fishes in the water, crocodiles in the sea, birds from the sky, from India, Arabia, Greece, Orientals and Occidentals, Russians, Persians, Franks and Egyptians from Misret'hi[1].

---

[1] Misret'hi–Egypt.

XL

Of Avt'handil's Going to P'hridon's When He Parted From Tariel

967. WEEPING the knight went seventy days along the road to the seashore. Afar off he saw in the sea boatmen approaching; he waited and asked: "Who are you, I beg you to tell me this: Whose realm is this or whose voice doth it obey?"

968. THEY answered: "O fair of face and form, strange and pleasing to us thou seemest, therefore with praise we address thee; hereunto is the boundary of the Turks, marching with the border of P'hridon, whose men we are; of him shall we tell thee, if we faint not from gazing on thee.

969. "NURADIN P'hridon is king of this our land, a knight brave, generous, mighty, on horseback a swift racer; none has power to harm so fair a sun; he is our lord, he like the beams spread forth from heaven."

970. THE knight said: "My brethren, in you have I happed upon good men. I seek your king, teach me whither I should go. How shall I go, when shall I come thither, how long is the road?" The boatmen guided him; they left not the shore.

971. THEY reported to him: "This is the road going to Mulghazanzar, there our king will meet thee, he of the swift arrow, the keen sword. Thou shalt arrive there ten days hence, O thou of the cypress form, ruby in hue. Alas! why dost thou, a stranger, burn us strangers, why consumest thou us like a flame of fire!"

972. THE knight said: "I marvel, brethren, why you are heart-slain for me, or how the faded winter roses can please you thus! If you had seen us then when we sat proud, uncrippled, we charmed them that gazed on us, with us they sat joyful."

973. THEY departed, the knight turned to pursue his road, he whose form is like the cypress, whose heart is like iron. He puts his horse to a canter, he discourses, he speaks aloud to comfort himself; the narcissi thunder, it rains tears, they lave the crystal and the enamel.

974. WHATEVER strangers he met on the road served him, were subservient to him; they came to gaze on him, they courted him, it was hard for them to let him go, scarce could they bear parting, they gave him a guide for the road whatever he asked they told him.

975. HE neared Mulghazanzar; soon he ended the long road. In the plain he saw an army of soldiers, and they were seen to be destroying game; on all sides a chain was formed, they encircled the outside of the field; they shot and shouted, they mowed down beasts like standing corn.

976. HE met a man, he asked him tidings of that host; he said: "Whose is this sound of trampling and stir?" He

answered: "P'hridon the monarch, King of Mulghazanzar, hunts, he holds the edge of the sedgy plain engirt."

977. MATCHLESS in mien he went towards the troops, he became merry, how can I ever tell the beauty of that knight! Those who are parted from him he makes to freeze, like the sun he burns them that are met with him; he maddens, if they look on him, those who gaze, his form sways like a tree.

978. IN the very midst of the hosts an eagle soared from somewhere. The knight urged on his horse, he emboldened himself, he feared not; he drew his bow and let the arrow fly; the eagle fell and blood flowed from it; he dismounted and clipped its wings; calmly he remounted, he panted not

979. WHEN they saw him, the archers ceased to shoot; they broke the circle, they came, they pressed upon him, they fainted, from all sides they surrounded him, some followed behind. They dared not ask him: "Who art thou?" nor could they say aught to him.

980. IN the meadow was a hill, on it stood P'hridon; forty men worthy to shoot with him attended him; thither Avt'handil made his way, after him followed the centre of the host. P'hridon marvelled. "What are they doing?" said he; he was angry with his armies.

981. P'HRIDON sent out a slave, saying: "Go, see the armies, what they are doing, why they have broken the circle, whither blind-like they go." The slave swiftly reached

them, he saw the cypress, the sapling form; he stood, his eyes became dazed, he forgot the words he had to say.

982. AVT'HANDIL perceived that this man was come to learn news of him. He said: "I beg thee to convey this message to thy lord from me: 'I am a stranger, wanderer, far removed from my home, sworn brother to Tariel, sent to you.'"

983. THE slave went to P'hridon to tell him his message. He said: "I have seen a sun arrived, he seems like the lightener of day. I think even sages would be maddened if they saw him anywhere. Quoth he: 'I am Tariel's brother, come to join the brave P'hridon.'"

984. WHEN he heard the name of Tariel, P'hridon's woes were lightened, from his eyes tears sprang forth, his heart grew more agitated, a blast froze the rose, from his eyelashes whirled snowstorms. They met each other, each was praised by the other, not dispraised.

985. HASTILY P'hridon came down from the ridge; he descended to meet Avt'handil. When he looked on him he said: "If this be not the sun, who is it?" Avt'handil outdid the praise P'hridon had heard from the slave. They both dismounted; joy made tears gush up.

986. THEY embraced; they were not shy for being strangers. The knight seems peerless to P'hridon, and P'hridon pleases the knight. Any onlookers who saw them would despise the sun. Slay me! if another like them will ever be bargained for or sold in the bazaar.

987. WHAT knights are there like P'hridon! But near him is one whom praises still more benefit; the sun makes the planets invisible when they come near; a candle gives no light by day, but its rays shine by night.

988. THEY mounted their horses and set out for P'hridon's palace. The chase was broken up; they made an end of the slaying of beasts. From all sides the troops thronged to gaze on Avt'handil; they said: "What creature can compare with him?"

989. THE knight said to P'hridon: "Thou art eager, I know, to hear my tidings. I will tell thee who I am, whence I come inasmuch as thou wishest to know, also whence I know Tariel and why I spoke of our brotherhood. He calls me brother; 'Thou art my brother,' quoth he, though I am scarce worthy to be his slave.

990. "I AM King Rostevan's vassal, a knight nurtured in Arabia, Spaspeti; by name they call me Avt'handil, I am a noble of great family, reared as son of the king, one to be respected, bold, none dares meddle with me.

991. "ONE day the king mounted, went forth to hunt; in the plain we saw Tariel, he poured forth tears watering the fields; we were astonished, he surprised us, we called and he came not, he made us angry; we knew not how fire consumed him.

992. "THE king shouted to the troops to seize him, and he was irritated; without trouble he slew, battle was not hard for him; of some he broke the arms and legs, some he slew

outright; there they learned that the course of the moon is not to be turned back.

993. "THE king, greatly indignant, perceived that the troops could not capture him; himself he mounted and went against him, the haughtily unfearing. When Tariel knew it was the king, then he avoided his sword, he gave the bridle to his horse, he was lost to our eyes.

994. "WE sought and could find no trace; we believed it devilry. The king was sad, forbad drinking, feast and banquet. I could not endure lack of certainty about his story. I stole away in quest of him, fire burned me, and smouldered.

995. "THREE years I sought him; I enjoyed not even sleep. I saw Khatavians he had mauled; they showed him to me. I found the yellowish rose, faint-rayed, pale-tinted; he welcomed me and loved me like a brother, like a son.

996. "HE took the caves from the Devis after great bloodshed. There Asmat'h attends the solitary, none else is with him; ever the old fire burns him, it is not newly roused. Groaning befits one parted from him, a black-mourning kerchief bound round the head.

997. "ALONE in the cave tearful, tear-stained damsel weeps. The knight hunts game for her as a lion for its whelp; he brings it and thus he feeds her. He cannot rest in one place. Save Asmat'h he desires not the sight of any of man's race.

998. "TO me, a stranger, he pleasantly narrated his wondrous
and pleasing story; he told me his tale, and his beloved's.
What woe he has suffered this tongue of a madman cannot
now tell; longing slays him, and lack of the sight of his
grave-digger.

999. "LIKE the moon he unceasingly roams, he rests not; he
sits on that horse thou gavest him, he never alights; he
sees no speaking being, like a wild beast he shuns men.
Woe is me, remembering him; alas for him dying for her
sake!

1000. "THE fire of that knight burns me, I am consumed with
hot fire: I pitied him, and I became mad, my heart grew
furious; I wished to seek remedies for him by sea and land.
I returned and saw the sovereigns, whose hearts were
gloomy.

1001. "I ENTREATED leave of absence; the king was enraged
at me, and fell into sadness. I deserted my soldiers, therefore
they there cried, 'Woe!' I stole away, I freed myself from
the flood of tears of blood. Now I seek balm for him; I turn
about hither and thither.

1002. "HE told me tidings of thee, how he had made brotherhood
with thee. Now have I found thee, peerless, worthy to be
praised by the tongue, counsel me where it is better to seek
that heavenly sun, the joy of those who gaze on her, the
disturber of those that cannot see her."

1003. NOW P'hridon speaks, utters the words spoken by that
knight; both in unison lamented in a threnody worthy of

praise; sobbing, they wept with impatient hearts, there
the roses were sprinkled by the water of tears dammed up
in the jungle.

1004. AMONG the soldiers there arose the sound of great weeping,
the scratching of the face by some, the casting away of
the veils. P'hridon weeps, laments aloud the seven years'
separation. Alas! the inconstancy and falsity of this vain
world!

1005. P'HRIDON laments: "How can we tell forth thy praise,
thou who canst not be praised, thou inexpressible one!
O sun of the earth, who transferrest the sun of the
firmament from its course, joy, life, quickener of them that
are near thee; light of the planets of heaven, consumer and
swallower up!

1006. "SINCE I was removed from thee, life has been hateful to
me. Though thou hast no leisure for me I long for thee; to
thee lack of me seems joy, it oppresses me greatly. Life
without thee is empty; the world is become hateful to me."

1007. P'HRIDON uttered these words in a beautiful lament.
They grew calm, they were silent; they rode with no sign
of song. Avt'handil is fair to beholders in his ethereal
loveliness; he covers the inky lakes of his eyes with the jet
ceiling of his lashes.

1008. THEY entered the city, there they found the palace
adorned in perfection, with all the officers of state mustered

the slaves delicately apparelled were in faultless order;
they were enraptured and ravished in heart with Avt'handil.

1009. THEY entered and held a great court, not a privy council;
on this side and on that side ten times ten lords were
ranged; apart sat the two together; who can tell forth their
praise? Here enamel, there jet, adorned the crystal and ruby
of their faces.

1010. THEY sat, they banqueted, they multiplied the best
liquor; they entertained Avt'handil as kinsman treats
kinsman; they brought beautiful vessels, all quite new.
But the heart of those who looked on that youth, alas! was
given to flame.

1011. THAT day they drank, they ate, there was a banquet for
the tribe of drinkers. Day dawned; they bathed Avt'handil;
there lies abundance of satin; they clad him in raiment
worth many thousands of drachmas; they girded him with a
girdle of inestimable worth.

1012. THE knight tarried some days, though he could not brook
delay; he went out hunting with P'hridon and sported, he
slew alike from far and near whatever offered itself to his
hand; his archery put every bowman to shame.

1013. THE knight said to P'hridon: "Hear what I have now to
tell thee. Parting from you seems to me like death, and
thereby shall I harm myself; but I, unhappy, have not time
to stay; another fire also consumes me. A long road, an
urgent deed I have to do, I shall be very late.

1014. "RIGHT is he who sheds tears at parting from thee. Today
without fail I depart, therefore it is that another fire burns
me; to tarry is a mistake of a traveller, he will do well
to teach himself this; lead me to the seashore where thou
sawest that sun."

1015. P'HRIDON answered: "Nothing shall be said by me to
hinder thee. I know thou hast no more time; another lance
pierces thee. Go! God will guide thee, may thy foes be
destroyed! But tell me, how shall I bear the lack of thee?

1016. "THIS I venture to tell thee: It is not fitting that thou
go away alone, I will give thee knights with thee to serve
and attend thee, armour and bedding, a mule, a horse.
If thou take not these thou wilt have trouble, tears will
flow on the rose cheeks."

1017. HE brought out four slaves, trustworthy in heart,
complete armour for each man, with armpieces and
greaves, sixty pounds of the red gold, full weight, not with
any shortage, a peerless stallion with complete harness.

1018. ON a strong-legged mule he packed bedding. He set out,
and P'hridon mounted and went forth with him also. Now
fire burned and consumed him who awaited the parting.
He laments: "If the sun were near us, winter could not
freeze us!"

1019. THE rumour of the knight's departure spread, they gave
themselves up to grief; the burgesses flocked together, those

who sold silk goods like those who sold fruit; the voice of
their lamentation was like thunder in the air; they said:
"We are removed from the sun; come, let us close our eyes."

1020. THEY passed through the city, they went on, they came
to the seashore where P'hridon had formerly seen the sun
seated; there they shed a rivulet of blood from the lake of
tears. P'hridon tells the story of that shining captive.

1021. "HITHER the two Negro slaves brought by ship the sun,
white-teethed, ruby-lipped—a black sight! I spurred my
horse, I determined to steal her by sword and arm; they saw
me from afar, they soon fled from me, the boat seemed like a
bird."

1022. THEY embraced each other, they multiplied the springs
of tears; they kissed, and both their fires were renewed;
the inseparable sworn brothers parted like brothers.
P'hridon remained, the knight went away, the form the
slayer of gazers.

XLI

Avt'handil's Departure From P'hridon to Seek Nestan-Daredjan

1023. THE knight speaks as he goes on his way like the full moon; there is the thought of T'hinat'hin to gladden his heart. He says: "I am far from thee; alas! the falseness of the cursed passing world! Thou hast the healing balsam for my wound.

1024. "WHY doth the ardour of grief for the heroes continually burn me? Why is my heart of rock and cliff become a hard rock? Even three lances cannot show a bruise on me. Thou art the cause that this world is thus envenomed for me."

1025. AVT'HANDIL fares on alone to the seashore with the four slaves, with all his might he seeks balm for Tariel; weeping by day and night he pours forth pools of tears; all the world seems to him as straw, even as straw in weight.

1026. WHEREVER he sees travellers walking by the shore he addresses them, he asks tidings of that sun. He roamed a hundred days. He went up a hill; camels loaded with stuff appeared; merchants distressed stood in perplexity on the shore.

1027. A COUNTLESS caravan was there on the seashore, they were distressed, they were gloomy, they could neither stand nor go forward. The knight greeted them; they hailed him with praise. He asked: "Merchants, who are ye?" They began to converse.

1028. USAM was the chief of the caravan, a wise man. He uttered respectfully a perfect eulogy, he invoked blessings on Avt'handil and praised his manners; he said: "O sun, thou art come as our life and comforter. Dismount; we will tell thee our story and business!"

1029. HE dismounted. They said: "We are Bagdad merchants, holders of the faith of Mohammed; we never drink new wines; we haste to trade in the city of the Sea-King; we are rich in wholesale goods, we have no cut pieces of stuff.

1030. "HERE on the seashore we found a man lying senseless; we succoured him till he could speak clearly with his tongue We asked him: 'Who art thou, stranger? What business dost thou follow after?' He said to us: 'If ye go on they will slay you. It is well that I still live!'

1031. "HE said: 'From Egypt we set out with a caravan and a guard, we embarked upon the sea laden with many kinds of stuff, there pirates in ships with sharp iron-pointed wooden rams slew us. All was lost; I know not how I came hither.'

1032. "O LION and sun, this is the reason of our standing here. If we return, our loss will be a hundredfold; if we embark, alas! they may slay us, we have no strength for battle. We cannot stay, we cannot go, the power to maintain ourselves is gone from us."

1033. THE knight said: "Whoever grieves is nought, and strives
in vain; whatever comes from above, we cannot avoid its
coming. I am surety for your blood, I take upon myself
what you shall shed; whoever fights with you, my sword will
wear itself out on your foes."

1034. THEY of the caravan were filled with great joy; they
said: "He is some knight, some hero, not timid like us, he
has self-confidence, let us be calm in heart." They
embarked, they went on board ship, they set out from the
coast.

1035. WITH pleasant weather they journeyed without hardship;
their convoyer, Avt'handil, leads them with brave heart. A
pirate ship appeared with an exceedingly long flag; that ship
had an iron-shod ploughshare with beam of wood for
shattering ships.

1036. THE pirates yelled and came on, they shouted and
trumpeted; the caravan was afraid of the multitude of
those warriors. The knight spoke: "Fear not their hardihood;
either I slay them all or this is the day of my death.

1037. "NOUGHT undecreed can they do to me, even if all the
hosts on earth engage me; if it be decreed, I shall not
survive, the spears are ready for me, neither strongholds nor
friends, not even brothers, can save me; who knows this
is stout-hearted like me.

1038. "YOU merchants are cowards, unskilled in war. Lest they
slay you with the arrow from afar, shut the doors behind

you. Behold me alone how I fight, how I use my lion-like arms; see how I make the blood of the corsair's crew flow."

1039. WITH gesture like a swift tiger he clad his form in armour; in one hand he held an iron mace. He stood forth with dauntless heart in the front of the ship, and as he slew onlookers with his gaze, so he slew foes with his sword.

1040. THOSE warriors yelled; their voices were uninterrupted. They thrust the beam upon which was the ploughshare. The knight stood fearless at the head of the ship, he trembled not; he struck with the mace, he broke the beam, the lion's arm swerved not.

1041. THE beam was destroyed, and Avt'handil remained with ship unshattered. Those warriors feared, they sought a way to shelter, they could not contrive it in time; he leaped on his foes, threshing them down round about him; there was not left there living man unhacked by him.

1042. WITH intrepid heart he slew those warriors like goats; some he threw down on the ship, some he cast into the sea; he threw one upon another, eight upon nine and nine upon eight; those who were left were hidden among the corpses, they stifled their cries.

1043. AS much as his heart desired was he victorious in the fight with them. Some humbly adjured him: "Slay us not, by thy faith!" Those he slew not, he enslaved them, whoever survived his wounds. Truly saith the Apostle: "Fear makes love."

1044. O MAN! boast not of thy strength, brag not drunken like! Might is of none avail if the power of the Lord aid thee not. A tiny spark overcomes, and burns up great trees. If God protect thee, it cuts alike well whether thou strike with a log or a sword.

1045. THERE Avt'handil saw their great treasures. He grappled twin-like ship to ship. He called the caravan. Usam was merry when he saw, he rejoiced, he lamented not, he spoke a eulogy in his praise, he gave form to great imaginings.

1046. PRAISERS of Avt'handil need even a thousand tongues; even they could not tell how fair he appeared after the fight. The caravan shouted, saying: "Lord, thanks to Thee! The sun has shed down on us his beams; the dark night has broken into day for us."

1047. THEY came up to him, they kissed his head, face, feet, hand; they spoke praise unstinted to the fair, the praiseworthy; the sight of him maddens the wise man as well as the fool! "We all are saved by thee in so hard a mischance."

1048. THE knight said: "Thanks to God, the Creator, Maker of all, by whom the heavenly powers decree what is to be done here; 'tis they that do all deeds hidden and some revealed. It is necessary to everyone to believe; a wise man has faith in the future.

1049. "GOD hath deigned to spare your blood, so many souls! I, alas! vain earth, what am I? Of myself, what can I do?

Now I have slain your foes, I have fulfilled what I spoke;
I have brought you the ship complete with its wealth as a
gift."

1050. PLEASANT it is when a good knight has won the battle,
when he has surpassed his comrades who were with him.
They congratulated him, they praised him, in this state they
were ashamed. The wound becomes him well, but little
was he hurt.

1051. THAT day they looked at that ship of the corsairs, they
put not off till the morrow. How could they count the
quantity of treasure lying there! They conveyed it to
their ship, they completely emptied the pirate ship; they
smashed it up and burned some of it; the wood they
bartered not for the drachma.

1052. USAM conveyed to Avt'handil a message from the
merchants: "We are strengthened by thee; we know our
baseness. Whatever we have is thine, of this there can be
no doubt; whatever thou givest us, let it be ours, we have
made an assembly here."

1053. THE knight announced: "O brothers, but now ye heard it:
the stream which flowed from your eyes has been perceived
by God, He hath saved you alive. What am I? What joy,
alas! have I given you? What could I do with whatever
you gave me? I have myself and my horse!

1054. "AS much treasure as I desired to amass I had of mine
own, countless priceless coverlets of silk. What use could I

make of yours? What do I want? I am but your companion
Moreover, I have some other dangerous business.

1055. "NOW, of this countless treasure I have found here, take
what you each wish; I shall be a claimant against none.
One thing I entreat: grant my request, one not to be
mistrusted; I have a certain matter to be kept hidden
within you.

1056. "TILL the time comes, speak not of me as if I were not
your master. Say, 'He is our chief,' call me not knight.
I will clothe myself as a merchant, I will begin chaffering;
keep the secret, by the brotherhood between us."

1057. THIS thing very greatly rejoiced the caravan; they came
and saluted him, saying: "It is our hope–the very request
we should have made to you, you yourself have made to
us–that we may serve him whose face we acknowledge as
the face of the sun."

1058. THENCE they departed and travelled on, they wasted no
time; they met fair weather, they sailed ever pleasantly;
they delighted in Avt'handil, they sang his praises; they
presented him with a pearl of the tint of the knight's
teeth.

XLII

The Story of Avt'handil's Arrival in Gulansharo

1059. AVT'HANDIL crossed the sea; with stately form went he.
They saw a city engirt by a thicket of garden, with
wondrous kinds of flowers of many and many a hue. In
what way canst thou understand the loveliness of that land

1060. WITH three ropes they moored the ship to the shore of
those gardens. Avt'handil clad his form in a cloak and sat
on a bench. They brought out men that were porters, hired
with drachmas. That knight bargains, acts as chief of the
caravan, and thereby conceals himself.

1061. THITHER came the gardener of him at whose garden
they had landed; with ecstasy he gazes at the knight's face
flashing like lightning. Avt'handil hailed him, he spoke to
the man with faultless words: "Whose men are ye, who are
ye? How call they the king reigning here?

1062. "TELL me all in detail," quoth the knight to that man;
"what stuff is dearer, or what is bought up cheap?" He
said: "I see, thy face seems to me like the face of the sun.
Whatever I know I will tell thee truly; I will by no means
inform thee crookedly.

1063. "THE Sea Realm is this, ten months' travel in extent, this is the city of Gulansharo, full of much loveliness. Hither everything fair cometh by ships sailing from sea to sea. Melik Surkhavi rules, perfect in good fortune and wealth.

1064. "EVEN if he be old, a man is rejuvenated by coming hither; drinking, rejoicing, tilting and songs are unceasing; summer and winter alike we have many-hued flowers; whoever knoweth us envieth us, even they who are our foes.

1065. "GREAT merchants can find nought more profitable than this: They buy, they sell, they gain, they lose; a poor man will be enriched in a month; from all quarters they gather merchandise; the penniless by the end of the year have wares laid by.

1066. "I AM gardener to Usen, chief of the merchants. I shall tell thee somewhat of the manner of his ordinance: This is his garden, your resting-place for the day; first it is necessary to show him all the fairest of your goods.

1067. "WHEN great merchants arrive they see him and give him gifts, they show him what they have, elsewhere they cannot unpack their goods; for the king they set aside the best, they straightway count out the price; thereupon he frees them to sell as they please.

1068. "HIS duty it is to receive such honourable folk as you, he orders the caterers how to entertain them fitly; he is not now here, what avails it me to speak of him? To meet you and carry you away with him, pressing you politely, is the way he should treat you.

295

1069. "P'HATMAN Khat'hun, the lady, his wife, is at home,
a hospitable hostess, amiable, not rough. I shall inform her
of your arrival, she will take you in as one of her own folk,
she will send a man to meet you, you shall enter the city
by daylight."

1070. AVT'HANDIL said: "Go, do whatever thou desirest."
The gardener runs, he rejoices, sweat pours down to his
breast. He tells his tidings to the lady: "I boast of this:
a youth comes, to them that look on him his rays seem like
the sun.

1071. "HE is some merchant, chief of a great caravan, wellgrown
like a cypress, a moon of seven days, his coat and the fold
of his coral-hued turban become him; he called me, asked
me tidings and the tariff for the purchase of goods."

1072. DAME P'hatman rejoiced; she sent ten slaves to meet him;
they prepared the caravanserais, she stored their wares.
The rose-cheeked, crystal and ruby, enamel, jet, entered;
they who looked on him compared his feet to the tiger's, his
palms to the lion's paws.

1073. THERE was a hubbub, the hosts of the town all assembled
they pressed on this side and on that, saying: "How shall
we gaze on him?" Some were carried away by desire, some
had their souls reft from them; their wives grew weary of
them, their husbands were left contemned.

XLIII

Avt'handil's Arrival at P'hatman's;
Her Reception of Him and Her Joy

1074. P'HATMAN, Usen's wife, met him in front of the door,
joyful she saluted him, she showed her pleasure; they
greeted each other, they went in and seated themselves. As
I have observed, his coming annoyed not Dame P'hatman.

1075. DAME P'hatman was attractive to the eye, not young but
brisk, of a good figure, dark in complexion, plump-faced,
not wizened, a lover of minstrels and singers,
a wine-drinker; she had abundance of elegant gowns and
head-dresses.

1076. THAT night Dame P'hatman entertained him right well.
The knight presented beautiful gifts; they that received
them said: "They are worthy!" P'hatman's entertainment
of him was worth while; by God! she lost not. When they
had drunken and eaten, the knight went out to sleep.

1077. IN the morning he showed all his wares, he had them all
unpacked; the fairest were laid aside for the king, he had
the price counted out; he said to the merchants: "Take

them away!" He loaded them, and had them carried away He said: "Sell as ye will; reveal not who I am!"

1078. THE knight was clad as a merchant; he was by no means dressed in his proper raiment. Sometimes P'hatman calls on him, sometimes he visits P'hatman. They sat together; they conversed with refined discourse. Absence from him was death to P'hatman, as Ramin's was to Vis.

XLIV

P'hatman Becomes Enamoured of Avt'handil; Writes Him a Letter and Sends It

1079. BETTER, for him who can bear it, is aloofness from woman; she plays with thee and pleases thee, she wins thee over and trusts thee; but in a trice she betrays thee, she cuts whatever pierces; so a secret should never be told to a woman.

1080. DESIRE of Avt'handil went into the heart of Dame P'hatman, love grew from more to more, it burned her like fire, she essayed to conceal it, but could not hide her woes, she said: "What am I to do, what will avail me?" She rained, she poured forth tears.

1081. "If I tell him this, alas! he will be worth, even the sight of him will become rare to me; if I tell him not, I cannot endure it, the fire will become more intense. I will speak, let me die or live, let one or other be my lot! How can the physician cure him who tells not what hurts him?"

1082. SHE wrote a piteous letter to be presented to that youth concerning her love, revealing her sufferings, moving and shaking the listeners' heart, a letter to be kept, not to be idly torn up.

XLV

The Letter of Love Written by P'hatman to Avt'handil

1083. "O SUN, since it pleased God to create thee a sun, thus
a joy and not a desirer of woes to them removed from thee,
a burner of those near united, a consumer of them with fire,
thy glance seems sweet to the planets, a thing to be boasted
of.

1084. "THEY that gaze on thee become enamoured of thee; for
thy sake piteously they faint. Thou art the rose; I marvel
why nightingales quiver not on thee. Thy beauty withers
the flowers, and mine too are fading. If the sunbeams reach
me not timely I am quite scorched.

1085. "GOD is my witness that I fear to tell you this, but,
luckless, what can I do for myself? I am quite parted from
patience; the heart cannot constantly endure the piercing
of the black lashes! If by any means thou canst help me,
then help, lest I lose my wits.

1086. "TILL an answer to this letter reaches me, till I know if
thou wilt slay me or reassure me–till then shall I endure life

however much my heart pains me. Oh for the time when life or death will be decided for me!"

1087. DAME P'hatman wrote and sent the letter to the knight. The knight read it as if it were from a sister or kinswoman; he said: "She knows not my heart. Who is she who courts the lover of her whose I am? The beloved I have—how can I compare her beauty to this one's?"

1088. SAID he: "What hath the raven to do with the rose, or what have they in common? But upon it the nightingale has not yet sweetly sung. Every unfitting deed is brief, and then it is fruitless. What says she? What nonsense she talks! What a letter she has written!"

1089. THIS kind of thought he thought in his heart. Then said he to himself: "Save thee I have no helper. For the sake of that for which I am a wanderer, since I wish to seek her I will do everything by which I can find her; what else should my heart heed!

1090. "THIS woman sits here seeing many men, a keeper of open house and a friend to travellers coming hither from all parts. I will consent, she will tell me all; however much the fire burns me with its flames, perchance she will be of some use to me; I shall know how to pay my debt to her."

1091. HE said: "When a woman loves anyone, becomes intimate with him and gives him her heart, shame and dishonour she weighs not, being wholly accursed; whatever she knows she declares, she tells every secret. It is better for me, I will consent; perchance I shall somewhere find out the hidden thing."

1092. AGAIN he said: "None can do aught if his planet favour him not; so what I want I have not, what I have I want not. The world is a kind of twilight, so here all is dusky. Whatever is in the pitcher, the same flows forth."

XLVI
Avt'handil's Letter in Answer to P'hatman's

1093. "THOU hast written to me; I have read thy letter in
praise of me. Thou hast anticipated me, but the burning of
the fire of love afflicts me more than thee. Thou wishest,
I too want thy company uninterrupted. Our union is agreed
since it is the desire of both."

1094. I CANNOT tell thee how P'hatman's pleasure increased.
She wrote: "The tears I, absent from thee, have shed
suffice. Now I shall be unaccompanied, here shalt thou
find me alone; hasten my union with thee, to-night when
evening falls. Come!"

1095. THAT very night when the letter of invitation was
presented to the knight, when twilight was falling and he
was going, another slave met him on the way with the
message: "Come not to-night; thou shalt find me unready
for thee." This vexed him, he turned not back, he said:
"What sort of thing is this?"

1096. THE invited guest went not back again on the withdrawal
of his invitation. P'hatman sits troubled. Avt'handil the
tree-like went in alone. He perceived the woman's

uneasiness, he saw it forthwith on his going in; she could not reveal it from fear, and also out of complaisance for him.

1097. THEY sat down together and began to kiss, to sport pleasantly, when a certain elegant youth of graceful mien appeared standing in the doorway. He entered; close behind followed a slave with sword and shield. When he saw Avt'handil he felt afraid as before a rocky road.

1098. WHEN P'hatman saw, she was afraid, she shook and fell a-trembling. The stranger gazed with wonder at them lying caressing; he said: "I will not hinder, O woman ... but when day breaks I shall cause thee to repent that thou hast had this youth.

1099. "THOU hast shamed me, O wicked woman, and made me to be despised, but to-morrow thou shalt know the answer to be paid for this deed; I shall make thee to devour thy children with thy teeth; if fail to do this, spit upon my beard, let me run mad in the fields!"

1100. THUS he spake, and the man touched his beard and went out of the door. P'hatman began to beat her head, her cheeks were scratched, the gurgling of her tears flowing like a fountain was heard. She said: "Come, stone me with stone let the throwers approach!"

1101. SHE laments: "I have, alas! slain my husband, I have killed off my little children, I have given away as loot our

possessions, the peerless cut gems! I am separated from my
dear ones! Alas! the upbringer! Alas! the upbrought! I have
made an end of myself; shameful are my words!"

1102. AVT'HANDIL hearkened to all this in perplexity. He said:
"What troubles thee, what say'st thou, why dost thou thus
lament, why did that youth threaten thee, what fault found
he in thee? Be calm; tell me who he was and on what errand
he roved!"

1103. THE woman replied: "O lion! I am mad with the flow of
tears; ask me no more tidings, nought can I tell thee with
my tongue. I have slain my children with mine own hand,
therefore can I no more be gay; impatient for thy love
I have slain myself.

1104. "THIS kind of thing certainly should happen to the utterer
of idle words, the chatterer who cannot hide a secret, the
witless, mad, raving. 'Help me with your lamentations!'
This will I say to all who see me. A physician cannot cure
one who drinks his own blood!

1105. "DO one thing of two: desire nothing more than this: If
thou canst kill that man, go, slay him secretly by night;
thus shalt thou save me and all my house from slaughter;
return, I will tell thee all, the reason why I shed tears.

1106. "IF not, take away thy loads on asses this very night,
escape from my neighbourhood, gather everything for

flight. I doubt my sins will fill thee too with woe. If that knight go to court he will make me eat my children with my mouth."

1107. WHEN Avt'handil, the proud, gifted with bold resolve heard this, he arose and took a mace—how fair, how bold is he! "To ignore this matter would be remissness on my part!" said he. Think not any living is his like; there is none other like unto him!

1108. TO P'hatman he said: "Give me a man as instructor, as guide, let him show me the road truly, else I want no helper I cannot look on that man as a warrior and mine equal. What I do I shall tell thee; wait for me, be calm!"

1109. THE woman gave him a slave as guide and leader. Again she cried out: "Inasmuch as the hot fire is to be cooled, if thou slay that knight to assuage the irritation of my heart. he has my ring, I entreat thee to bring it hither."

1110. AVT'HANDIL of the peerless form passed the city. On the seashore stood a building of red-green stone; in the lower part fair palaces, then above terrace upon terrace, vast, beautiful, numerous, hanging one over the other.

1111. THITHER is the sun-faced Avt'handil led by his guide, who says to him in a low voice: "This is the palace of him thou seekest." He shows it to him, and says: "Seest thou him standing on yonder terraced roof? Know this, there he lies to sleep; or thou shalt find him sitting."

1112. BEFORE the door of that luckless youth lay two guards.
       Avt'handil passed, he stole in without making a sound; he
       put a hand on each of their throats, forthwith he slew them
       he struck head upon head, brain and hair were mingled.

XLVII

Here Is the Slaying of the Chachnagir and His Two Guards by Avt'handil

1113. THAT youth lay alone in his chamber with angry heart.
Bloody-handed Avt'handil, strong in stature, entered, he
gave him no time to rise, privily he slew him, we could not
have perceived it; he laid hold of him, struck him on the
ground, slew him with a knife.

1114. HE is a sun to them that gaze on him, a wild beast and
a terror to those that oppose him. He cut off the finger with
the ring, he hurled him down to the ground; he threw him
from the window towards the sea, he was mingled with the
sands of the sea; for him nowhere is there a tomb, nor spade
to dig his grave.

1115. NOT a sound of their slaughter was heard. The sweet rose
came forth; whereby could he have been so embittered?
This is a marvel to me, how he could thus steal his blood!
As he had lately come, by the same road went he away.

1116. WHEN the lion, the sun, the sweetly-speaking knight, came
into P'hatman's house, he announced: "I have slain him;
no more will that youth see sunny day; thy slave himself I
have as witness; make him swear an oath in God's name

309

that I did the deed; behold the finger and the ring, and I have my knife bloodied.

1117. "NOW tell me of what thou spakest, why thou wert so furiously enraged. With what did that man threaten thee? I am in great haste to know it." P'hatman embraced his legs: "I am not worthy to look on thy face; my wounded heart is healed; now am I ready to extinguish my fires.

1118. "I AND Usen with our children are now born anew. O lion how can we magnify thy praises! Since we may boast that his blood is spilt, I will tell thee all from the beginning; prepare to listen."

XLVIII

P'hatman Tells Avt'handil the Story of Nestan-Daredjan

1119. "IN this city it is a rule that on New Year's Day no merchant trades, none sets out on a journey; we all straightway begin to deck and beautify ourselves; the sovereigns make a great court banquet.

1120. "WE, great merchants, are bound to take presents to court; the sovereigns must give gifts befitting us. For ten days there is heard everywhere the sound of the cymbal and tambourine; in the moedan, tilting, ball-play, the stamping of horses.

1121. "MY husband, Usen, is the leader of the great merchants, I lead their wives; I need none to invite me; rich or poor, we give presents to the queen; we entertain ourselves agreeably at court, we come home merry.

1122. "NEW Year's Day was come, we gave our gifts to the queen; we gave to them, they gave to us, we filled them, we were filled. After a time we went forth merry, at our will; again we sat down to rejoice, we behaved as we wished

1123. "AT eventide I went into the garden to sport; I took the ladies with me, it behoved me to entertain them; I brought with me minstrels, they discoursed sweet song; I played and gambolled like a child, I changed veil and hair.

1124. "THERE in the garden were fair mansions beautifully built, lofty, with a prospect on every side, overhanging the sea. Thither I led the ladies, them that were with me; anew we made a banquet, we sat pleasantly, joyously.

1125. "MERRY, I entertained the merchants' wives, pleasantly, in a sisterly way. While drinking, without any cause a distaste came upon me. When they perceived me thus, they separated, all that sat at meal. I was left alone; some sadness fell on my heart like soot.

1126. "I OPENED the window and turned my face to the road, I looked out, I shook off the sadness growing within me. Far away I saw something small, it floated in the sea, methought a bird or beast; to what else could I liken it?

1127. "FROM afar I could not recognize it; when it came near it was a boat; two men clad in black, and black also of visage, on either side stood close; only a head appeared; they came ashore, that strange sight astonished me.

1128. "THEY beached the boat; they landed in front of the garden. They looked thither, they looked hither, if any anywhere observed them, they saw no creature, nothing alarmed them. Secretly I watched them; I was quiet indoors.

1129. "WHAT they landed from the boat in a chest—they took off the lid—was a maiden of wondrous form, who stepped forth; on her head was a black veil, beneath she was clad in green. It would suffice the sun to be like her in beauty.

1130. "WHEN the maiden turned towards me, rays rose upon the rock; the lightning of her cheeks flashed over land and sky; I blinked mine eyes, I could no more gaze on her than on the sun; I closed the door on my side; they could not perceive that they were watched.

1131. "I CALLED for slaves who waited upon me; I pointed: 'See what beauty the Indians hold captive! Steal down, go forth, quietly, not racing hastily. If they will sell her to you, give them the price, whatever they may be wanting.

1132. "'IF they will not give her to you, let them not take her away, capture her from them, slay them, bring hither that moon, do the errand well, use your best endeavour!' My slaves stole down from above as if they flew; they chaffered, they sold not. I saw the blacks looked right ill pleased.

1133. "I STOOD at the window; when I saw they would not sell her, I cried: 'Slay them!' They seized them and cut off their heads, they threw them out into the sea; they turned back, they guarded the maiden. I went down to meet her, I took her, she had not tarried long on the seashore.

1134. "HOW can I tell thee her praise! what loveliness! what delicacy! I swear she is the sun; 'tis untrue that the sun is sun! Who can endure her rays, who can delineate her! If she consume me, lo! I am ready, no preparation is needed for this."

1135. WHEN she had ended these words, P'hatman rent her face with her hands; Avt'handil, too, wept, he shed hot tears; they forgot each other, for her sake they became as mad; the spring of tears flowing down from above melted the slight new-fallen snow of the cheek.

1136. THEY wept. The knight said: "Break not off! Conclude!" P'hatman said: "I received her; I made my heart faithful to her. I kissed her every part, and thereby I wearied her. I seated her on my couch, I caressed her, I loved her.

1137. "I SAID to her: 'Tell me, O sun, who thou art or of what race a child! Whither were those Ethiops taking thee, lady of the Pleiads of heaven?' To all these words she made no answer. I saw a hundred springs of tears dropping from her eyes.

1138. "WHEN I pressed her with questions, with much discourse, she wept with gentle voice, sobbing from the heart; a stream flowed through the jetty trough of her lashes from the narcissi, upon the crystal and ruby. Gazing at her I burned, I became dead-hearted.

1139. "SHE said to me: 'To me thou art a mother, better than a mother. Of what profit can my story be to thee? It is but the tale of chatterer. A lone wanderer am I, overtaken by an unhappy fate. If thou ask me aught, may the might of the All-Seeing blame thee!'

1140. "I SAID to myself, 'It is not fitting untimely to summon
and carry off the sun; the captor will become mad and
wholly lose his wits. A request should be timely, the making
of every entreaty. How know I now that it is not a time to
converse with this sun!'

1141. "I LED away that sun-faced one already praised, I cannot
call her upraised. By the longing I have for her, and by her
sun, I hardly could hide the ray of that sun! I enveloped
her in many fold of heavy brocade, not thin stuff." The tear
hails down, the rose is frost-bitten, from the lashes blows
a snowy blast.

1142. "I LED into my home that sun-faced one, an aloe-tree in
form. For her I furnished a house, therein I put her very
secretly, I told no human being, I kept her privily, with
precaution; I caused a Negro to serve her; I used to enter,
I saw her alone.

1143. "HOW, alas! can I tell thee of her strange behaviour! Day
and night weeping unceasing and flowing of tears! I
entreated her: 'Hush!' For but one moment would she
submit. Now without her how do I live; alas! woe is me!

1144. "WHEN I went in, pools of tears stood before her; in the
inky abyss of her eyes were strewn jetty lances, from the
inky lakes into the bowls full of jet there was a stream, and
between the coral and cornelian glittered the twin pearls of
teeth.

1145. "BY reason of the ceaseless flow of tears I could not find time for inquiry. If I asked even, 'Who art thou? What brought thee into this plight?' like a fountain, a rivulet of blood gushed forth from the aloe-tree. No human being could endure more, unless made of stone.

1146. "NO coverlet she wanted, nor mattress to lie upon, she was ever in her veil and one short cloak, her arm she placed as a headrest and reposed thereon. With a thousand entreaties I could scarce persuade her to eat a little.

1147. "BY-the-by, I will tell thee of the wonder of the veil and cloak: I have seen all kinds of rare and costly things, but I know not of what sort of stuff hers were made, for it had the softness of woven material and the firmness of forged metal.

1148. "THUS that lovely one tarried long in my house. I could not trust my husband; I feared he would inform. I said to myself: 'If I tell him, I know the rascal will betray my secret at court.' Thus I thought at my frequent goings in and comings out.

1149. "I SAID to myself: 'If I tell him not, what am I to do, what can I do for her? I know not in the least what she wants, nor what any could do to help her. If my husband finds out, he will slay me, nothing can save me; how can I hide that sun-like light!

1150. "'I, ALAS! what can I do alone! The burning of my fires increases. Come, I will trust him, I will not wrong Usen; I will make him swear not to betray me; if he give me full assurance, he cannot doom his soul, he will not be an oath-breaker!'

1151. "ALONE I went to my husband; I frolicked and fondled him. Then I said to him: 'I will tell thee something, but first swear to me thou wilt tell no human being, give me a binding oath.' He swore a fearful oath: 'May I beat my head on the rocks!

1152. "'WHAT thou tellest me I will reveal to no soul, even unto death, neither to old nor young, friend nor foe!' Then I told all to that kindhearted man, Usen: 'Come, I will lead thee to a certain place here; come, I will show thee the sun's peer.'

1153. "HE rose to accompany me, we departed, we entered the palace gates. Usen marvelled; he even quaked when he saw the sunbeams. He said: 'What hast thou shown me, what have I seen, what is she, of what stuff? If she be verily an earthly being, may God's eyes look upon me with wrath!'

1154. "I SAID: 'Nor know I aught of her being a creature of flesh; I have no knowledge more than I have told thee. Let me and thee ask who she is, and who is at fault that such madness afflicts her; perchance she will tell us somewhat, we will pray her to do us this great kindness.'

1155. "WE went in, we both had a care to show her respect. We said: 'O sun, for thy sake a furnace of flame burns us. Tell us what is the cure for the waning moon, what hath ensaffroned thee who art ruby-like in hue?'

1156. "WHETHER she heard or hearkened not to what we said we know not; the rose was glued together, it showed not the pearl; the serpents of her locks were twined in disorder; when she turned her face away, the sun was eclipsed by the dragon, it dawned not upon us.

1157. "BY our converse we could not induce her to answer. The tiger-panther sits sullen-faced, we could not comprehend her wrath; again we annoyed her, she wept tears flowing like a fountain, and, 'I know not! Let me alone!' quoth she this only with her tongue she said to us.

1158. "WE sat down and wept with her and poured forth tears. What we had spoken to her made us sorry; how could we venture to say aught else? We could scarce persuade her to be quiet, we calmed her, we soothed her; we offered her some fruit, but we could not make her eat at all.

1159. "USEN said: 'She has wiped away a multitude of woes from me. Those cheeks are fit for the sun; how can they be kissed by man! Most right is he who sees not her if his sufferings be increased a hundred-and-twenty-fold. If I prefer my children may God slay them!'

1160. "A LONG time we gazed at her, then we went forth with sighs and moans; to be with her seemed to us joy, parting grieved us greatly. When we had leisure from affairs of trade we used to see her. Our hearts were inextricably prisoned in her net.

1161. "AFTER some time had passed, and nights and days were sped, Usen said to me: 'I have not seen our king since the

day before yesterday; if thou advisest me, I will go and see
him, I will go and pay my court and present gifts.' I replied
'Certainly, by God, since such is your desire.'

1162. "USEN set out pearls and gems on a tray. I entreated him,
saying: 'At court thou wilt meet the drunken court folk.
Kill me! if thou be not wary of the story of that maid.'
Again he swore to me: 'I will not tell it, may swords strike
my head!'

1163. "USEN went; he found the king sitting feasting. Usen is
the king's boon companion, and the king is his well-wisher.
The king called him forward; he accepted the gifts he had
brought. Now behold the tipsy merchant, how hasty, rash
and ill-bred he is!

1164. "WHEN the king had drunk before Usen many
double-goblets, still they quaffed and again filled more
tankards and beakers; he forgot those oaths; what to him
were Korans and Meccas! Truly is it said: 'A rose befits not
a crow, nor do horns suit an ass!'

1165. "THE great king said to the witless, drunken Usen: 'I
marvel much whence thou gettest these gems to give us,
where thou findest huge pearls and peerless rubies. By my
head! I cannot return thee one-tenth for thy gifts!'

1166. "USEN saluted, and said: 'O mighty sovereign, shedder
of beams from above, O nourisher of creatures, O sun!
Whatever else I have, whose is it, be it gold or treasure?
What brought I forth from my mother's womb? By you it
has been granted to me.

1167. "'BY your head! I make bold to say that gratitude for gifts beseems you not. I have somewhat else, a daughter-in-law for you, a bride to unite to your son; for this undoubtedly you will thank me when you see the sun's like; then will you oftener say: "Happiness is ours!"'"

1168. "WHY should I lengthen speech? He brake his oath, the power of religion; he told of the finding of the maid portrayed by gazers as a sun. This pleased the king greatly; it gave gaiety to his heart. He ordered her conveyance to court and the fulfilment of Usen's utterance.

1169. "PLEASANTLY I was sitting here at home; hitherto I had not sighed. At the door appeared the chief of the king's slaves, he brought with him sixty slaves, as is the custom of kings; they came in, I was much astonished, I said: 'This is some high affair of state.'

1170. "THEY greeted me: 'P'hatman,' said he, 'it is the command of the equal of the sun: that maid like two suns whom Usen presented to-day, now bring her to me, I shall take her with me; we have not far to go.' When I heard this, the heavens overwhelmed me, with wrath hill struck hill.

1171. "THEREUPON in amazement I inquired: 'What maid do you want, which?' They said to me: 'Usen presented one with a face flashing with lightning.' There was nought to be done; the day of the taking away of my soul was fixed. I trembled, I could not rise, neither could I remain sitting.

1172. "I WENT in; I saw that lovely one weeping and flooded in
tears. I said: 'O sun, seest thou fully how black Fate hath
played me false! Heaven is turned towards me in wrath,
I am despoiled, I am wholly uprooted; I am denounced, the
king asketh for thee, therefore am I heartbroken.'

1173. "SHE said to me: 'Sister, marvel not, however hard this
may be! Luckless Fate hath ever been a doer of ill upon me;
if some good had befallen me thou mightest have wondered,
what marvel is evil? All kinds of woe are not new to me,
old are they.'

1174. "HER eyes poured forth frequent tears like pearls. She
rose as fearless as if she were a tiger or a hero; joy no longer
seemed joy nor did woe seem woe to her. She begged me to
cover her form and face with a veil.

1175. "I SENT into the treasure-house on which no price was set;
I took out gems and pearls as much as I could, every single
separate one was worth a city. I went back; I girded them
round the waist of her for whose sake my heart was dying.

1176. "I SAID: 'O my dear one! Perchance this sort of thing
may somewhere be of use to thee!' I gave that face, the
sun's peer, into the hands of the slaves. The king was
warned, he met her; the kettledrum was beaten, there was
hubbub. She went forward with bent head, calm, saying
nought.

1177. "ONLOOKERS flocked upon her, there was trampling and
uproar; the officers could not hold them back, there was no
quiet there. When the king saw her, cypress-like, coming

towards him, he said in amazement: 'O sun, how art thou brought hither?'

1178. "SUN-like, she made those who gazed on her to blink. The king deigned to say: 'I have seen, she hath turned me into one who has seen nought. Who but God could imagine her? Right is he who is in love with her if he, alas! roam mad in deserts!'

1179. "HE seated her at his side, he talked to her with sweet discourse; quoth he: 'Tell me who art thou, whose art thou, of what race art thou come?' With her sun-like face she gave no answer; with bowed head, of gentle mien, sorrowful she sits.

1180. "WHATEVER he said, she hearkened not to the king. Elsewhere was her heart; of somewhat else she thought. The roses were glued together; she opened not the pearl. She made them that looked on her wonder, what else could they think.

1181. "THE king said: 'What can we think of? With what can we comfort our heart? There can be no opinion save these two: Either she is in love with someone, she is thinking of her beloved, save him she has no leisure for any, to none can she speak.

1182. "'Or she is some sage, lofty and high-seeing; joy seems not joy to her, nor sorrow when it is heaped on sorrow, as a table she looks on misfortune and happiness alike; she is elsewhere, elsewhere she soars, her mind is like a dove's.

1183. "'GOD grant my son come home victorious. I will have for his homecoming this sun ready for him; perchance he will make her say something, and we also shall know what is revealed; till then, let the moon rest with waning ray far sundered from the sun.'

1184. "OF the king's son I will tell thee: a good, fearless youth, peerless in valour and beauty, fair in face and form; at that time he was gone forth to war, there had he tarried long; for him his father prepared her, the star-like one.

1185. "THEY brought her and apparelled her form in maidenly garb; on it was seen many a ray of glittering gems, on her head they set a crown of a whole ruby, there the rose was beautified by the colour of the transparent crystal.

1186. "THE king commanded: 'Deck the chamber of the princess royal.' They set up a couch of gold, of red of the Occident. The great king himself, the lord of the whole palace, arose and set thereon that sun, the joy of the heart of beholders.

1187. "HE commanded nine eunuchs to stand guard at the door. The king sat down to a feast befitting their race; to Usen he gave immeasurable gifts as a return for that peer of the sun: they made trumpet and kettledrum to sound for the increasing of the noise.

1188. "THEY prolonged the feasting; the drinking went on exceeding long. The sun-faced maiden says to Fate: 'What a murderous Fate have I! Whence am I come hither, to whom shall I belong, for whose sake am I mad? What shall

323

I do? What shall I undertake? What will avail me? A very hard life have I!'

1189. "AGAIN she says: 'I will not wither the rose-like beauty. I will attempt somewhat; perchance God will protect me from my foe. What reasonable man slays himself before death comes? When he is in trouble, then it needs that the intelligent should have his wits!'

1190. "SHE called the eunuchs, and said: 'Hearken, come to reason! You are deceived, mistaken as to my royalty; your lord is in error in desiring me for a daughter-in-law. In vain, alas! sounds he for me the trumpet, the kettledrum and clarion.

1191. "'I AM not suited to be your queen; elsewhither leads my path. God keep man far from me, be he sun-faced, cypress-formed! You beg of me something different; my business is of another kind. With you my life beseems me not.

1192. "'WITHOUT fail I shall slay myself, I shall strike a knife into my heart; your lord will kill you, you will have no time of tarrying in the world. This then is better: I will give you the weighty treasure wherewith my waist is girded, let me steal away, let me go free, lest you regret.'

1193. "SHE undid the pearls and gems that girdled her; she doffed, too, the crown, transparent, of a whole ruby; she gave them, she said: 'Take them, with burning heart I implore you; let me go, and you will have paid a great debt to your God!'

1194. "THE slaves were greedy for her costly treasure, they forgot the fear of the king as of a bellman, they resolved to let her of the peerless face escape. See what gold doth, that crook from a devilish root!

1195. "GOLD never gives joy to them that love it; till the day of death greed makes them gnash their teeth. Gold comes in and goes out, they murmur at the course of the planets when it is lacking; moreover it binds the soul here, and hinders it from soaring up.

1196. "WHEN the eunuchs had ended the matter as she wished, one took off his garment and gave it to her; they passed through other doors because the great hall was full of drunken men. The moon remained full, unswallowed by the serpent.

1197. "THE slaves, too, disappeared; they stole forth with her. The maiden knocked at my door, and asked for me, P'hatman. I went, I knew her, I embraced her, was I not surprised! She would not come in with me at all, saying: 'Why dost thou invite me!' I regretted it.

1198. "SHE said to me: 'I have bought myself with what thou gavest me. May God in return reward thee with heavenly favour! No longer canst thou hide me, let me go, send me off swiftly on horseback ere the king get wit and send men to gallop in pursuit.'

1199. "SWIFTLY I entered the stable, I loosed the best steed, I saddled it, set her upon it; cheerful was she, not sighing. She was like the sun, the best of heaven's lights, when it mounts the lion. My labour was lost; I could not harvest what I had sown.

1200. "THE day drew down to evening, the rumour spread, her pursuers came; inside the city was a state of siege, they raised a hue and cry; they questioned me, I said: 'If you find her there in the house where I am, may I be guilty towards the kings and answerable for their blood.'

1201. "THEY sought, nought could they discover, they returned abashed. From that time the king and all his familiars mourn. Behold the palace folk; they are clad in raiment dyed violet colour. The sun went away from us; since then we lack light.

1202. "NOW I shall narrate to thee anon the whereabouts of that moon, but first of all I will tell thee why that man threatened me. I, alas! was his she-goat; he was my he-goat Timidity slurs a man, and wantonness a woman.

1203. "I AM not content with my husband, for he is lean and ill-favoured; this man, the Chachnagir,[1] was a gentleman high at court; we loved each other, though I shall wear no mourning weeds for him; would that one might give me a cup of his blood to sip!

1204. "LIKE a woman, like a fool, I told him this story of the coming of that sun to me, and of her stealing away like

---

[1] *Chachnagir*—official taster of food and wine at the king's court.

a fox; he threatened me with exposure, not like a friend, like a foe. Now when I think of him as a corpse, ah! how relieved am I!

1205. "WHENEVER we quarrelled alone he menaced me. When I called thee I did not think he was at home; he had arrived, he told me of his coming. Thou also wert coming; I was afraid, so I begged thee: 'Do not come!' I sent a slave to meet thee.

1206. "YOU turned not back, you came, you brought beams of light to me; you both met, you were assembled to fight over me, so I feared, I could think of no way. He, alas! desired my death in his heart, and not only with his tongue.

1207. "IF thou hadst not slain him, and if he had gone forthwith to court, in his wrath he would have denounced me, for his heart was burned as with fire; the angry king would have cleared away my house at one swoop, he would, O God! have made me eat my children, then he would have stoned me with stone.

1208. "GOD reward thee in return—what thanks can I render thee! thee who hast delivered me safe from that serpent's gaze! Now henceforth I can be happy in my star and Fate! No longer do I fear death! Ha! ha! What has befallen me!"

1209. AVT'HANDIL said: "Fear not! Even in the book it is thus written: 'Of all foes the most hateful is the friend-foe; if a man be wise, he will not heartily confide.' Fear no more from him, now is he corpse-like.

1210. "TELL me the same story—since thou spedst the maiden all the tidings thou hast learned or heard of her." Again P'hatman spoke weeping; again the tear flowed from her eyes. Quoth she: "The ray which sun-like illumined the fields was brought to nought."

XLIX

The Story of the Capture of Nestan-Daredjan by the Kadjis, Told by P'hatman to Avt'handil

1211. WOE, O passing world, in falsehood thou art like Satan, none can know aught of thine, where thy treachery is. That face apparent as a sun—where hast thou it hidden? Whither hast thou taken it? Therefore I see that in the end all seems vain, wherever anything may be.

1212. P'HATMAN said: "The sun was departed from me, the light of all the world, life and existence, the gain of my hands; from that time unceasingly the burning of hot fires afflicted me, I could not dry the spring of tears flowing forth from mine eyes.

1213. "HOUSE and child became hateful to me, I sat with cheerless heart; waking I thought of her, when I fell asleep I thought of her in my drowsiness. The oath-breaker Usen seems to me of the infidels in faith; the accursed one cannot approach me, to be near me with his cursed face.

1214. "ONE day at eventide, just at sunset, I passed the guards, the door of the asylum caught mine eye; I was in a reverie,

sadness at the thought of her was slaying me; I said:
'Cursed is the vow of every man!'

1215. "FROM somewhere there came a wandering slave with
three companions, the slave clad as a slave, the others in
coarse travelling garb; they brought food and drink which
they had bought in the city for a drachma. They drank,
they ate, they chattered, thus they sat merry.

1216. "I HEARKENED to them, I watched them. They said:
'Pleasantly we rejoiced, but though here we are joined as
comrades, yet are we strangers, none of us knows who
another is or whence we are come; we must at least tell one
another our stories with our tongues.'

1217. "THOSE others told their tales as is the wont of wayfarers.
The slave said: 'O brothers, providence is a celestial thing;
I harvest for you pearls, you sowed but millet; my story
is better than your stories:

1218. "'I AM the slave of the exalted king, the ruler of the
Kadjis. It chanced that he was struck by a sickness which
prevailed over him; the helper of the widow, the comforter
of the orphan, was dead to us; now his sister, better than
a parent, rears his children.

1219. "'DULARDUKHT is a woman, but a rock, like a cliff, her
slave is wounded by none, but he wounds others. She had
little nephews: Rosan and Rodia; now she is seated as
sovereign of Kadjet'hi, "the Mighty" is she called.

1220. "'WE heard news of the death overseas of her sister. The viziers were distressed, they refrained from assembling a privy council: "How can we venture to report the extinction of a face which was the light of the lands?"– Roshak is a slave, the chief of many thousand slaves.

1221. "'ROSHAK said: "Even if I be killed for mine absence, I shall not be at the mourning! I go into the plain, I will reave, I will fill myself with booty; I shall come home enriched, I shall be back in good time. When the sovereign goes forth to bewail her sister, I too will accompany her."

1222. "'HE said to us, his underlings: "I will go, come with me!" He took of us a hundred slaves, all chosen by him. By day in the sunlight we reaved, by night also we watched; many a caravan we broke up, we unloaded the treasure for ourselves.

1223. "'ONE very dark night we were wandering over the plains; there appeared to us certain great lights in the midst of the field; we said: "Is it the sun strayed down from heaven to earth!" Perplexed, we gave our minds to torturing thought

1224. "'SOME said: "It is the dawn!" Others said: "It is the moon!" We, drawn up in fighting array, moved towards it–I saw it from very near–we made a wide circuit round it, we came and surrounded it. From that light came a voice speaking to us.

1225. "'IT said to us: "Who are you, O cavaliers? Tell me your names! From Gulansharo I go, a messenger to Kadjet'hi have a care of me." When we heard this we approached, we formed a circle round about. A certain sun-faced rider appeared before our eyes.

1226. "'WE gazed at the brilliant face flashing out lightning, its glittering spread itself over the surroundings like the sun; rarely she spoke to us with some gentle discourse, then from her teeth the ray lighted up her jetty lashes.

1227. "'AGAIN we addressed that sun with sweet-discoursing tongue; she was not a slave, she spoke falsely, this we perceived. Roshak discovered that it was a damsel; he rode by her side; we did not let her go, we made bold to keep her in our hands.

1228. "'AGAIN we asked: "Tell us the true story of that sun-like light of thine. Whose art thou, who art thou, whence comest thou, enlightener of darkness?" She told us nought; she shed a stream of hot tears. How pitiable is the full moon swallowed by the serpent!

1229. "'NEITHER plain tale nor secret, she told us nought, neither who she was, nor by whom she had been treacherously treated; angrily she spoke with us, sullen, on the defensive, like an asp attacking onlookers with her eye.

1230. "'ROSHAK ordered us: "Ask not, it seems nought is to be said now; her business is a strange one and difficult to be told The good fortune of our sovereign is to be desired by creatures, for God giveth her whatever is most marvellous.

1231. "'"THIS damsel has been destined to us by God that we might bring her; we will take her as a gift, Dulardukht will render us very great thanks; if we conceal it, we shall be found out, and our sovereign is proud: first, it is an offence to her, then it is a great disgrace."

1232. "'WE agreed, we prolonged not the discussion. We returned, we made for Kadjet'hi, leading her with us; we ventured not to speak directly to her, nor did we annoy her. She weeps; with embittered heart she laves her cheeks in flowing tears.

1233. "'I SAID to Roshak: "Give me leave; soon again shall I attend you. At present I have some business in the city of Gulansharo." He granted me leave. Hereabout I have some stuff to be carried off, I will take it with me, I will go and overtake them.'

1234. "THIS story of the slave greatly pleased those men. I heard it; the stream from the pool of tears dried up in me. I guessed, I recognized every sign of her who is my life; this gave me a little comfort, like a drachma's weight.

1235. "I LAID hold of that slave and set him close before me. I asked him: 'Tell me what thou wert saying; I, too, wish to hear.' He told me again the same as I had heard thence. This story enlivened me; me, struggling in soul, it preserved alive.

1236. "I HAD two black slaves full of sorcery, by their art they go and come invisible; I brought them out, I despatched them to Kadjet'hi, I said: 'Tarry not; give me tidings of her by your deeds.'

1237. "IN three days they came and told me, swiftly had they
trod the road: 'The queen, who was ready to go over the
sea, has taken her. None can fix his eyes to gaze upon her,
as upon the sun. The queen has betrothed her as wife to the
little boy Rosan.

1238. """WE shall wed her to Rosan," this is the decree of Queen
Dulardukht, "at present I have not leisure for the wedding,
now is my heart consumed with fire; when I return home
I will make a daughter-in-law of her who is praised as
heaven's sun." She has set her in the castle; one eunuch
attends her.

1239. "'DULARDUKHT took with her all those skilled in
sorcery, for perilous is the road, her foes are ready for the
fray; she has left at home all her bravest knights. She will
tarry; but little time has already passed.

1240. "'THE city of the Kadjis has hitherto been unassailable by
foes; within the city is a strong rock, high and long; inside
that rock is hollowed out a passage for climbing up. Alone
there is that star, the consumer of those who come in touch
with her.

1241. "'AT the gate of the passage are continually on guard
knights not ill-favoured, there stand ten thousand heroes
all of the chosen knights, at each of the three city gates
three thousand.' O heart, the world hath condemned thee;
I know not, alas! what binds thee."

336

1242. WHEN Avt'handil, the sun-faced but woeful, heard these tidings he was pleased, he showed nothing else. The lovely creature rendered thanks to God: "Somebody's sister has told me joyful news!"

1243. HE said to P'hatman: "Beloved, thou art worthy to be loved by me, thou hast let me hear a welcome story, not with louring looks; but let me hear more fully about Kadjet'hi; every Kadj is fleshless, how can it become human?

1244. "PITY for that maiden kindles me and burns me with flame; but I marvel what the fleshless Kadjis can do with a woman!" P'hatman said: "Hearken to me! Truly I see thee here perplexed. They are not Kadjis, but men who put their trust in steep rocks," quoth she.

1245. "THEIR name is called Kadji because they are banded together, men skilled in sorcery, exceeding cunning in the art, harmers of all men, themselves unable to be harmed by any; they that go out to join battle with them come back blinded and shamed.

1246. "THEY do something wondrous, they blind the eyes of their foes, they raise fearful winds, they make the ship to founder midst the seas, they run as on dry land, for they clean dry up the water; if they wish they make the day dark, if they wish they enlighten the darkness.

1247. "FOR this reason all those that dwell round about call them Kadjis, though they, too, are men fleshly like us."

Avt'handil thanked her: "Thou hast extinguished my hot flames; the tidings just told me have pleased me greatly."

1248. AVT'HANDIL, shedding tears, magnifies God with his heart; he said: "O God, I thank Thee, for Thou art the Comforter of my woes, who wast and art, Unspeakable, Unheard by ears: Your mercy is suddenly spread forth over us!"

1249. FOR the knowledge of this story he magnified God with tears. P'hatman thought of herself; therefore she was again burned up. The knight kept his secret, he lent himself to love; P'hatman embraced his neck, she kissed his sun-like face.

1250. That night P'hatman enjoyed lying with Avt'handil; the knight unwillingly embraces her neck with his crystal neck; remembrance of T'hinat'hin slays him, he quakes with secret fear, his maddened heart raced away to the wild beasts and ran with them.

1251. AVT'HANDIL secretly rains tears, they flow to mingle with the sea; in an inky eddy floats a jetty ship. He says: "Behold me, O lovers, me who have a rose for mine own! Away from her, I, the nightingale, like a carrion-crow, sit on the dungheap!"

1252. THE tears which flowed there from him would have melted a stone, the thicket of jet dammed them up, there is a pool on the rose-field. P'hatman rejoiced in him as if she were a nightingale; if a crow find a rose it thinks itself a nightingale.

1253. DAY dawned; the sun whose rays were soiled by the world went forth to bathe. The woman gave him many coats, cloaks, turbans, many kinds of perfumes, fair clean shirts. "Whatsoever thou desirest," said she, "put on; be not shy of me!"

1254. AVT'HANDIL said: "This day will I declare mine affair." The wearing of merchant garb had hitherto been his resolve. That day wholly in knightly raiment he apparelled his brave form; he increased his beauty, the lion resembled the sun.

1255. P'HATMAN prepared a meal, to which she invited Avt'handil. The knight came in adorned, gaily, not with louring looks. P'hatman looked, she was astonished that he was not in merchant garb; she smiled at him: "Thus is it better for the pleasure of them that are mad for thee."

1256. P'HATMAN exceedingly admired his beauty. He made no answer, he smiled to himself: "It seems she does not recognize me!" How did he consider P'hatman foolish! He looked on her as on an equal, for he had no choice.

1257. WHEN they had eaten they separated, the knight went home; having drunk wine, he lay down merry, pleasantly he fell asleep. At eventide he awoke; he shed his rays across the fields. He invited P'hatman: "Come, see me, I am alone, quite alone!"

1258. P'HATMAN went, Avt'handil heard her voice making moan; she said: "Undoubtedly I am slain by him whose form is like an aloe-tree." He set her at his side; he gave her

339

a pillow from his carpet. The shade from the eaves of the eyelashes overshadows the rose-garden.

1259. AVT'HANDIL said: "O P'hatman, I know thee; thou wilt tremble at these tidings like one bitten by a serpent; but hitherto thou hast not heard the truth concerning me; my slayers are black lashes, trees of jet.

1260. "THOU thinkest me some merchant, master of a caravan; I am the Spaspeti of the exalted King Rostevan, chief of the great host befitting him; I have the mastery over many treasures and arsenals.–

1261. "I KNOW thee to be a good friend, faithful, trusty.–He has one daughter, a sun the enlightener of lands; she it is who consumes me and melts me; she sent me, I forsook my master, her father.

1262. "THAT damsel thou hadst–to seek that same damsel, that substitute for the sun, I have gone over the whole world; I have seen him who roves for her sake, where he, pale lion, lies wasting himself, his heart and strength."

1263. AVT'HANDIL told all his own tale to P'hatman, the story of the donning of the tiger hide by Tariel. He said: "Thou art the balm of him thou has not yet seen, the resource of him of frequent eyelash, ruffled like a raven's wing.

1264. "COME, P'hatman, and aid me, let us try to be of use to him, let us help them, perchance those stars shall receive joy. All men who shall know it, all will begin to praise us. Surely again will it befall the lovers to meet.

1265. "BRING me that same sorcerer slave, I will send him to Kadjet'hi, we will make known to the maiden all the tidings known to us, she also will inform us of the truth, we will do what she chooses. God grant you may hear that the kingdom of the Kadjis is vanquished by us."

1266. P'HATMAN said: "Glory to God, what things have befallen me! This day I have heard tidings equal to immortality!" She brought the sorcerer slave, black as a raven, and said: "I send thee to Kadjet'hi; go, thou hast a long journey.

1267. "NOW will appear advantage for me from thy sorcery, speedily quench the furnace of the burning of my fires, tell that sun the means for her cure." He said: "To-morrow I shall give you full news of what you wish."

L

The Letter Written by P'hatman to Nestan-Daredjan

1268. P'HATMAN writes: "O star, heavenly sun of the world,
consumer and griever of all them that are afar from thee,
elegant and eloquent in words, lovely, fair-tongued,
crystal and ruby both welded in one!

1269. "THOUGH thou gavest me not to hear thy story, I have
learnt the truth, thereby hath my heart been comforted.
Console with news Tariel, who is become mad for thee!
May you both attain your desire, may he be a rose and thou
a violet!

1270. "HIS sworn brother is come in quest of thee, Avt'handil,
an Arab knight renowned in Arabia, Spaspeti of King
Rostevan, to be contemned of none. Write news of thyself,
thou proud one, wise in understanding!

1271. "FOR this purpose have we sent this slave to your
presence: We would know tidings of Kadjet'hi. Have the
Kadjis come home? We wish to know in detail the number
of warriors there. Who are thy guards, and who is their
chief?

1272. "WHATEVER thou knowest concerning that place, write to us, make it known. Then send some token for thy lover. All the sorrow thou hast had hitherto, change it into joy! May it please God that I unite the lovers so befitting each other!

1273. "GO, O letter, hasten, if swift be thy knee! I envy thee, thou goest to see the crystal, jest and rubies. In Fate thou art happier than I, O letter; the eyes of her who consumes me will look upon thee. If thou hearest of my life after thee, shalt thou not pity me!"

1274. P'HATMAN gave the letter to that cunning sorcerer: "Give this letter to the sun-like maiden!" The wizard donned a certain green mantle over his form: in that very moment he was lost to view, he flew over the roofs.

1275. HE went like an arrow shot by a swift-bowed archer. When he reached Kadjet'hi it was just dusk twilight. Invisible he passed the multitude of knights guarding the gates. He gave to that sun the greeting of her who longed for her.

1276. HE passed the closed gates of the castle as if they had been open; the Negro entered, the black-faced, long-haired, cloaked; that sun was affrighted, she thought it was somewhat to harm her; the rose was changed to saffron and the violets to sky blue.

1277. THE Kadj said: "Whom think'st thou me to be, and why swoonest thou thus? I am P'hatman's slave despatched to thy presence, this letter will justify me, I speak not falsely to thee. Let the sun's rays come forth, O rose, fade not so soon."

343

1278. THE sun-faced marvelled at P'hatman's wonderful news;
she split her almonds, the jets quivered with the rod of jet.
The slave gave her the letter with his own hand. She sighs,
she reads the letter, she wets it with her hot tears.

1279. SHE asked the slave: "Tell me, who is my seeker, or who
knows me to be alive, treading the earth?" He said:
"I will venture to tell you only what I know. When thou
wentest forth, since then hath our sun been darkened.

1280. "HENCEFORTH P'hatman's heart hath been torn by
lances; the tears she shed are such as to be united to the
seas. Once already I brought news of thee to her. I call
God to witness that for her since then the tear hath not
ceased.

1281. "NOW there came a certain knight, fair of face; in detail
she told him all, what trouble you are in; he with hero-like
arm is thy seeker; they sent me, they entreated me to
hasten with ceaseless haste."

1282. THE maiden said: "What thou hast said, O man, seems to
me to be truth. How could P'hatman know from whom I
was carried away! Doubtless somewhere is he who burns me
with fire. I will write to her; thou also shalt tell how my
heart boils."

LI

The Letter Written by Nestan-Daredjan to P'hatman

1283. THE sun-faced writes: "O dame, O mother, better than a mother to me! See what the world hath done to me, its thrall! Alas! there is added to those griefs of mine still another! Now that I have seen thy missive it hath greatly encouraged me.

1284. "THOU didst save me from two sorcerers; thou didst alleviate my woes. Now I am thus held here by the whole force of the Kadjis; a whole realm, many thousand heroes, guard me alone. Ill befell me, my counsels and resolves.

1285. "WHAT other tidings hence can I write to thee? The Queen of the Kadjis is not come, nor will the Kadjis yet come; but countless hosts guard me, and with what bravery! What! the quest for me! It is not possible, believe me!

1286. "WHOEVER is come seeking me is wearied in vain; he suffers, he is consumed, he is kindled for me, a flame like fire burns him. But I envy him, he hath seen the sun, thus is he not frozen. Without him, alas! what great pity my life is!

1287. "FORMERLY I told thee not my story, I hid it from thee for that my tongue could not speak it; I spared myself woes. I entreat thee, beg my beloved to have pity and not come in search of me, write to him, send him a message.

1288. "WHAT afflicts me is enough, let him not slay me with a woe equal to this: I should see him a corpse, I should die a double death. None can help me, I know this for a truth; this is no gossip. If he will not hearken to thee, stone me with a heap of black stone!

1289. "THOU didst ask me to send a token, show this: I send a cutting from the veils he gave me; these veils for his sake are a fair sight to me, though in colour they are black, like my Fate."

LII

The Letter Written by Nestan-Daredjan to Her Beloved

1290. NOW she sobbing, weeping, writes to her beloved; quenching with her tears the intense fires that consumed him. She wrote a letter piercing the heart of the hearers. She splits the rose; there appears the translucent crystal.

1291. "O MINE own! this letter is the work of my hands; for pen I have my form, a pen steeped in gall; for paper I glue thy heart even to my heart; O heart, sad heart, thou art bound, loose not thyself, now be bound!

1292. "THOU seest, O mine own! of what deeds the world is a doer. However much light shines, for me it is but darkness. The wise know the world, therefore they despise it, to them it is contemptible. My life without thee, woe is me! how exceeding hard it is!

1293. "THOU seest, mine own! how Fate and cursed time hath parted us; no longer do I glad see thee, my glad loved one; what, indeed, can the heart rent by thee do without thee! My thought manifests now to thee what was hidden.

1294. "BY thy sun! until now I thought not thou wert alive; as for me, methought my life and all my resource had passed away. Now when I hear news of thee, I magnify the Creator and humble myself before God. All mine erstwhile grief I weigh as joy.

1295. "THY life is sufficient for my heart to hope in, a heart all wounded and so consumed! Think of me, remember me as one lost to thee; I sit nursing the love I planted.

1296. "NOW, O mine own, my story is not to be written to thee by me; the tongue will tire, none that hear will believe! P'hatman took me from sorcerers; may God protect her! Now again the world hath done what befits it.

1297. "WORLD hath now added worse woe to my woe, my ill luck was not appeased by these manifold afflictions; and again it delivered me into the hands of the Kadjis, hard to combat; Fate hath done to us, mine own, all that hath befallen us.

1298. "I AM sitting in a castle so lofty that eyes can scarce see the ground; the road enters by a passage, over it stand guards; day and night knights miss not their turn as sentries, they will kill those that engage them, like fire will they envelop them.

1299. "SURELY thou thinkest not that these are of the same kind as other warriors? Slay me not with woes worse than the present! I shall see thee dead, I shall be burnt up like

tinder by steel. Since I am sundered from thee, renounce
me with a heart harder than rock itself.

1300. "BELOVED, sorrow not with such grief! Tell me, can
there be for me another with the form of an aloe-tree! Life
without thee is nought for me, henceforth I should be full
of regret; either I would cast myself down from the rock
or slay myself with a knife.

1301. "BY thy sun! thy moon will fall to the lot of none save
thee! By thy sun! to none shall she fall though triple suns
shone forth! Here would I dash myself down; the great
rocks are very nigh to me. To thee would I commit my
soul; perchance wings would be given to me by Heaven.

1302. "ENTREAT God for me; it may be He will deliver me
from the travail of the world and from union with fire,
water, earth and air. Let Him give me wings and I shall fly
up, I shall attain my desire—day and night I shall gaze on
the sun's rays flashing in splendour.

1303. "THE sun cannot be without thee, for thou art an atom
of it; of a surety thou shalt adhere to it as its zodiac, and
not as one rejected. There shall I seek thee; I shall liken
thee to it, thou shalt enlighten my darkened heart. If my
life was bitter, let my death be sweet!

1304. "DEATH is no longer grievous to me, since it is to thee
I commit my soul; but I have laid thy love in my heart,
and there it rests. When I think of parting from thee, for me
wound is added to wound. Weep not and mourn not for me,
O mine own, for love of me!

1305. "GO, betake thyself to India, be of some help to my
father, who is straitened by foes, helpless on all sides;
comfort the heart of him who suffers separation from me.
Think of me weeping for thy sake with undrying tears.

1306. "WHATEVER complaint I have made against my Fate is
sufficient complaint. Know this, that true justice goeth
from heart to heart; for thy sake will I die, the ravens will
call me! I shall suffice for thy weeping and suffering.

1307. "LO, mark the token from the veil that was thine; from
one end I have cut off a strip, O mine own; this is all that
is left to me in place of that great hope; in wrath the
wheel of the seven heavens hath turned upon us."

1308. WHEN she had finished this letter written to her beloved,
she cut off a fringe from those veils; bareheaded, the
thick, long locks of her hair became her well, the scent
blows from the aloe, breathing through the raven's wings.

1309. THAT slave departed, journeying to Gulansharo; in one
instant he reached P'hatman's, he travelled not many
days. When this matter so dear to him had been
accomplished, Avt'handil with hands upraised thanks God
with full understanding, not as one bemused.

1310. HE said to P'hatman: "The thing desired is timely
finished for me; thy great zeal for my sake is still
unrecompensed. I go, I have no leisure to tarry longer,
last year's time is come. Swiftly shall I lead into Kadjet'hi
him who will annihilate and destroy them."

1311. THE lady said: "O lion, the fire now becomes hotter; my
heart will be sundered from its light, thereby will it be

350

darkened; hasten, grieve not for me, the madman will still remain mad. Should the Kadjis arrive before you, going thither will be made difficult for you."

1312. THE knight called P'hridon's slaves who attended him. He said: "Corpses hitherto, now indeed are we enlivened; we are renewed by the hearing of what we wished. I shall show you our enemies wounded and thereby woe-stricken.

1313. "GO and tell P'hridon this unvarnished story. I cannot see him, I am hurried, my road is one of haste. Let him strengthen his great voice to make it still more bold. I will give you all the precious tissues taken by me as booty.

1314. "GREAT is the debt laid upon me by you; I will show my gratitude in another way when I join P'hridon again. For the nonce, take away all that was reft from the pirates; I can give you no more than this, I know that so I shall seem to you niggardly.

1315. "I HAVE no home near; I have no power to dispense gifts." He gave them a ship full, beautiful things, a host in number. He said: "Go, take them away, travel the road to that same region. Give this letter from me, his sworn brother, to P'hridon."

LIII

Avt'handil's Letter to P'hridon

1316. HE wrote: "Exalted P'hridon, supremely blest, king of kings, lion-like in stout-heartedness, O sun, recklessly shedding rays, mighty, joyous, spiller of the blood of foes—thy youngest brother from far, far away barks thee a greeting.

1317. "I HAVE seen troubles, and I have, too, received recompense for what pains I have suffered. Well hath fallen out the matter planned by me: I have truly learned the story of that face likened to a sun, the sustainer of that lion who was buried under the earth.

1318. "THE sovereign of the Kadjis has that sun; she is captive in Kadjet'hi. To go thither seems to me sport, though the road is one of battle. From the narcissi a rain of crystal falls; the rose is wet with rain. The Kadjis are not yet with the maid, but countless is their host.

1319. "GLAD in heart I rejoice, for this my tear will not flow in channels. Wherever thou and thy brother are the difficult will be made easy; whatever you may desire you will certainly do it, you shall not fail; not only no man can stand against you, I trow that even a rock will soften before you.

1320. "NOW pardon me, I cannot see thee, so I have passed afar off; I have no leisure to linger on the road, for that moon is captive. Soon shall we come merry; rejoice at the sight of us! What more than this can I say to thee: help thy brother in brotherly fashion.

1321. "THE attachment of these slaves is beyond reward; pleasantly have they served me, and your heart, too, will be pleased at this. Why should he be praised who hath sojourned long with you? Every like gives birth to like; this is a saying of the sages."

1322. HE wrote this letter, he tied it up and rolled it; rose and violet he gave it to P'hridon's slaves; he communicated through them by word of mouth all that was needful, how he should do; the open door of coral showed its pearls to them.

1323. AVT'HANDIL searched; he found a ship of that region where Tariel was. That sun with the face of a full moon prepared to set out; but to leave the woeful-hearted P'hatman was a heaviness to him; those who parted from him shed a rivulet of blood.

1324. P'HATMAN, Usen and the slaves weep with hot tears. They said: "O sun, what hast thou done to us? Thou didst burn us with hot fires, why darkenest thou us with the gloom of thine absence? Bury us with the hands that must bury us by thy departure."

LIV

Avt'handil's Departure from Gulansharo, and His Meeting With Tariel

1325. AVT'HANDIL has crossed the seas in a certain ship for travellers. He rides glad-hearted all alone. To meet Tariel with such tidings rejoices him. With hands uplifted, with his heart he hopes in God.

1326. SUMMER was come, from the Earth came forth verdure, the token of the rose bursting into bloom, the time of their tryst, the change of course by the sun, its sitting on the Cancer. He sighed when he saw the flower long time unseen by him.

1327. The sky thundered and the cloud rained crystal dew; he kissed the rose with his rose-like lips; he said: "I gaze on you with tenderly-observant eye; I rejoice to have converse with you in her stead."

1328. WHEN he thought on his friend, the bitter tears flowed; he travelled those weary ways towards Tariel, deserted and pathless, unknown regions; lion and tiger of the reedy thickets he slew wherever he saw them.

1329. THE caves came in sight, he was glad, he recognized them. He said: "These be the rocks where my friend is, he for whom my tears have flowed. I am indeed worthy to see him face to face, to relate to him what I have heard. If he be not come, what shall I do? Vain will have been my travail.

1330. "IF he be come, doubtless he would not tarry within; he would go somewhere into the plain, like a wild beast he would roam in the fields; it is better for me to go round by the rushes." He bethought himself, he looked about; thus he spoke and turned, he went towards the plains.

1331. HE canters along and sings with merry heart; he shouts to him by name with cheerful voice. He went a little farther, there appeared the sun in full splendour, at the edge of the rushes stands Tariel with sharp sword.

1332. TARIEL had slain a lion; its blood anointed his sword. He stood dismounted at the edge of the rushes; his horse was not with him. He heard Avt'handil's shout, he was astonished; he looked at him, recognized him, started, ran towards him, bounded.

1333. TARIEL flung aside his sword and went towards his adopted brother. The knight alighted from his horse; he seemed more radiant than the sun. They kissed each other; their necks were as if riveted together. There was the sugary sound of the rose frequently opening.

1334. TARIEL, weeping, uttered polished, exquisite words—the tear of blood dyed the jetty thickets crimson, the fountain of tears, many streams, waters the aloe: "Since I have seen thee, what matters it to me if eight pains oppress me?"

1335. TARIEL weeps and Avt'handil was speaking to him laughing, he smiles, he opens his coral, the flash from his teeth quivers; he said: "I have learned tidings which will please thee; now the flower will be renewed, the rose hitherto fading."

1336. TARIEL said: "O brother, what which rejoices me to-day is enough, in seeing thee I have seen all my comfort, whatever other balm God gives; hast thou not heard: How can man find in the world that which is not of Heaven's doing!"

1337. WHEN Tariel was not convinced, Avt'handil was ill at ease, he could no longer delay to tell the tale; he hastened, he drew forth the veil of her on whose lips the rose blooms; when Tariel saw, he recognized it, seized upon, started.

1338. HE recognized the letter and the fringe of the veil and unfolded them, he pressed them to his face; he fell, a rose pale in hue, his spirits fled, he drooped his lashes of jet. Neither Quaissi[1] nor even Salaman[2] could bear sorrows like his.

---

[1] Quaissi, i. e., Madjnun, the lover of Leila, in the poem *Leila and Madjnun*, by Nizami.
[2] Salaman, the hero of the Arabian story *Salaman and Absal*.

1339. AVT'HANDIL gazes at Tariel lying lifeless; he flew to him, he set about helping him, the sweetly-speaking; he could not be of avail to the consumed one, completely burned up with fire; her tokens had laid hold of his life.

1340. AVT'HANDIL sat down to weep; he mourns with melodious voice, full of the tears his raven locks, he sweeps them from the crystal roof, he brake the ruby polished with a hammer of adamant, thence issue streams which I likened to coral in hue.

1341. HE scratches his face; blood flows from his cheeks while gazing at Tariel. "What I have done neither madman nor fool hath done. Why did I in my haste pour water on a fire difficult to quench! The heart struck hastily by exceeding joy cannot bear it.

1342. "I HAVE slain my friend! What befits me disgraced? I blame myself for a deed not thought out with heed. A stupid man cannot do well in a difficult matter. It is said: 'Chidden slowness is better than praised haste.'"

1343. TARIEL lay unconscious, as if scorched. Avt'handil rose, he passed through the rushes in search of water; he found the lion's blood, he carries it to quench the flame, he sprinkled it on Tariel's breast; the lapis lazuli became ruby-hued.

1344. AVT'HANDIL sprinkled the breast of that lion with the lion's blood. Tariel started up, the ranks of the race of India moved, he opened his eyes, he received power to sit up; blue seems the ray of the moon diminished in ray by the sun.

1345. WINTER makes the roses fade, their leaves fall; the ardour of the summer sun burns them, they bemoan the drought, but upon them nightingales complain with lovely voice; heat consumes, frost freezes; the wounds hurt them in either case.

1346. EVEN so is it hard to deal with the heart of man; it is mad alike both in grief and in joy; it is always wounded, the passing world is never whole for him. He only can trust this world who is his own foe.

1347. TARIEL gazed again on the writing of his slayer; he reads, though the reading of her letter maddens him; his tears blind him to the light, dark seems the beam of day. Avt'handil rose, he began to speak with rough words.

1348. HE said: "Such behaviour is unworthy of an instructed man! Why should we weep now? It behoves us to set about the making of smiles. Arise, let us go in quest of that lost sun. Soon shall I lead thee to her; I must bring thee to thy desired one.

1349. "WHAT joy befits us, therewithal let us first rejoice. Then let us mount and set out, let us go towards Kadjet'hi. Be our swords our guides, let us make them turn their backs; untroubled shall we return, we shall reduce them to carrion."

1350. THEN Tariel asks for tidings; he no longer swooned. He looked up, he raised his eyes, the black and white lightning glittered, as a ruby by the sun so was his colour increased. Who is worthy that towards him the sky turn ever in mercy?

1351. TO Avt'handil he gave thanks; he conversed with him: "How shall I speak thy praise, worthy to be praised by the wise! Like a spring up on a mountain thou hast watered the flower of the plain; thou hast cut off for me the flow of tears of the pool of the narcissi.

1352. "I CAN never make thee a return; may the God of heaven repay thee! May He in my stead reward thee from His height!" They mounted and went home; they made great rejoicing. Now the world will indeed state Asmat'h so long hungering.

1353. AT the door of the cave Asmat'h sits alone, not fully dressed; when she had looked she recognized Tariel, and with him a knight on a white horse; both were sweetly singing like songster nightingales. Immediately she recognized them, she rose hastily, bare but for her smock.

1354. HITHERTO she had ever seen him come to the cave weeping, now she wondered to behold him singing, laughing seized with fear she rose, her understanding was like a drunkard's; she heard not yet the news she so longed for.

1355. WHEN they saw her they shouted to her, laughing and showing their teeth: "Ho! Asmat'h! God's mercy is come down on us from on high; we have found the lost moon;

what we desired that have we done; now we shall have our
fires quenched by Fate, our sorrows turned to joy."

1356. AVT'HANDIL alighted from his horse to embrace Asmat'h
she laid hold of the aloe, pliant to the touch was its branch;
she kisses his neck and face; she sheds tears. "Tell me what
thou hast discovered, what thou hast done. Beseeching
thee, I weep on the field."

1357. AVT'HANDIL gave to Asmat'h the letter of her charge,
the aloe with faded branch, the pale moon. He said: "See
the writing of her who hath passed through troubles; the
sun approaches us, it hath given us the putting away of
shadow."

1358. WHEN Asmat'h saw the letter she knew Nestan's hand;
she marvelled, fear seized her, she quakes like one possessed
from head to foot overwhelming wonder laid hold on her;
she says: "What have I seen, what do I hear, is it indeed
true?"

1359. AVT'HANDIL said: "Fear not, this story is true, joy is
given to us, all sore grief is put away from us, the sun is
come nigh us, darkness is no longer dark for us. Good hath
overcome ill; the essence of good is lasting."

1360. THE King of the Indians merrily spoke somewhat with
Asmat'h; they embraced each other, joy made them weep;
the raven's tail dropped light dew upon the rose. God
forsaketh not man if man comprehend this.

1361. THEY gave God great thanks. They said: "Thou hast done to us what was best; now we recognize that your mouth would not have adjudged to us the worst." The King of the Indians, with uplifted hand, joyously shouted this. Merry they went into the caves; Asmat'h made ready somewhat for their refreshment.

1362. TARIEL said to Avt'handil: "Hearken to these words: I will tell thee something, think me not a tedious narrator. Since the time when I captured the caves and slew droves of Devis, their precious treasury lies here.

1363. "NEVER have I seen it, for I have not wished to do so. Come and let us open it; let us see how much treasure there is." It pleased him; both arose, nor did Asmat'h stay seated. They broke down forty doors; it was no great struggle for them.

1364. THEY found unequalled treasure, hitherto unseen by their eyes. There stood a heap of jewels of fair workmanship. There were seen pearls each as big as a ball for play. Who could make account of the gold not to be numbered by any!

1365. INSIDE those forty rooms were full. They found an armoury built for storing armour; there all kinds of armour were placed like preserves; therein was a coffer, sealed, unopened.

1366. UPON it was written: "Here lieth wondrous armour: chain helmet, habergeon, steel-cutting sword. If the Kadjis attack the Devis it will be a hard day. Whoever openeth at any other time is a slayer of kings!"

1367. THEY opened the coffer; they found in it three suits of armour fit for three warrior knights to don; coats of mail, swords, helmets, greaves of like sort; they were in emerald nests, as it were shrines.

1368. EACH clothed himself with each, they tested them on themselves; chain helmet and habergeon nought could dent; they struck the swords on iron, they cut it like cotton-thread. I tell you they prize them more than all the world; they would not barter them for it.

1369. THEY said: "As a sign this is enough for us; we are in good luck. God has gazed on us with His eye, looking down from above." They took up that armour, each put it on his neck; they bound up one set with leather thongs to present to P'hridon.

1370. THEY took with them some gold, some rare pearls; they went forth, they sealed up the forty treasuries. Avt'handil said: "Henceforth will I fasten my palm to the sword; nowhere shall I go to-night, when day dawns I shall not tarry."

1371. NOW, painter, limn the sworn brothers more steadfast than brothers, these lovers of stars, excelled by none, both heroic knights renowned in bravery. When they go to Kadjet'hi you shall see a battle of piercing lances.

LV

Tariel and Avt'handil Go to P'hridon

1372. WHEN day dawned they set out; they took Asmat'h with them. Till they came to Nuradin's land they mounted her behind them; there a merchant gave them a horse for a price in gold, he made not a gift of it. As guide Avt'handil sufficed; whom else need he take!

1373. THEY wended their way and met with Nuradin's herdsmen they saw the herd of horses; it pleased them, who had come for P'hridon. There said the Hindoo to Avt'handil: "I will have thee do a good piece of fooling: Come, let us play a joke on P'hridon, let us chase his herd.

1374. "WE will carry off the herd, he will come and hear that the herd is reaved; he will prepare to do battle, to dye the plain with gore. Suddenly he will recognize us, he will be surprised, he will calm his heart. Pleasant is good joking; it makes even the proud merry."

1375. THEY began to seize the steeds, P'hridon's finest. There the herdsmen made a torch, they struck steel. They shouted: "Who are ye, knights, who do such high deeds?

This herd is his who strikes the foe with his sword without making him to sigh."

1376. THEY seized their bows, they pursued the herdsmen; the herdsmen shrieked aloud, they raised their voices: "Help, help! Brigands are massacring us!" They made an outcry, they united, they appealed to P'hridon, they were not bashful.

1377. P'HRIDON arrayed himself, he mounted, he rode forth in full array. They made an outcry, they united, the regiment covered the fields. Those suns whom winter could not freeze came forward; they were covered up, helmets hid their faces.

1378. WHEN Tariel knew P'hridon, "Now have I seen him I want," said he; he raised his helm, he smiled, he laughed; he said to P'hridon: "What dost thou wish? Why doth our coming annoy thee? Bad host! Thou meetest us to fight."

1379. P'HRIDON swiftly dismounted; he fell down and saluted. They also alighted, they embraced—ay, kissed him. P'hridon with upraised hand gave God measureless thanks. The lords also kissed them, whoever knew them.

1380. P'HRIDON said: "Why tarried ye? I expected ye sooner. I am ready; I shall not lag in any service of yours!" It seemed as if two suns and a moon were united there; they beautified one another. They set out, they departed.

1381. AT P'hridon's fairly-builded house they both alighted;
he sits down beside his sworn brother Avt'handil; Tariel sat
on a throne covered in cloth of gold. To P'hridon, renowned
as a hero, they presented that armour.

1382. THEY said: "At this time we have no other gifts for
thee, but we have many other fair things lying in a place
we wot of." He laid his face to the ground, he wasted no
time: "Such a gift to me is worthy of you."

1383. THAT night they rested as P'hridon's guests; baths he
gave them, he gave them gifts of garments in plenty, he
clad their beauty in beauty, each garment fairer than the
other; he gave them rare jewels and pearls in a golden
basin.

1384. HE said: "This is the speech of a bad host; 'tis as if
hospitality to you, wise ones, wearied me as if you were
mad; but tarrying now avails not, it is better to travel the
long road; if the Kadjis outstrip us there is a risk of trouble.

1385. "WHY should we use great hosts? We want good and few;
three hundred men suffice us, let us go swift like runaways;
in Kadjet'hi for fighting the Kadjis we shall put basket-hilts
on our swords; soon shall we find her whose pleasant aloe
form will slay us.

1386. "ONCE aforetime I was in Kadjet'hi; you shall see it,
and you, too, shall find it strong; on all sides round about
is rock, a foe may not come up to it; if we may not go in
privily, it is impossible to engage openly; so we need no
army, the squadron cannot follow us secretly."

1387. WITH what he said, they too agreed. They left there the maiden Asmat'h; P'hridon bestows a gift upon her. They took with them three hundred horsemen equal to heroes. At the last God will give the victory to all who have been distressed.

1388. ALL three sworn brothers crossed the sea. P'hridon knows the way; going day and night they travel. P'hridon said: "Now are we coming nigh the regions of Kadjet'hi; henceforth we must travel by night so that we be not discovered."

1389. THE three behaved according to this advice of P'hridon's; when it was daylight they stopped, and by night they went swiftly on. They arrived; the city appeared; they could not count the guards; outside was a rock, the noise of the sentinels in crowds increased.

1390. AT the gate of the passage ten thousand braves kept guard. Those lions saw the city; the shining moon stood upon it. They said: "Let us advise what is best, now is choice difficult; a hundred can overcome a thousand if they choose the best way."

LVI
The Counsel of Nuradin-P'hridon

1391. P'HRIDON said: "I will speak a word, I think I am not at fault: We are few, the city is only expungable by many; we have not strength for a direct attack—this is no time for boasting—in a thousand years we could not anywhere win in if they shut the gate against us.

1392. "IN my childhood my tutors instructed me in rope dancing, they taught me their tricks, they made me leap, they trained me, I used to go along a rope so that eyes could not follow me; whatever little boys looked at me they also desired to do it.

1393. "NOW, whichever of you knows best how to cast a noose, let us throw the end of a long rope to that tower, it seems as easy for me to cross as a field; I shall make it a trouble to you to find a sound man inside.

1394. "TO me it seems nought to cross in armour, no trouble to bear a shield; nimbly shall I leap down inside, strike like a wind, slay the soldiers; I shall open, you will see the opening of the gate, you too come thither where you hear the uproar of alarm."

LVII

The Counsel of Avt'handil

1395. AVT'HANDIL said: "Ha, P'hridon! friends cannot complain of thee; thou hast hope in thy lion-like arms, wounds hurt not thee; thou counsellest hard counsel to make foes lament; but hearest thou not how very near the garrison shouts!

1396. "WHEN thou goest over, the garrison will hear the clatter of thine armour, they will perceive thee, they will cut the cord, of this thou must be assured. Everything will turn out ill for thee; only the vain attempt will remain to thee. That counsel is of no value; let us help ourselves in some other way.

1397. "THIS is better; you stay hidden in ambush. These men will not lay hands on a traveller coming into the town. I will dress myself as a merchant, I will do a treacherous deed; I will load a mule with helmet, hauberk and sword.

1398. "IT is of no use for the three of us to go in, there is risk that they would perceive it; I shall go alone as a merchant and well shall I win in unnoticed; secretly shall I don mine armour, I shall appear, I shall deceive them. God grant that I may make channels of blood to flow generously in there!

1399. "WITHOUT any difficulty I shall remove the guards inside: you strike outside the gate, all like heroes; I shall shatter the locks, I shall open, stone and mortar will not stop me. If aught else would be better, say so; I am for a plan of this sort."

LVIII

The Counsel of Tariel

1400. TARIEL said: "I recognize your heroism exceeding that of heroes; your counsel and advice is like your own stout-heartedness; I know you desire fierce fight, not a vain brandishing of swords, when the battle becomes perilous then are ye men.

1401. "BUT let me too have some choice in the matter. The sound will be heard by her who maddens me; like the sun she will be standing aloft; you will have fierce fight, she will see me as a non-combatant! This will be a slur on me. Nay, speak no flattering words!

1402. "BETTER than that counsel is this—let us do as I say: Let us divide the men by hundreds; when night turns to dawn let the three of us start out from three places, swiftly let us urge on our horses; they will send out to encounter us, we shall seem insignificant to them, we shall lend a powerful palm to the sword.

1403. "SWIFTLY shall we engage them, we shall get round them they will not be able to shut the gates against us; one of the three will go in, the others from outside will strike the foe that is outside; that one who is inside will fall on those within, making their blood flow; again let us lay hold of the arms mightily used by us!"

1404. P'HRIDON said: "I understand, I perceive, I know what it is. None could forestall at the gates that horse that once was mine; when I gave it I knew not that we should want to mount guard over the Kadjis in Kadjet'hi; if so, I tell thee I would by no means have given it to thee, such is mine avarice!"

1405. P'HRIDON, the gay, jests with such discourse as this; thereupon they, the eloquent, wise-worded ones, laugh, they joke one with another, with merriment beseeming them. They dismounted and arrayed themselves; they mounted their excellent steeds.

1406. AGAIN they interchanged words, not tart to the mouth. They resolved on that plan proposed by Tariel. They divided among them by hundreds the men, all equal to heroes. They mounted their horses; they covered their heads with their helmets.

LIX

The Taking of the Castle of Kadjet'hi and the Saving of Nestan-Daredjan

1407. I SAW those heroes shining with rays excelling the sun; those three are covered by the seven planets with a column of light. Tariel with slender form sits on the black horse; they consumed their foes in fight as their admirers by gazing.

1408. NOW, this is what I shall say is their image and likeness: When clouds rain down, and the stream pours from the mountains, it comes and glides through the glens, turmoil and uproar is heard; but when it unites with the sea then is it even so calm.

1409. THOUGH P'hridon and Avt'handil are unrivalled in valour yet to engage with Tariel is to be desired of none; the sun hides even the planets, nor do the Pleiads shine. Now give heed, O listener; thou shalt hear of fierce fights.

1410. THE three split up into three, one for each gate; with them they had three hundred men all equal to heroes. That night they hastily made a reconnaissance, not illusory. Day dawned, they appeared, they set forth, they each had his shield.

1411. FIRST they went quietly in the guise of some travellers; those inside could not perceive, they could not meet them alertly, they had no fear in their hearts, quietly they stood at ease. They approached; for the time being they covered over their helmets.

1412. SUDDENLY they spurred their horses, their whips swished. When they saw, they opened the gates, a tumult came forth from the city. The three set out in three different directions, thus risking their lives. They played on fifes and drums; they made the trumpets sound shrill.

1413. THEN the measureless wrath of God struck Kadjet'hi. Cronos,[1] looking down in anger, removed the sweetness of the sun; to them also in wrath turned round the wheel and circle of heaven. The fields could not contain the corpses; the army of the dead was increasing.

1414. THE sound of Tariel's mighty voice made men unwounded faint, he rent the armour, the strength of the chain-mail was brought to nought; they attacked the gates on three sides, they found no difficulty in cutting them down; when they entered the city they began swiftly to destroy the castle.

1415. AVT'HANDIL and the lion P'hridon met inside, they had wholly destroyed the enemy, whose blood flowed in

---

[1] Cronos–Saturn (Greek).

378

streams; they shouted and saw each other, they rejoiced greatly; they said: "How goeth it with Tariel?" Their eyes roved round seeking him.

1416. NONE of them knew; they could hear nought of Tariel. They wended to the castle gate, no care had they for the foe; there they saw a bank of armour, shattered chips of sword-blades, the ten thousand guards lifeless, like dust.

1417. ALL the castle guard lay like sick men, every one wounded from head to foot, their armour rent in pieces, the castle gates open, the fragments of the gates flung aside. They recognized Tariel's handiwork, they said: "This is his doing."

1418. THEY found the roads prepared, they entered and crept up the passage; they saw: the moon was freed from the serpent to meet the sun; he raised his helmet, his reedy hair thrown back became him well, breast was glued to breast, neck was riveted to neck.

1419. THEY embraced each other, they kissed and shed tears; they were like when Musht'har and Zual are united. When the sun surrounds the rose it becomes fair and reflects the rays. They that have hitherto seen griefs will henceforth rejoice.

1420. THEY kissed each other, they stood neck-welded; again full oft they glued the roses of the opened lips. Now Avt'handil and P'hridon came forth also, the three sworn brothers were gathered together; they gave greeting to that sun, they presented themselves as they were called on.

1421. THE sun met them with lovely, laughing face, the proud
one kissed her helpers with gentle mien, she humbly gave
them thanks with dainty words; both together talked with
fair discourse.

1422. THEY greeted Tariel too, that tree like an aloe sapling,
they wished him joy of the victory, they asked news of one
another; it irked them not, they regretted not, for their
armour had not failed them; they themselves had quit
themselves as lions, those that fought against them had been
as hinds and goats.

1423. OUT of the three hundred men, a hundred and sixty came
in with them; it grieves P'hridon for his troops, but on the
other hand he rejoiced; they sought out and suffered not
to live whatever adversaries were left. What treasures
they found, now how can their number be told!

1424. THEY collected mules, camels, whatever they could find
that was swift, they loaded three thousand with pearls and
gems, every gem cut, jacinths and rubies; they placed that
sun in a palanquin, precautions are taken by them.

1425. THEY appointed sixty men to guard the castle of
Kadjet'hi. They led away that sun—hard would it be to
ravish her from them—they set out for the City of the Seas,
though long is the way thither. They said: "We must see
P'hatman; we owe her a due recompense."

LX

The Going of Tariel to the King of the Seas

1426. TO the presence of the King of the Seas he sent a messenger of good tidings; he bade him announce: "I, Tariel, come, vanquisher of foes, their destroyer and slayer; from Kadjet'hi I bring my sun, piercer of me with lances; I desire to see thee with honour, as father and parent.

1427. "NOW I have the land of the Kadjis and their hoards. O king, all that is good hath happened to me from you: my sun was freed by P'hatman, she was a mother and a sister to her. What can I give thee in return for this? I hate vain promises.

1428. "COME, see us before we have passed thy land. I present to thee outright the kingdom of the Kadjis, accept it from me; let thy men be posted there, hold castle strongly. I am in haste, I cannot come to see thee, come thou forth, wend towards me.

1429. "ON my behalf tell Usen, P'hatman's husband, to send her, the sight of her will please her she freed; whom else can she desire to see more than her who is brighter than the sun, even as a crystal is brighter than pitch!"

383

1430. WHEN Tariel's man was received by the ruler of the seas—it is the custom that the heart is agitated by startling tidings—he gave thanks and glory to God the Just Judge. Straightway he mounted; he needed no other messenger.

1431. HE loaded baggage, he appointed the making of their wedding, he takes a number of pretty things, a great quantity of jet. He has P'hatman with him, they made a journey of ten days: the sight of the lion and the sun, the light of the lands, rejoices him.

1432. AFAR off the three met the great King of the Seas, they dismounted, he humbly kissed them, they were encompassed by a host of troops; they rendered praise to Tariel, he gave a thousand thanks, when they saw the damsel the King of the Seas was fascinated by her crystal-halo rays.

1433. SLOW fire consumed Dame P'hatman at the sight of her, she embraced her, she covered with kisses her hand, foot, face, neck; she said: "O God, I will serve Thee, since my darkness is lightened for me; I recognize the shortness of evil, Thy goodness is everlasting."

1434. THE maiden embraced P'hatman; sweetly she speaks, not angry: "God hath enlightened my rent, faded heart; now am I as full as formerly I was waning; the sun hath shed his beams upon me, therefore I appear a rose unfrozen."

1435. THE King of the Seas celebrated there an exceeding great wedding; he thanked Tariel too for Kadjet'hi; he would not let them go for seven days; generously he dispensed gifts, the treasure he had loaded; they wore out by treading upon it the scattered gold coin as if it were a bridge.

1436. THERE stood a heap of silk, brocade and satin. He gave to Tariel a crown, a price could not be set on it, of a whole jacinth, yellow, exceeding pure, likewise a throne of gold, red, refined.

1437. HE presented to Nestan-Daredjan a mantle adorned with gems, red jacinths, rubies of Badakhshan and rubies; they both sat, the maid and the youth, with faces flashing lightning; they that looked on them burned with new fire.

1438. HE presented to Avt'handil and P'hridon measureless great gifts, a valuable saddle, an excellent horse, to each a jewelled coat shedding rare-hued rays; they said: "What thanks can we utter! Prosperous be your state!"

1439. TARIEL rendered thanks with his tongue in fair words: "Greatly have I been pleased, O king; first at seeing you, then you have filled us with many fair kinds of gifts; I wot we did well not to pass by afar off from you."

1440. THE King of the Seas says: "O king, lion, valorous, life of those near you, slayer from afar of those that cannot look on you, what can I give you like unto yourself, O fair to look upon! When I am away from you what shall avail me, O desirable to be gazed on!"

1441. TARIEL said to P'hatman: "I adopt thee as my sister. O sister, great is mine unpayable debt to thy heart! Now whatever treasure of the Kadjis I have brought with me from Kadjet'hi I give it to thee, take it, I sell it not."

1442. DAME P'hatman made obeisance, she proffered exceeding great thanks: "O king, thy sight burns me with unquenchable fire. When I shall be away from thee what shall I do! Thou wilt leave me like one bereft of sense. Ah, blessed are those near thee; woe to him that cannot gaze on you."

1443. THE three radiant ones spoke to the King of the Seas; their teeth were crystals, their lips as pearl-shells. "When we are deprived of you we desire not merrymakings, flutes, harps and kettledrums. But give us leave, it is time, let us depart, we are in haste.

1444. "BE our father, parent and hope! But this indeed we beseech of thee: grant us a ship!" The king said: "I grudge not to give myself to earth for you; since thou art in haste, what can I say to thee! Go! Thine arm be thy guide!"

1445. THE king fitted out a ship on the shore. Tariel set out; those who were parted shed tears, they beat their heads, they tore their hair and beards and cast them away. P'hatman's tears in their flow even augmented the sea.

1446. THE three sworn brothers crossed the seas together, again they confirmed by their word what they formerly affirmed; singing and laughter were beseeming to them, who were not ignorant thereof; the ray from their lips shone upon the planks of crystal.

1447. THENCE they sent a man to Asmat'h as a messenger of good tidings; also to P'hridon's chief to tell them of the fight: "He comes hither, as the sun he rises high, reinforcing the planets; we erstwhile frozen shall be frozen now no more."

1448. THEY seated that sun in a palanquin; they wended their way along the coast. They sported like children; the passing away of woe gladdened them. They came where was the land of the hero Nuradin, they were met, they heard the sound of frequent song.

1449. THERE all P'hridon's lords met them. Asmat'h, full of joy, whose wounds no longer appeared, was riveted to Nestan-Daredjan so that axes could not unloose them. Now she had ended all her faithful services.

1450. NESTAN-DAREDJAN embraces her, kisses her face with her mouth. She said: "Mine own, woe is me, I have filled thee too with grief. Now God hath granted us grace, I acknowledge His boundless bounty. I know not with what I can repay so great a heart as thine!"

1451. ASMAT'H said: "Thanks be to God, I have seen the roses unfrozen. At length understanding hath thus revealed things hidden. Death itself seems to me life when I see you happy. Better than all friends are suzerain and vassals that love one another!"

1452. THE lords did homage, they rendered great praise: "Since God hath caused us to rejoice, blessed is His divinity; He hath shown us your face, no longer doth the burning of fires consume us; even He that gave the wound, He hath the power to heal it."

1453. THEY came and put their mouths on their hands; thus they kissed them. The king Tariel said: "For our sake have your brethren sacrificed themselves. They have found joy in eternity, a reality and no dream. They have attained communion with the One; their glories are increased a hundred-and-twenty-fold.

1454. "THOUGH their death is sore to me and grievous, yet the great immortal gift hath there fallen to their lot." This he spake, gently he wept, and the rain of tears was mingled with the snow. Boreas blows from the narcissi; January freezes the rose.

1455. THERE all wept when they saw him in tears; whoever had lost any kinsman moaned, weeping and sobbing. All were hushed. Then they said respectfully to Tariel: "Since sages liken thee to the sun, it befits them that look upon you to be merry; wherefore should they lament!

1456. "WHO is worthy of your so great weeping and sorrow? Death for your sake is far better than walking upon the earth!" Then P'hridon said to the king: "Make not bitterness to thyself from aught. May God in return render to thee a thousand joys!"

1457. AVT'HANDIL also sympathized; he speaks with great sorrow. They rendered praise, and said: "Let us now yield ourselves to smiling; since the lost lion has found the vanished sun, no more will we weep what is deplorable, no longer will we set canals in our eyes."

1458. THITHER they went where is the great city Mulghazanzar They played trumpet and kettledrum, there was trampling and uproar; the sound of drum and copper drum blended fairly; the burgesses crowded round, they left the bazaar.

1459. THE merchants came from their rows, on all sides there is a host of onlookers: the officers kept a wide space round them, they had arms in their hands; families came crowding in, causing trouble to the officers; their entreaty is to be allowed there to look upon them.

1460. AT P'hridon's they alighted, they saw a pleasing palace, many slaves with golden girdles met them, they have nought but gold brocade as a carpet for their feet; they threw up gold above their heads, the crowd marching there picked it up in heaps.

LXI

The Wedding of Tariel and Nestan by P'hridon

1461. THEY placed for the maid and the youth a throne white
and coral-hued, prettily sprinkled with red and yellow gems
for Avt'handil one of mingled yellow and black; they came,
they sat down. The spectators, I ween, were impatient for
them.

1462. THE minstrels came forth; the sound of sweet singing was
heard. They made the wedding; the presentation of soft silk
stuffs was multiplied by P'hridon, the good entertainer, not
an abashed host. A smile, a tooth-glimpse, beautifies
Nestan-Daredjan.

1463. THEY brought out incomparable gifts from the wealthy
P'hridon: nine pearls in size like a goose's egg; also one
gem like to the sun with augmented ray: before it at night
a painter could have painted a picture.

1464. LIKEWISE he presented to each a necklace to throw over
the neck, of gems cut into spheres, of whole jacinths. He

also brought a tray scarcely to be held in the hand, a gift
for the lion Avt'handil from the generous P'hridon.

1465. THAT tray is full of plump pearls; he gave all to
Avt'handil, with not unseemly words. The house was filled
with brocade and soft cloth of gold; Tariel the proud gave
thanks with sweet words.

1466. FOR eight days P'hridon made measureless wedding
festivities, every day they offer priceless presents prepared;
day and night castanets and harp cease not to sound.
Behold a youth and a maiden worthy each of the other have
attained each other.

1467. TARIEL one day spake to P'hridon words of the heart:
"Your heart is more mine than that of a born brother; my
life would not be a fitting return, nor the gift of my soul;
dying I found from you the balm for my wound.

1468. "THOU knowest of Avt'handil's self-sacrifice for my sake;
now I would serve him in return; go, ask, he will reveal
what he wants; as he hath quenched my furnace, even so
hath his burned enough.

1469. "SAY to him: 'O brother, what will repay thee for the
grief thou hast seen for my sake? God will grant thee His
grace imaged forth from on high. If I cannot do something
desirable for thee, contrived for thy sake, I will not see my
house, nor hall, nor hut.

391

1470. "'NOW tell me what thou wishest of me, or in what I can help thee. I choose that we go to Arabia; be thou my guide. Our swords and sweet words will arrange our business. If thou be not united to thy wife I will be not husband to mine.'"

1471. WHEN P'hridon told Avt'handil Tariel's message, he laughed, he smiled, mirth beautified him. He said: "Why want I a helper? I am not hurt by a wound from any. The Kadjis possess not my sun, nor doth lack of joy afflict her.

1472. "My sun sits upon a throne, powerful by the will of God, respected and honoured, proud, harmed by none, she is by no means oppressed by Kadjis, nor by the sorcery of wizards Why should I want help with regard to her? Expect me not to speak flattering words.

1473. "WHEN Providence shall come for me, heavenly being from above, if God wills, shall visit my heart, consolations for the furnace; then indeed the radiances of the flashing of the sun will be my lot when I am dying; till that time be come, vain are my runnings to and fro.

1474. "GO and report to Tariel the answer spoken by me: 'What thanks are needed, O king, however great is thy compassion; even from my mother's womb am I born to be your servant, and, by God, let me be but earth till thou be recognized as king.

1475. "'THOU hast said: "I desire thy union to thy beloved!" This is like your compassionate heart. There my sword cuts not, nor breadth of tongue. It is better for me to await the deed of yon celestial Providence.

1476. "'THIS is my wish and my desire, that I may see thee powerful in India, enthroned upon the thrones, the heavenly planet, too, sitting by thy side, the face flashing lightning; that your foes be exterminated, that no adversary appear there.

1477. "'WHEN these the desires of my heart have been fulfilled to me, then indeed shall I go to Arabia, it will befall me to be near that sun; when she wills she shall quench the burnings of this fire for me. Nought else do I wish from you, I hate all kinds of flattery.'"

1478. WHEN P'hridon reported to Tariel these words of the knight, he said: "That will I not do; for that it needs no wizard. As he found the cause of the existence of my life, even so he too shall see the valour of a brother in his favour.

1479. "GO, speak on my behalf words not of adulation: 'I will not remain without seeing thy foster-father. I suspect I slew many servants beloved by him. I will only beg forgiveness, and so I shall return.'

1480. "SPEAK thus: 'Send me no more messages. Tomorrow I shall not fail to set out; I shall have no more of the word "if"; the King of the Arabs will not make my words to be of no avail; pleasantly shall I beg his daughter, I shall entreat of him, I shall persuade him.'"

1481. P'HRIDON told Avt'handil Tariel's message: "He will not stay," quoth he; "vain is it for thee to speak of waiting!" It oppressed him; again the smoke and glow burned his heart. Thus respect is due to kings, devotion from knights.

1482. AVT'HANDIL went to beseech Tariel on bended knee; he
embraces his feet, he kisses them, he no longer looks up to
his waist. He says: "What I have sinned against Rostevan
this year is enough; make me not again to be a breaker,
a shatterer of loyalty.

1483. "WHAT thou desirest God's justice will not give thee. How
can I dare do a treacherous deed to my foster-father, how
can I undertake aught against him who for my sake is
become pale, how can the servant use his sword upon his
master!

1484. "SUCH a deed will make discord between me and my
beloved. Woe is me if she become angry, displeased, if
wrath compel her heart! Then will she even stint me of
tidings, and make me languish for a sight of her. No man of
flesh can exact forgiveness for me."

1485. TARIEL, that radiant sun, spake laughing. He took
Avt'handil's hand, raised him, set him on his feet: "Thy
help hath done me every good, but it is better that thou
also shouldst rejoice my joy with thine.

1486. "I GREATLY hate too much fear, respect and ceremony
in a friend, I hate unbroken sternness, gloominess, majesty;
if one be a hearty friend let him tend towards me; if not,
I for myself, he for himself, separation is much better.

1487. "I KNOW the heart of thy beloved with regard to thee;
the visit of me who have met thee will not displease her.
Now I can venture to speak somewhat plausibly to the
king: I only desire to see the desirable sight of them.

1488. "THIS only will I say to him entreatingly and respectfully that he should give thee his daughter of his free will. Since the end is union, how can you endure separation? Beautify each other; fade not apart."

1489. WHEN Avt'handil knew from Tariel that he would not be hindered from going, he ventured not to dispute, he added thereto assent, P'hridon counted over select men as a convoy; he set out with them, of course he travelled the road with them.

1490. THIS hidden thing Divons[1] the sage reveals: "God sends good, He creates no evil, He shortens the bad to a moment, He renews the good for a long time, His perfect self He makes more perfect, He degrades not Himself."

1491. THOSE lions, those suns, set out from P'hridon's country. They lead with them the sun-faced, the maiden, the amazing to beholders; the raven's tail, ordered, hangs coiled by the crystal; beauty, tenderness, there adorned the ruby of Badakhshan.

1492. THAT sun sat in a palanquin, and thus they made her fare. They followed the chase; there caused they blood to flow. Wherever they came upon a land they were the joy of beholders, they went forth to meet them, gave gifts, eulogized, reviled them not.

1493. IT was as if the sun sat in the firmament amid moons. Many days they journeyed, merry, sagely discoursing,

---

[1] Dionysius, the Areopagite.

within those great plains on all sides unattained of men. They reached the neighbourhood of that rock where Tariel had been.

1494. TARIEL said: "It is seemly that I should be your host this day. Thither will I go where I was while madness afflicted me. There will Asmat'h entertain us; she hath store of smoked meat. When I give you fair gifts you shall praise the variety of the treasure."

1495. THEY went in; they dismounted in that cave of the great rocks. Asmat'h had venison; she carves it for the guests. They were merry, they joked at the passing of those deeds; they thanked God that He had turned their days of woe to joy.

1496. THEY explored the hill abounding in caves, merry they played; they found those treasures sealed up by Tariel, uncounted by any, apprehended by none; they say not with dissatisfied hearts: "We lack!"

1497. HE gave many fair gifts, to each what was fitting; then he enriched P'hridon's people, army and generals alike; every man was enriched, all those who came with them, but there lay so much treasure it seemed still untouched by man.

1498. HE said to P'hridon: "Hard will it be for me to pay the debt I owe thee; but it is said: 'A man who is a doer of good loseth not in the end.' Now the treasure, as much as lieth here or is to be found, let it all be thine, take it away, as it belongs to thee."

1499. P'HRIDON humbly did homage, he expressed exceeding gratitude: "O king, why thinkest thou me stupid and thus mazed? Every enemy seems to thee as straw, however much he may be like a thick cudgel. My joy lasts but so long as I shall be a gazer on thee."

1500. P'HRIDON made men go back to bring camels to take away all this treasure to his home. Now they set out thence on the road leading to Arabia. Avt'handil is a minished moon by longing to be united with the sun.

1501. WHEN many days were passed they reached the boundaries of Arabia; they saw villages, castles, frequent, uninterrupted; those dwelling therein had clothed their forms in blue and green, all are bathed in tears for Avt'handil.

1502. TARIEL sent a man to the presence of King Rostevan to say: "I venture, O king, to wish you the fulfilment of your desires; I, King of the Indians, come to your royal court; I will show thee the rosebud, unfaded, unplucked.

1503. "FORMERLY the sight of me—the ground under your feet—made you angry: thou didst ill in attempting to capture me, to urge thy horse against me; I showed thine armies some sign of anger, I massacred many slaves, servants of your palace.

1504. "NOW therefore I come before you, I have gone out of my way; you will pardon me that in which I sinned against thee, let thy wrath be sufficient. We have no offerings, as

398

P'hridon and his knights can testify; the only gift I have brought you is your Avt'handil."

1505. TONGUE cannot shortly tell how they rejoiced when the messenger of these good tidings come to the king; the brilliancy of three rays was added to T'hinat'hin's cheeks, the shadow of eyebrows and lashes makes fairer the crystal and ruby.

1506. THEY beat the kettledrums and peals of joyous laughter were heard, the soldiers ran hither and thither, they desired to run to meet them, they began to lead out the horses and to bring out saddles, a multitude of knights, swift-armed, stout-hearted, mounted.

1507. THE king mounted, the princes and the armies entire go to meet them; whoever hears, others from diverse parts come to his presence; all give thanks to God, they raise their voices, they say: "Evil hath no existence; good things are ever ready for thee!"

1508. WHEN they met and the meeters perceived each other, Avt'handil said with tender words to Tariel: "Behold, seest thou the dust-dyed plains? Therefore a furnace consumes me, my heart is fevered and sad.

1509. "THERE is my foster-father; he is come to meet you. I cannot go thither, I am ashamed, a furnace consumes my heart; living man hath never been shamed as I am. What you intend to do for me you know, also P'hridon who is beside you."

1510. TARIEL said: "Thou dost well to show respect to thy lord. Now stay, come not thither, stay alone without me. I will go; I will tell the king of thy hiding. With God's help I think I shall soon unite thee to that sun with the form of an aloe."

1511. THE lion Avt'handil tarried there; a little tent was put up. Nestan-Daredjan also stayed there, the amazer of beholders the zephyr of her eyelashes is wafted like a north-east wind. The King of the Indians departed, straight, not secretly.

1512. P'HRIDON went with him; of a truth they were a long time crossing the field. Tariel went forward alone, his figure swayed. The king knew of their coming; he dismounted and did homage to the bold one strong as a lion; he does honour to the King of the Indians as a father.

1513. TARIEL also did homage; he goes to kiss, to greet. The king kissed his neck to give pleasure to his lips; in wonder he speaks, in order to embolden him: "Thou art the sun; separation from thee turns day into night."

1514. THE king marvelled at his beauty and good looks, he gazes with wonder on his face, he praises the hardihood of his arms. Then P'hridon also greeted him; he did homage to the king, to the king eager for the sight of Avt'handil.

1515. THE king shrinks from praising Tariel, and is discouraged. Tariel says: "O king, hereby is my heart subjected to thee; I marvel how you can think thus of my worth; since Avt'handil is thine, how can any other please thee!

1516. "DOST thou not wonder at not seeing him, and at his tarrying! Come and let us sit down, O king, pleasant is this meadow of verdure; I will venture to tell you the reason why I could not bring him before you; I have a favour to ask of you, now I must beg leave of you."

1517. THE kings sat down; the multitude of the host stood round. A smile brighter than a lamp flits over Tariel's face; the sight maddens the beholders of his bearing and gestures. He began to relate to the king a speech wisely chosen:

1518. "O KING, I hold myself unworthy to mention this, but I am come before you to entreat, to beg; he himself beseeches who seems a sun-like shedder of rays, he who is my light and enlightener.

1519. "NOW we both venture to approach thee with prayer and entreaty. Avt'handil gave me balm befitting him; he forgot that woes quite equal to ours afflicted him. I will not weary thee; a long story is beyond our powers.

1520. "YOUR children love each other, the maid loves him and he the maid; therefore I think on him pitiful, tearful and wan, on bended knee I entreat thee, let them no longer be consumed by flame, but give your daughter to the strong-armed, stout-hearted one.

1521. "NO more than this will I ask of thee, neither short nor long." He drew forth his handkerchief, tied it round his neck, rose up, bent his knee, besought him as a teacher. It astonished all men who heard this story.

1522. WHEN he saw Tariel on his bended knees, the king was dismayed; he went back a long way, he did homage, he fell down to the earth. He said: "O monarch, all my joy is blown away from me; this abasement of you thus has saddened for me the sight of you.

1523. "HOW could it be that man should not grant thee whatever thou desirest, or that I should grudge my daughter if thou didst wish to devote her to death or slavery even! If you had ordered it from your home, not even then would my tears flow; none other can she find like him if she fly up even to heaven!

1524. "I COULD not find a better son-in-law than Avt'handil. Myself I have given the realm to my daughter, she has it and it befits her; the rose blooms anew, my flower is blown. What objection can I make? Only let him be satisfied!

1525. "IF thou wert to marry her to some slave, even then I would not grudge her to thee. Who could refuse thee, how could any save a madman quarrel with thee! If I loved not Avt'handil, why did I thus yearn for him? Verily, O God, I am in Thy presence, this is confirmed by me."

1526. WHEN Tariel heard this speech from the king, he bowed himself, humbly did homage, fell on his face. Then the king did homage to him, he came forward, he stood before him. They thanked each other, nor were they at all annoyed.

1527. P'HRIDON mounted, he galloped as herald of good tidings to Avt'handil—indeed, he also rejoiced at this great joy—he went and took him, led him and accompanied him; but he is abashed before the king, darkly he shed his beam.

1528. THE king arose, met him; the knight dismounted when the king came; in his hands he had a handkerchief, therewith he hid his face. The sun was concealed by a cloud, it grew gloomy, the rose was chilled; but how could anything hide his beauty!

1529. THE king would have kissed him, tears no longer flow, Avt'handil embraced his feet, the ray streams down; the king said: "Arise, be not ashamed, thou hast revealed thy prowess; since thou art loyal to me, be not ashamed; why shouldst thou be ashamed before me?"

1530. HE embraced him, he kissed him all over his face; he said: "Thou hast quenched my hot fire, though tardily hast thou appeared to me as water; to her who has herded in the jet and the vicinity of the eyelashes to-morrow I shall unite thee, O lion, with the sun, come quickly to her."

1531. THE king embraced the neck of that lion and hero-like one, he seats him close, he speaks to him, kisses him, gazes on his face. That sun so met royalty, as he was worthy of it. Then is joy pleasant, when a man hath passed through grief.

1532. THE knight says to the king: "I marvel that thou speakest of something else, why thou desirest not to see the sun, or why thou delayest! Meet her gaily, conduct her to your house; be clothed in her rays, set them around as a light."

1533. HE told Tariel also; they mounted and went to meet the lady. The cheeks of those three Goliaths were dyed to sun colour; they met what they desired, they found what they sought; they had handled their swords, not girded them idly on their loins.

1534. DISMOUNTING afar off, the king greeted the lady, the lightning flashing from her cheeks blinded his eyes; she met him, sitting in the palanquin she kissed him. The king began a eulogy; he was wholly bereft of his wits.

1535. HE said: "O sun, how shall I praise thee, O light, and maker of good weather! For thy sake understandings are mad, and not for nought. O sun-like and moon-like, to what planet do they liken thee! No longer do I wish to look on you, O ye roses and violets!"

1536. ALL they that saw her marvelled at the shedding of her rays. Like a sun she blinded the eyes of the onlookers by the sight of her light; wheresoever she appeared crowds came running towards her; burned by her they found the comfort of their hearts in gazing.

1537. THEY mounted, they all went homewards, they have the seven planets to compare with that sun; her beauty is incomprehensible, it is beyond their understanding. Soon they came to the place of the king's dwelling-house.

1538. THEY came in, they saw T'hinat'hin, the bestower of woe on them that look on her; the wearing of the purple beautified the sceptre and crown-bearer; the radiance of her face rested on the faces of the new-comers. The King of the Indians entered, that hero-like sun.

1539. TARIEL and his wife humbly saluted the maid, they met, kissed and held pleasant converse, they illumined that hall, they made not the light to fade; they turned crystal and ruby of Badakhshan into cheeks, jet into eyelashes.

1540. T'HINAT'HIN invited them up to the lofty royal throne. Tariel said: "Sit thou; it is desired by the Supreme Judge; this day more than all days thy throne benefits thee, I seat the lion of lions beside thee, the sun of suns."

1541. BOTH took him by the hand and set him on her throne; they placed Avt'handil by the side of her for desire of whom he was slain; she is better than the seen and the unseen, better than all sights. Think not any were like them in love, not even Ramin and Vis.

1542. THE maiden was bashful and astonished to have Avt'handil seated by her side; her colour paled and her heart shot forth a tremor from within. The king said: "Child, why art thou so bashful before me? The sages say that love in its end will not fail.

1543. "NOW, children, God grant you a thousand years' length of life, happiness, prosperity, glory, and, moreover, freedom from ills; may heaven not make you fickle, may it fall to your lot to be steadfast like it, may my fate to be have the earth heaped over me by your hands."

1544. THEN the king commanded the armies to do homage to Avt'handil: "This is your king," quoth he, "such was God's will. This day he hath my throne, I have old age like an infection. Serve him as well as you have served me, keep my command."

1545. THE soldiers and the lords bent, humbly they did homage; they said: "Let us be as the earth to them that dispose of our lives, them who magnify those of us who are obedient, who liken the disobedient unto corpses, who make the arms of foes to fail and encourage our hearts!"

1546. TARIEL too spoke with a eulogy the glorification of hope; he said to the maiden: "You are united, no longer the heat of fires burns thee, thy husband is my brother, I desire too that you be my sister, I will bring to nought those who are false and opposed to thee."

LXIII

Here Is the Marriage of Avt'handil and T'hinat'hin by the King of the Arabs

1547. THAT day Avt'handil sits as lord and is high king; tendernesses beautify Tariel who sits with him. Nestan-Daredjan, the amazer of onlookers, is with T'hinat'hin; it is as if heaven had bent down to earth, and two suns are united.

1548. THEY began to bring bread to plenish the armies; beeves and sheep are slain more abundant than moss. There was made an offering of presents, fitting to them. The ray of the faces of them all lightens like the sun.

1549. THE bowls were of jacinth, the cups were of ruby; moreover, wondrously coloured vessels bear passing wondrous seals. The panegyrist of that wedding would be praised by the sages. O inlooker, thou wouldst have said unto thy heart: "Be not loosed, be bound there!"

1550. THE minstrels approached from all sides, there was heard the sound of the cymbal; heaped like a hillock of gold and cut rubies of Badakhshan; for drinkers flows a fountain of wine from a hundred runlets, like a canal; from twilight to dawn, there was noise, the time of mourning passed.

1551. NONE remained without a gift, neither lame nor crippled; pearls rolled to and fro, scattered, thrown about; satin and solid gold were of none account, to be carried away. For three days the King of the Indies was as a groomsman to Avt'handil.

1552. ON the morrow the King of the Arabs again entertains; he is not listless. He said to Tariel: "Pleasant it is to gaze on thy sun! Thou art king of all kings, and she queen. It behoves us to be your slaves, to pierce our ears for earrings.

1553. "NOW, O king, it is not fitting that we should sit on a level with you!" The royal throne Rostevan placed for Tariel, and another couch apart; he placed Avt'handil and his wife lower down, according to their rank. First of all they present gifts for Tariel; they lie in a heap.

1554. THE King of the Arabs plays the host, he does nothing but entertain; sometimes he approaches these, sometimes those, he stands not upon his royal dignity; he gives, and all praise his ungrudging generosity. P'hridon sits near Avt'handil, as one accustomed to kingship.

1555. THE King Rostevan did honour to the daughter of the Indies and her husband, he gave them love and gifts, as to a son and daughter-in-law; it is impossible to tell even a tenth of what he gave, to each a sceptre, purple and jewelled crowns.

1556. STILL he gave to both gifts fitting their fate; a thousand gems like the eggs of a Romany hen; then a thousand pearls like a dove's egg; a thousand steeds, in size each like a hill.

1557. TO P'hridon he gave nine trays full to the brim with pearls, nine steeds richly saddled. The King of the Indians does homage with dignity, wise, not drunkenly; he gave thanks soberly though he had drunk of the wine.

1558. WHY should I lengthen speech? The days of one month passed. They sported, they ceased not at all from drinking. To Tariel they presented wondrous jewels of ruby stone. Their radiance like the sun's covers them all.

1559. TARIEL was like a rose, and a light snow shower fell from his eyes; he sent Avt'handil to Rostevan to ask for leave; he gave him this message: "To be near thee is enough for me as full joy, but enemies hold my kingdom, I know they are eating up the land.

1560. "THE knowledge and art of the learned destroy the unlearned. I think any hurt to me would bring somewhat of sadness unto you too. I go that tarrying here may not bring evil upon me, soon again may I see you happy, may God's will grant it!"

1561. ROSTEVAN said: "O king, why art thou so bashful? Whatever is best for you do it, look into it, examine it. Avt'handil will accompany thee, go with a great host; rend in pieces and cut up your enemies and them that are traitors."

1562. AVT'HANDIL said to Tariel those two words that Rostevan had said. Tariel said: "Speak not thus; guard the rows of crystal. How canst thou, O sun, depart from the newly united moon!" Avt'handil said: "I shall not be seduced by thee with this.

1563. "OF a truth thou wishest not to forsake me while thou goest away slandering me, saying: 'He loveth his wife, forsooth; he hath forsaken me, 'twas like him!' Am I to remain sundered from thee and an object of pity to myself! For a man to forsake his friend!... Ugh! Ugh! he will do ill!"

1564. TARIEL'S smile is like the sprinkling of crystal from roses. He said: "Absent from thee I bewail myself more than thou. Since thou wishest it, come away with me, accuse me not of flattery." Avt'handil commands troops to be summoned to him from all sides.

1565. HE assembled the armies of Arabia, no time is wasted; eighty thousand men were all arrayed, man and horse clad in armour of Khvarazmia. The King of the Arabs eats the gall of bitterness at their separation.

1566. PARTING each from other, both maidens, the adopted sisters, sworn with the oath of sisterhood, trusting in each other's word, with breast welded to breast, with neck riveted to neck, wept. The onlookers, too, had their hearts consumed.

1567. WHEN the moon is on a level with the star of dawn, both shine equally; should one go away, the other also is

410

removed; if it go not away, the sky will make it remove; to look at them the inlooker must become a hill and a mountain.

1568. HE who created them such, He Himself shall sunder them, though of their own will they desire not parting. They glue together and cleave the rose, they weep and tears flow; all those who parted from them thought their lives of no account.

1569. NESTAN-DAREDJAN said: "Would that I had never come to know thee! Separated from the sun I should not now be thus melted by parting. Thou shalt know tidings of me; let me have news of thee, speak to me in letters. As I am burned up for thy sake, thou shalt melt for mine."

1570. T'HINAT'HIN said: "O sun, delight of them that gaze on thee! How can I give thee up, or how can I endure parting! Instead of praying for days from God, I shall desire death. Mayst thou have as many days as I shall shed tears!"

1571. AGAIN they kissed each other, those ladies parted; she who was left there could not take her eyes away from her who was gone; she too looks back, therefore flames consumed her. I cannot write down a tenth part of that I could wish!

1572. ROSTEVAN at their departure was made more mad than madmen; a thousand times he says, "Woe is me!" not merely once doth he sigh; hot flows the spring of tears, as if a cauldron were being heated. Tariel's face is drawn, the soft snow falls gently, it wastes away.

1573. THE king crushed Tariel's rose with embracing and kissing. Quoth he: "Your presence hitherto seems like a dream to me; when thou art gone afar from me I shall remain with my sufferings twentyfold increased. Life was given to us by thee; by thee also shall we be slain."

1574. TARIEL mounted and parting from the king gave him a farewell greeting; all the soldiers shed tears moistening the meadows, they said: "The sun hastes to greet thee, haste thou too to meet him." He said: "For your sake I weep more than Sala."[1]

1575. THEY set out and departed with many troops and much baggage—Tariel, P'hridon, Avt'handil, all elegant in form; he had eighty thousand men with worthy steeds; the three went on, helpful one to another.

1576. THE three went their way—God can never create their like again! They were met; none dared withstand them. In the plain they tarried for dinner when morning was past. As was fitting they feasted; they drank wine, not buttermilk.

---

[1] Sala—Salaman.

LXIV

Tariel Hears About the Death of the King of India

1577. ON the summit of the mountain, a great caravan appeared, men and mules were all in black; the tresses of their hair were woven round their heads. The king commandeth: "Bring them here, we must tarry yet a while."

1578. THEY brought those merchants and their chief. The king asked: "Who are you, why are your bodies robed in black?" The men answered: "Such is the custom in the countries from which we come. We came to India from Egypt and have travelled a long way."

1579. TARIEL, P'hridon and Avt'handil rejoiced to hear that those merchants had come from India; they feigned indifference and abandoned themselves not to their feelings. Tariel began to speak to them in a foreign language they did not understand Indian and they also answered in Arabian.

1580. THEY said: "Give us, O merchants, some tidings from India." Those answered: "The wrath of God has fallen on India from on high, and great and small shed tears which fall from their eyes drop by drop; the sages living among them have lost their minds."

1581. THE chief of the merchants spake to them in words of great eloquence: "P'harsadan, King of India, was a happy king. He had a daughter, a star, more sun than the sun. Her teeth were pearls, her form the aloe-tree, her cheeks were rubies from Badakhshan, her hair was raven black.

1582. "DEARLY did that maid and the Amirbar love one another. The Amirbar killed the bridegroom, news of it spread rapidly. A tempest raged devastating all of India. From her childhood this maiden had been reared by her aunt.

1583. "HER aunt was a Kadj, most cunning in matters of sorcery Thus she undertook a most fearful task, depriving the earth of sun. And she, unfortunate one, died being unworthy of life. The maiden disappeared, she planted elsewhere the shoot of the aloe-tree.

1584. "HAVING learned this, the Amirbar, the lion, set forth in quest of the sun. He disappeared, the sun was dimmed in India, the moon was tarnished; both are lost, there is no hope of finding them. The king said: 'O God, why dost thou burn me on a slow fire!'

1585. "THE king was wrathful, to find them was beyond his power; the sound of the cymbals and harps gave place to woe. A brief time more he endured the burning of the furnace. Now he too is dead, the processions and the sound of footsteps have come to an end."

1586. HAVING conveyed these tidings the merchant continued to speak. The woman cried out violently, and tore the veil from her head. Tariel too cried out, disclosing what had been hidden. A torrent flowed from the narcissi, the snow melted.

1587. KILL me, if the sun could disobey the bare-headed woman! Her fragrance is like unto the perfume of the rose, she, the bare-headed one, is like a poppy. If even the sage praiseth her, they will tell him: "Stop!" as to a donkey. Her teeth are like twin-pearls set in a crystal shell.

1588. BITTERLY the woman laments her father's death, she is like a nightingale. She tears her hair which streams about her, her eyes are filled with tears; the rose become saffron. the ruby is like moss. A cloud covers the sun, dimming its rays.

1589. SHE scratches her face, she tears her hair, she weeps and wails in a clamorous voice. Blood and tears flow in torrents from her eyes. "O father, let me die for thy sake! I, thy unworthy child, I have done nought for thee, in nothing have I pleased you.

1590. "MY father, who is no more, was the light of my eyes. Who will bring thee my tidings, consoling thy heart therewith! O sun, of what use is thy light, why dost thou shine of the world! O world, why dost not perish! O mountain, why yearn to rise aloft!"

1591. TARIEL laments weeping: "O master, what is this I hear! I marvel that the sun still shines, that it manifests no grief!

417

You are dead, sun of everything living, the world is no longer yours. For God's sake be merciful, forgive me the grief I have brought upon you!"

1592. ONCE again they spake: "Tell us the rest of this tale!" The merchants answered: "O protector, a great battle is being fought in India. The troops of the Khatavians came, they surrounded the town, a certain King Ramaz is their lord.

1593. "ALTHOUGH the queen is still alive, she is more dead than the dead. The Indian troops are fighting, yet have they already abandoned all hope. All the fortresses on the boundaries are taken and destroyed. O sun, shed your rays, see how unclement is the weather.

1594. "ALL those living there and we amongst them made ourselves black robes. We presented ourselves to Ramaz and made ourselves known as Egyptians; our king is great, and therefore Ramaz wished to maintain peace with him. He released us, we set forth, he caused us no harm."

1595. HAVING heard this Tariel set forth in haste; in one day he traversed a three days' journey; he raised his banner, nor did he shield himself. Now look how staunch is his giant's heart!

LXV

The Arrival of Tariel in India
and His Conquest of the Khatavians

1596. TARIEL arrived in India; hills were there and the crest of a great mountain; countless troops appeared, he marvelled at their number. Tariel said: "O knights, what hope do you give me! I swear by God and by your happiness that I shall soon be free of them.

1597. "THESE troops have already felt the edge of my sword: once they engaged in battle with me, I pierced their armour, I crushed them utterly." Avt'handil said: "Why speak words of violence? We shall make dust of them and trample them under our feet."

1598. PROUDLY they made ready for battle, acting most dexterously; they mounted their best steeds and gave rein to them; they urged the steeds to outdistance one another. Those who looked on them praised. They galloped down the slope over the crest of the mountain, flinging up columns of dust.

1599. THE front ranks of the warriors came upon the guard of the Khatavians. Tariel's warriors put them to flight, they pursued them, they threw them from their horses and brought them to Tariel and Avt'handil. Those cried: "Whose men are ye?"

1600. THEY answered: "O, lord, we have been deceived, we were sent here as guards, we are warriors of King Ramaz." Tariel commanded: "Go, ye wrathful fools, go, inform your master: 'They come, those brave of heart.'

1601. "SAY: 'It is the order of Tariel, the proud and mighty king, the courageous lord who strikes fear into his enemies: thine own guards will bring thee tidings of me, fear will not save thee from death, grief is of no avail.

1602. "'WHO but a madman would think of intimidating the great! How didst thou dare to make an assault on India, thou maddest of the mad! I have come—the fire that shall utterly consume thee. I shall blunt my sharpened steel on thy body.'"

1603. THE guards went, each trying to outdistance the other. They related everything to Ramaz, they could hold back nothing: "The king of India has come, he commands excellent warriors; who can hide himself from them? One of them alone is worth two of any other."

1604. TARIEL raised his banner and the flag of his country. The banner of the Arabian king was also raised: all know that the lance is the weapon of the Arabs. P'hridon, the sun, is there too, the knight who spilled a pool of blood.

1605. THEY went a little farther, five hundred horsemen appeared. The Arabian knights who were there wished to engage in battle. Tariel said to them: "Do not thus." He made them to sue for forgiveness. The horsemen came up, Ramaz appeared, he had no armour, nor had he even a knife.

1606. HE embraced the legs of Tariel's horse; sinking to his knees he began to entreat Tariel. He said to him: "Pity me for the sake of Him who created thee; do not let me live, let them carry me away dead. Fate has so smitten my heart that it must belong to you.

1607. "TEN years have passed since you departed, since you disappeared. The birds are without a master, the eagle has broken its wings; that is why I have undertaken this affair over which we are contending. Long since has the world been lost to me as one loses at a game of dice."

1608. THEY all swore by the Almighty, fell on their knees before him: "For the sake of Him who created thee thus, do not kill." Tariel became pensive, Ramaz fell on his face before him. God giveth joy to repentant sinners, what man then can but forgive?

1609. STUDYING the writings of the sages, I found the following: The greatest courage for a man is not to kill his conquered enemy, but to stop in time—if you want to be truly brave, remember these words.

1610. THEREAT Tariel's heart softened, he was righteous, like unto God. He said: "I shall kill no more; if the conquered is seized with fear, he will twist aright what was wrongly twisted. Now I have set right all that was wrong."

1611. THEY all made obeisance to him and blessed him, they implored God to make greater their joy. They were saved from death, having received life from Tariel. Tariel's sword is unappeased, it hungers for the flesh of the warriors.

1612. MUSHT'HAR appeared in order to see Tariel. With his gentleness Tariel calmed the fire of his wrath. They came to gaze at him; the troops of Ramaz could scarce find place. In India a light like unto a column descended from the sky.

1613. A MAN came to these troops as a messenger: "He will not kill you, he has mercy on you." All blessed him. They sounded the bell and joyously they said: "He has come, that knight who single-handed has killed so many."

1614. THEY went forth to meet Tariel, they greeted him from afar. The Indians recognized their banner among the troops who raised their flag aloft, but they did not dare to trust them. They said: "They are plotting some treacherous deed." They expected not Tariel, they bathed in tears.

1615. TARIEL drew closer and cried: "It is I your king! My star is high, her eyes flashing lightning. From on high the Almighty has given the wings of an eagle—come forth, I cannot endure to have you so far."

1616. ONLY then did they recognize Tariel, they began to run up from all sides. The terraced roofs and great walls beamed with light. They conversed in loud voices, crying: "Our ailment has left us, now the Almighty, hitherto wrathful, has shown us His mercy!"

1617. THEY opened the door, they brought the keys: all those who came to look upon them were dressed in mourning. The woman and the knight both wept, the roses of the garden were moistened; they screamed, they beat their heads, their raven hair fell on the crystal.

1618. THE pupil, as was fitting, lost his senses for his master, the tears that fell from his eyes were more burning than fire; he beat his head, screamed, wept with fearful grief. He raked the thicket of jet with a crystal rake.

1619. WHEN he saw the viziers of the court apparelled in mourning, once again Tariel uttered a shrill cry. Blood and tears flowed from his eyes in torrents. The viziers came and embraced him as a brother, as a son.

1620. THE lords embraced him, they expressed their sympathy to the bridegroom and bride. The maid lost consciousness; she did not venture to lament for her father; the branches fell from the rose bush, no one could raise it. You could not meet there a laughing or a smiling man.

1621. THE queen ran forth to see them. "Who is weeping and why weep you?" quoth she. She was angry and said: "God hath changed His wrath to mercy, we must thank Him, we have no time for grief, no time to say 'Alas'."

1622. SHEDDING hot tears she embraced Tariel. She said: "My flaming fire is out, now a slow fire consumes me; be silent,

be calm, hear my tidings; God, who makes joyful the
orphans, hath rejoiced me sending thee back alive."

1623. THE weeping maiden addressed her mother: "O mother,
what must I do! When I left thee, in red and yellow raiment
wert thou clad, but now I see thee in black. My father has
abandoned his throne. Alas, no longer does he sit thereon!"
Her mother dried the maiden's tears: "Do not weep, be
silent, ill-omened one!"

1624. SHE kissed her face and the delicate roses of her lips. She
crushed the rose with her mouth, she drowned the aloe-tree.
She said to Nestan-Daredjan: "Why should we speak
ill-omened words? We must all enjoy a thousand felicities,
not merely one."

1625. WHEN some time had passed, the lords came to do homage,
presenting themselves. Those suns came forth to meet them
and embraced them with heartfelt love. They kissed and
greeted each one separately.

1626. AVT'HANDIL and P'hridon expressed their sympathy to
the queen. Tariel said: "O queen, you do not know them.
They are our saviours, we have no time at present for
lengthy discourse. We both have received life through
them."

1627. THEY rose and went into the town, they entered their
palace. The queen said a few words, addressing them as it

were: "God hath destroyed our foes, no more can they do us harm; therefore am I joyous and glad of heart."

1628. SHE commanded: "Put off your mourning, beat the drums and the cymbals, let a great noise and exultation come from our court, engirdle your brocades with golden belts. Laugh and sing, let the murmuring of your tears cease."

LXVI

The Wedding of Tariel and Nestan-Daredjan

1629. THE queen took the bride and the bridegroom by the hand,
she placed them together on the royal throne, she
abandoned her sadness, she made staunch her womanly
heart, she changed her grief into joy, she obliged no one
to weep any longer.

1630. TARIEL and his bride, sitting together on the royal throne,
suited each other, the woman suited the knight; whose
mind or whose tongue can express their praise—what son of
Adam can be like them?

1631. THE queen attired herself, she doffed her black garments,
she prepared gay robes for the lords, rejoicing the eye. She
dressed them all, augmenting their joy. Quoth she: "Let us
forget grief since joy has come to us."

1632. WHAT Tariel and his wife had desired fell to their lot,
seven royal thrones, seats of joy, incomparable; this present
solace makes them forget their sufferings. A man
unacquainted with sorrow cannot find pleasure in joy.

1633. SEE the two sitting together; even the sun could not be better! They blow the trumpet and proclaim him king, copper drums make the voices sound sweet; they give him the key of the treasuries, they gave themselves into his hands as subjects. "This is our king!" they cried, and they acclaimed him.

1634. THEY caused two thrones to be prepared for Avt'handil and P'hridon, they sat royally thereon, they extolled their majesty, what other human beings did God create like them! They related their sorrows; they revealed them to all.

1635. THEY drank, ate, made merry, they increased the household; as befits a wedding so did they celebrate it; to both they gave presents, equally to each. They gathered together treasure to give to the poor.

1636. ALL the Indians considered Avt'handil and P'hridon to be helpers. "From you every good happens to us," said they ceaselessly; they looked upon them as lords, whatever they willed that they did, they came before them continually to pay court to them.

1637. THE King of the Indians said to Asmat'h, the sharer of his sorrows: "What thou hast done, neither upbringer nor upbrought hath done. Now I enthrone thee over one-seventh part of the kingdom of India, thine let it be, serve us, sweet to the sweet!

1638. "WHOMSOEVER thou desirest as husband wed him, rule the kingdom, henceforth serve us, be subject to us." Asmat'h covered his feet with kisses. "From thee is my

427

power," quoth she; "what can I find, what better service can I have than thine!"

1639. THE three sworn brothers tarried together a few days. They sported, they received more incomparable gifts; what rare pearls, what excellent horses! But longing for T'hinat'hin made Avt'handil to show lines on his face.

1640. TARIEL perceived that longing of the knight for his wife. He said: "Of a truth thy heart is angered against me. Now woe is me! Thought hath made of thy seven griefs eight. I shall be separated from thee; the passing world grudges me my joy."

1641. THEN P'hridon begged leave of him. "I will go home," quoth he; "my foot will oft tread this court and land if thou wilt command me as an elder to a younger. I shall desire thee as the deer the fountain."

1642. AS presents for Rostevan, Tariel made Avt'handil take with him beautiful short robes, also a vessel full of cut gems, not spoons, not ladles. "Take them from me, go," quoth he, "disobey me not!" Avt'handil said: "I know not how I shall survive without thee!"

1643. THE lady Nestan sent to the lady T'hinat'hin a short cloak and a veil; who save her was worthy of such garments! A jewel—he who carried it off could not say: "I have carried it in vain!"—at night it gives light like the sun; it is visible wherever thou lookest.

1644. AVT'HANDIL mounted, he departed, he said farewell to Tariel, the flame of the fire of separation burned them both; all the Indians wept, the tear moistened the mead. Avt'handil said: "The poison of this world slays me!"

1645. P'HRIDON and Avt'handil journeyed together for a few days; the road separated them, each went his way weeping the things they had planned had turned out well for them; Avt'handil came to Arabia, he had not seen troubles in vain.

1646. THE Arabs came forth to meet him, he beautified the realm; he saw his sun, the affliction of his desires fled; he sat with her on the throne, he rejoiced at the joy of the onlookers. The Most High from above endowed his crown with sovereignty.

1647. THOSE three sovereigns loved one another, they visited one another, their desires were fulfilled, they that disputed their rule were put to the sword, they enlarged their kingdoms, they were sovereign, they increased their might.

1648. THEY poured down mercy like snow on all alike, they enriched orphans and widows and the poor did not beg, they terrified evil-doers; the lambs did not suck from strange ewes, within their dominions the goat and the wolf fed together.

Epilogue

1649. THEIR tale is ended like a dream of the night. They are
passed away, gone beyond the world. Behold the treachery
of time; to him who thinks it long, even for him it is of a
moment, I, a certain Meskhian bard, the bard Rust'hveli,
I write this.

1650. FOR David,[1] god of the Georgians, whom the sun serves in
his course, I have put this story into verse, for his
entertainment who strikes terror from East to West,
consuming those who are traitors to him, rejoicing those
who are loyal.

1651. HOW shall I sing David's deeds, heroic, loud-sounding,
these wondrous tales of strange, foreign monarchs! Old-time
customs and deeds, praises of those kings, have I found
and done into verse. Thus have we chattered!

1652. THIS is such a world as is not to be trusted by any; it
is a moment to the eyes of men, and only long enough for

---

[1] David–the consort of Queen T'hamar.

the blinking of the eyelashes. What seek you, what do you? Fate is an insulter. For him whom Fate deceives not it is better to be in both worlds.

1653. MOSE Khoneli praised Amiran, son of Daredjan; Shavt'heli whose poem they admired, praised Abdul-Mesia; Sargis T'hmogveli, the unwearying-tongued, praised Dilarget'h; Rust'hveli praised Tariel, for whom his tear unceasing flows.